D1187882

WAGON WHEELS TO DENVER

Marian McIntyre McDonough

WAGON WHEELS
TO DENVER

By

MARIAN McINTYRE McDONOUGH

Illustrated by
MANNING De V. LEE

THE GOLDEN BELL PRESS
DENVER, COLORADO

To
M. Y. M.
who lived this story

CONTENTS

CONTENTS

WAGON WHEELS
TO DENVER

I

Wheels West!

THIRTEEN-YEAR-OLD Marian Blane, dressed in the full skirt and tight basque of the fashion of 1871, stood on the plank walk before a Leavenworth hotel. She stared unhappily at the busy main street of the oldest town in Kansas.

The hot June sun shone on the ruffles and tilted hats of the women, gay splashes of color among the black broadcloth, somber wide hats and occasional buckskin garments of the men, over the sweating wagon teams, the rattling carriages and the stone and frame buildings across the way. The air was heavy with dust and the smell of horses and creaking leather. Already the sun

11

was high overhead and yet Father and Doctor Frank had not arrived with the camping outfit. Not that their delay mattered to Marian. She cared little when they started on the last lap of their journey West. She blinked back two nagging tears.

"See 'em, Marian?" cried Russell, her six-year-old brother, thrusting an eager brown head through the hotel doorway for the tenth time in that many minutes.

"No-o!" Marian faltered, pulling herself back from the ache of her thoughts.

"Why don't Father come? What's he doin'?" Russell questioned impatiently, running to join her.

"Goodness knows!"

Russell's dark eyes searched up and down the crowded thoroughfare. "He said he'd be right back. Didn't he?" The boy turned disappointed eyes to his sister. "Mummy says . . . What you cryin' for?"

"I'm no-ot!"

"You are too! I saw you Don't you want to go to Colorado? Don't you?" His fingers tugged at her flannel sleeve.

"No!" Marian answered.

She avoided the surprise in the snub-nosed face. No one understood—no one, least of all Russell!

Through the hotel window she could see her mother sitting wearily upon their sole-leather trunk. In spite of her high color, her face had a pinched look and there were shadowy half moons beneath her blue eyes. Mother didn't look quite herself in that practical flannel dress and plain traveling hat with her heavy brown hair drawn severely into a not in back. Somehow Marian missed her mother's ruffled silks and fringed capes. She seemed like everything else, since they had left Chicago, different— strangely different.

Marian had not wanted to come on the trip in the first place. However, old Doctor Wright had recommended the high dry air of Colorado Territory for Mother. He had advised them to make the journey slowly by wagon instead of by the Kansas Pacific Railroad which had been completed to Denver in September. Besides, he had told them, they would not feel the climb to the high elevation so much and it would be cheaper and far more healthful for Mother. He suggested that young Doctor Frank, his son, go with them. A new country was a good place, he thought, to start a medical practice.

Fortunately Mr. Blane was able to sell his hardware business and rent their comfortable, vine-covered home before the day set to leave. On the first of June the Blanes, accompanied by Doctor Frank, with Chase, Marian's Newfoundland dog tied in the baggage car, left Chicago for Leavenworth where they were to journey in wagons to Colorado.

Marian had been close to tears many times on that long train ride. The fact that she had never ridden on a train before failed to make her forget all that she was leaving.

It had been hardest of all to leave her best friend,

Lizzie Singleton. Saying good-bye to Lizzie had been worse than leaving Grandmother or Aunt Lily, even worse than parting with her own marble bust of Clytie, which she had proudly won at the Fair for disabled war soldiers; to say nothing of her tiny dolls, Lily and John. To be sure she didn't play with dolls any more, but these two were as much a part of her as the little vacant place between her upper front teeth. She loved them for their daintiness and their association with Lizzie. Clytie had to be left behind, but on the last day when no one was looking, Marian wedged the dolls and their set of furniture down in the trunk under the money box. After all, they were the only treasures small enough to take. They would always bring Lizzie and Chicago very near.

Marian became aware of Russell swaggering restlessly back and forth before her. At any other time his self-conscious pride in his new toy pistol slung man-fashion from the wide Morocco belt of his long blouse would have amused her. Russell felt so grown up since they had started on this journey.

"Do you see them yet?" It was Mother's voice calling from the doorway.

"No, Mother."

"But where can they be?" cried Mrs. Blane, as she joined the children. "We should have started ages ago." She turned her eyes to Marian. "Mercy, child! Don't look so solemn! Probably Doctor Frank's met a friend. You know how he is. I believe if he were on a desert

14

island, he'd meet someone he knew.'' Mother laughed. It was a standing joke now how frequently the young doctor ran into friends and acquaintances. Hadn't he met two friends on the train and a fellow student whom he had known at medical school that year, right here in Leavenworth?

Suddenly Russell cried out, ''Mummy! Look! Father's comin'!'' He jumped up and down in excitement.

Marian's quick glance followed her brother's pointing finger. A mule-drawn covered wagon, with a calico pony tied to the rear, lurched around the corner, followed by a shiny flat-topped carriage also drawn by sleek brown mules.

''Hurrah! Hurrah! They're here! They're here!'' Russell sing-songed happily. ''And looky!'' he shouted with the next breath. ''There's two wagons followin' 'em.''

The next minute the Blane wagon lumbered up, and red-headed Doctor Frank, who always grinned instead of smiled, pulled up the mules with a flourish and leaped to the ground. A large, curly black dog bounded after him and barked joyously at Marian. She knew Chase was trying to tell her how glad he was to be untied at last. She hugged him close.

''Bet you're all tired of waiting,'' the flushed young doctor apologized, ''but we met some people over at the blacksmith's who're going to Colorado. Mr. Blane thought it would be a good idea if we joined forces. They hadn't planned to leave until tomorrow, so we helped them pack up.''

"We did wonder what had become of you, Frank. But I was sure you'd met someone!'' Mother suppressed a smile as she gathered up her trailing skirts and stepped daintily toward the carriage.

Slowly Marian followed her mother. She stared at the two wagons which had pulled up directly behind their outfit. For the first time that day there was a flicker of interest in her corn-flower-blue eyes. However, she was unable to see who sat in the second wagon and there was but one occupant in the first, a soiled-shirted, red-faced man whose wide hat moved up and down to the rhythm of his jaws. Marian repressed a shudder and looked away.

Russell had already dashed to the carriage from which Mr. Blane had descended. Father looked almost a stranger in his new calfskin boots, buckskin trousers and dark flannel shirt as he towered above Marian, until she met the comforting brown of his eyes which could twinkle so unexpectedly in his grave face.

"Climb in, Russell,'' Father directed as he turned to Mother and swept off his dark camping hat in the way he reserved for her only. Just as if she were a queen, Marian always thought. "Sorry we kept you waiting,'' he said gently, helping Mother into the rear seat.

"Wait a minute!'' Father said. "Here're the Coopers now! I want you all to meet them.''

Marian turned quickly and confronted a man who would have made two of Father. Mr. Cooper had a jolly face with a great curly beard spread fan-wise across his enormous chest. His hairy hands felt rough and cal loused when she timidly shook hands.

Mrs. Cooper was a motherly bundle of dark calico, and her hair, in back, was braided rug-fashion. Her round face was a glow of kindness as she greeted Marian and beamed sympathetically at Mother.

"And this is Virginia Cooper," Father introduced.

"How-do-you-do," Marian murmured politely, unable to take her eyes from the girl's hat which resembled a pancake with streamers.

"Hello," Virginia giggled, staring in her turn.

Virginia was older, fifteen at least, Marian decided. Her dress of gray flannel hung unbecomingly from her shoulders, and the waist line sagged about her thin hips. Evidently Virginia was expected to grow. Her straight hair, the color of flax, framed a pointed white face and eyes the gray-green of Lake Michigan in a storm.

Suddenly Marian remembered her manners. She had been staring rudely. Flushing, she asked, "Are—are you glad to be going West?"

"Land, yes! I think it's going to be terribly exciting! Don't you?" Virginia smiled. Marian decided that she liked her better. She had a nice smile.

"No, I hate it!" Marian confided.

"You do! Well, of course I guess it'll be scary sometimes. I've read and heard about such terrible things happening to folks going West. You know, horse thieves and outlaws and dreadful Indian massacres.''

Marian's eyes widened. ''But—but Father says it's safer now. Besides we're going to follow the railroad. Surely . . .''

''Well, I hope so!'' Virginia broke in. ''But I bet a button we have a time getting there!'' Then she added mysteriously, ''I'll tell you some stories that'll give you goose flesh!''

''Honest? Oh, but if they're true ones I don't believe . . .''

''True! Of course they're true. Pa says so!'' Virginia interrupted. ''Why, just last year the Indians . . .'' she broke off suddenly. She had discovered Gypsy, the shaggy-hoofed, calico pony, which Father had purchased the day before with the rest of the camp outfit. ''Is that your own pony?''

''Yes—that is—she will be when I'm not afraid to ride her,'' answered Marian.

''Afraid! Good land! Don't you know how to ride?'' ''N-no!''

''Well, forevermore! Why, I ride Rusty all the time. I'll show you! It's as easy as that!'' Virginia snapped her fingers.

Marian decided that Virginia, in spite of her awkward clothes, thought herself a very superior young person. She didn't believe she was going to like her very well.

18

WHEELS WEST!

Mr. Cooper's hearty voice interrupted her thoughts. He was saying, "And I expect 'twould be an idea to camp hard by some farm-house. They're sure to have milk and butter. We'll follow you folks, Blane. Come along, Mom! Come, Virginia!"

"Good-bye! See you in camp!" said Virginia, hastening after her mother.

In the meantime a crowd of onlookers had gathered about the wagons. Under their curious stares, Marian felt as conspicuous as if she were in a circus parade. She was relieved when the porter carried out the trunk and they were ready to start.

"All ready! Go ahead!" Father shouted to Doctor Frank in the wagon. He clucked at the demure looking Dinah and Toby. Presently they left the Missouri River and the business section far behind and rattled along an avenue of shady trees.

Marian sat very still. She was thinking of this strange girl, Virginia, and her terrifying words. She recalled Russell's innumerable questions on the train about Indians and the life out West. At the time she had failed to be interested or heed the answers.

"Father," she broke out suddenly, "is it going to be scary going West? Will we really meet outlaws and Indians?"

"I hardly think likely. You see, Marian, we'll follow the Kansas Pacific and there'll be farms near by and later plenty of forts. Besides we have the Coopers and

19

their driver, Casper. I may pick up a man myself if I can find one who'll go for his board. It might be a good idea to have someone along who knows the roads. But we'll get along. Don't worry, child.''

Father was such a comforting sort of person, Marian thought. Somewhat relieved, she settled back in the seat and tried to imagine what camp life would be like. Presently they passed a group of soldiers in dusty blue, cantering toward Fort Leavenworth, which Father had pointed out to Marian the day before.

"Marian," Father said, lowering his voice and turning his gaze from the soldiers to her questioning face, "now that Mother is frail, you must be my little soldier. You must be brave and take what comes with head and shoulders up like those soldiers there. You must obey orders and never mutiny and take care of Mother and little Russell.'' He fondled one of her curls and gently pinched her cheek where that funny shadowy crease lay that Mother called a dimple. "How about it?''

"I—I'll try, Father!'' Marian promised solemnly. She squeezed his hard palm with her soft fingers and then looked quickly away to hide the sudden tears that stung her eyes. She thought of her mother, so strangely frail now. Oh, she would try hard to be a good soldier. Her blurred glance met the velvety eyes of her dog trotting beside the carriage. Chase wagged his tail as if he understood how hard that promise was going to be.

The travelers made camp that evening beside a tree-

lined stream not far from a neat farm-house. It felt good
to Marian to stretch her weary legs after the long tire-
some ride. Helplessly, she watched her father and Doctor
Frank unload the wagon. Russell scampered back and
forth asking questions. Further down the stream the
Coopers were putting up their tents and she could see
Virginia bustling about camp. Before the Blanes had
set up their sheet-iron stove, the smell of frying potatoes
floated over from the other camp.

"Come, Marian! Work to do!" called Father kindly.
"Give Frank a hand with supper. It'll be dark before
we know it." He led away Baby and Buck, the wagon
mules, to where the rest of the animals were picketed.

"You peel the potatoes, little lady, and unpack the
dishes," Doctor Frank directed from where he knelt
building a fire in the stove. "And you, Russie, hunt for
some more wood."

Awkwardly, Marian tackled the potatoes until there
was a small pan full, and a decidedly larger one overflowing with very thick peelings.

"Never mind!" consoled the young man at her look of
chagrin when he teased her about the amount of potatoes
she handed him. "You can do a better job next time.
I'll sharpen that knife."

"Oh, don't!" Marian protested. "I've already cut
myself once on the horrid old thing!"

Nursing her cut thumb she slowly unpacked the dishes.
Soon the smell of boiling coffee and the cheerful sputter-

ing of frying potatoes flavored the air. Marian realized suddenly that she was hungry. Perhaps it was going to be like a picnic after all, she thought, as she set down the last shiny new tin cup and plate on a cot near by.

"We would better use that cot for a table," Mother suggested, from her camp chair. "You'll find the table-cloth and napkins in the top tray of the trunk, Marian."

The dried beef was bubbling in its creamy sauce, the potatoes were browned to a turn and yet Father had not succeeded in putting up the square, fourteen-foot tent.

"Confound this contraption!" Father stormed at the yards of canvas. "Never dreamed it was such a job to put up a tent!" he muttered.

"Better have some supper first, William," Mother advised, smiling. "Then we'll help you on your 'confounded contraption,' as you call it."

Shortly they were seated about the clean tablecloth. Mother, Russell and Marian sat on the camp chairs and the men sat Turkish-fashion on the ground. Marian ate as hungrily as the rest. She was surprised how delightfully different it tasted from suppers at home—all but the plum preserves that Tillie, their cook, had insisted they bring. The preserves recalled Chicago, and Tillie queening it over the big Stewart range in the kitchen.

When they had finished, Father turned to Marian. "Now your job will be the dishes. If Doctor's to cook, it's only fair that you do them. Russell can be wood boy and general roustabout." Father leaped to his feet and

22

marched toward the tent. "Frank, you'd better give me a hand," he called over his shoulder.

Marian looked at the tin dishes on which the remains of cream sauce stuck like graying paste, at the grease-caked frying-pan and the boiled-over crust on the coffee-pot. She made a wry face.

Marian slowly rolled up her sleeves and tied a big apron of her mother's about her waist with a jerk. She set to work. Chase followed her back and forth, eagerly catching the scraps that she tossed him.

The water scorched her tender hands and then became too cool as she impatiently added more from the drinking bucket. Worst of all, the teakettle was empty now! The soap refused to lather, the water felt horrid, so did her hands. So absorbed was she that she failed to notice the overcast sky or the trees swaying beside the stream. Impatiently she pushed back her wind-blown curls and fastened them behind her ears with her round comb. She wished dishes weren't her job. She hated them! Mentally she counted up—three times a day for two months —why, that would be one hundred and eighty meals, and if it took them longer . . .

"For land sakes! Are you still doing dishes?" cried Virginia running to join her. "Hurry up, slow poke! I came over to tell you those stories I promised."

"I'm nearly through. Don't you hate dishes?"

"Sort of. But I've always done them back in Ohio.

23

If you think that's many you ought to see the mountains of 'em we have at harvesting time!''

"But it isn't so much the number, it's the feel!'' Marian complained. "Just look what those pots did to my hands! I'll never get that old black and grease off!'' she added in despair holding up her hands for Virginia's inspection.

"Why don't you try soap?'' Virginia suggested, perching herself on the water cask.

Marian stifled a quick retort. Hurriedly she put away the dishes.

Virginia watched her a moment in silence. "What did you bring along to amuse yourself?'' she asked, when Marian had straightened up from the dish box, and was smoothing back her tumbled curls.

"Oh some books, *'Nelly's Dark Days,'* and one of the *Juno* books, and that one that came out last year, *'An Old Fashioned Girl.'* And games of course.'' But of the dolls, Lily and John, Marian said nothing. After all, she told herself, she had only brought them along to comfort her when she was lonely. It had been a long time since she had really played with them in Lizzie's doll house. Somehow she felt Virginia would laugh if she knew. Only Russell understood about her feeling for them.

Marian turned away and picked up the table-cloth and shook it vigorously.

"Oh—do you use table-cloths—camping?'' Virginia asked in amazement.

24

"Why, of course! Mother says it's no use to act like savages even if we are going to a wild country."

Virginia flushed. She looked up at the darkened sky. "Goodness!" she cried suddenly. "It's going to rain this minute! Feel it? I'd better run back!"

As Virginia darted away, Marian glanced up. The sky was heavy with angry clouds. Whirls of dust danced toward her and whipped her skirts about her legs. Apprehensively she glanced at her father and Doctor Frank. They were struggling with the tent which the wind flapped playfully from their clutching hands.

The next instant the rain pelted them with giant drops. Father dropped his end of the canvas and ran toward her, shouting, "Quick! Hustle to the wagon "

Marian dropped the table-cloth and grabbed Russell who was playing beside the carriage. Quickly they scrambled into the wagon and wedged themselves down between the saddles, trunk and bedding.

In these uncomfortable quarters there was barely space for Mother and Marian and Russell, so the men protected themselves as best they could under a blanket on the high seat. Chase whined pitifully outside until Marian pleaded with her father to pull him up in front.

Presently the rain became a steady patter-patter upon their canvas roof. Already Marian's legs prickled with sleep. She longed to stretch them. Achingly she tried to slap them awake.

"Do you suppose we'll have to stay here all night?" she asked in exasperation.

"I'm afraid so," Mother answered. "But we're dry and that's more than the cots are. I don't believe we'll use night dresses tonight," she added ruefully.

When the storm had spent itself, Mr. Blane shoved the saddles and trunk out into the rain-soaked night. With this added room, Mother and the children lay down among the wadded quilts and blankets. Marian was grateful for the darkness that hid her misty eyes.

So this was camping! Well, now she knew she hated it!

Rain-soaked canvas, puddle-filled camp chairs, soggy bread and no dry wood greeted the bedraggled Blanes the next morning. To be sure the world about them was a freshly washed green and the sun smiled warmly. But no one noticed, least of all Marian. It had been her fault that the food box had been left open, the bread ruined. She felt heavy-eyed and just one hopeless wrinkle as she assisted Russell in scrubbing his hands in the muddy stream. With a grimace at the riled water she made her own sketchy toilet, watched from across the water by two solemn-eyed cows. Unnoticed a meadow-lark trilled sweetly from a leafy branch above.

With dry wood and bread borrowed from the obliging Coopers, breakfast was finally ready. But the sun was hot overhead before their belongings were dry and the wagon packed.

As Marian helped her father shove in the last cot, he

nodded toward the Coopers who had been packed and ready to start for some time. "Pshaw! I think we need a man like Casper! We're greenhorns. Just plain greenhorns at this camp life. I'm going to get that driver before I do another thing!"

"Oh do, Father!" cried Marian. Perhaps this hired man could do the dishes, she thought hopefully. Hadn't she seen Casper help with the Coopers' pots and pans that very morning?

However, two weeks slipped by and the Blanes found no driver. Days of jogging slow miles over rutted roads. Days of travel through rolling, wooded country along shallow streams. Days of mired down wagons, aching muscles and heavy-eyed exhaustion at night beneath a flapping tent. They passed through Topeka, Manhattan and Fort Riley. And then at Junction City, the Blanes discovered Jake. Or, rather, Jake discovered them.

Marian saw the man first. The girls were sitting in the carriage before a two-story frame hotel. They were waiting for the men to return with supplies. Across the wide dusty street a group of idlers had gathered in the shade of a false-fronted store, below a swaying Lager Beer sign. Suddenly a giant of a man in a wide tattered hat pushed his enormous shoulders through the group. Marian stared round-eyed at the six-shooter slung at his hip.

"Look!" she whispered to Virginia.

The man sauntered over past the Cooper wagons where

27

Mother and Russell were visiting with Mrs. Cooper. Still appraising the outfit, the man turned back and swaggered straight toward the girls, flicking at his dusty boots with a blacksnake whip.

It was the longest, blackest whip that Marian had ever seen. As he came nearer, she wondered if it was the wide black hat which made his eyes so small and narrow by comparison, or the jagged white scar through one drooping eyebrow.

"Why, he looks just like a walrus!" Marian whispered delightedly, noticing the dark droop of his mustache which partly hid his lips.

"Sh-h! He'll hear you! But he does, at that," Virginia giggled.

"Whar ya bound, gals?" The harsh voice made Marian jump. Chase growled, as the man leaned his powerful arms on the dashboard.

"Colorado," Virginia spoke up.

"Ain't that funny, so'm I!" The man's narrow gaze traveled over the carriage, then discovered Gypsy hitched to the rear.

"M'name's Jake Wolf. Need a driver?"

"Why . . ." Marian began.

"Of course you do!" cried Virginia. "Your father's been looking . . ."

"Fine!" broke in the man. "Maybe I'd do. Think so, gal?" The narrow black eyes were appraising Marian.

28

"But Father wants someone who's been to Colorado and knows the roads," Marian answered doubtfully.

"Know them trails! I was brung up on 'em! Been a skinner since I was no bigger'n you!"

"Skinner!" Marian echoed.

"You mean a buffalo skinner, don't you?" asked Virginia importantly.

"Ain't saying I don't. But now—I'm a mule skinner to the likes o' ya!"

Just then William Blane, heavily laiden with bundles, emerged from the store.

"There's Father now!" cried Marian. "You'd better talk to him."

Jake strode across the sun-baked dirt path. Marian failed to catch their words until Father wheeled sharply and reëntered the store, followed by Jake calling in his boastful voice, "Ask the bar-keep yonder. Ask the store-keeper. Ask anybody 'round these parts who Jake Wolf is!"

Just then Mother and Russell joined the girls. Marian and Virginia told them with much excitement about Jake Wolf, buffalo skinner.

Russell was wide-eyed. "Maybe he'll catch me a big buffalo," he suggested hopefully.

"Won't you be glad if your father hires him?" Virginia asked Marian presently.

"Well—ye-es. At least he looks powerfully strong and —and maybe we'll need someone like that when we get

29

really on the plains." Marian was thinking of Virginia's stories. "But I'd never ask him to do the dishes in a million years. No sir! Never!"

Virginia giggled. "Land, no! Jake looks handier with a gun than a dish-rag, I'm thinking."

A contemptuous snort startled the girls. They looked up quickly. Unnoticed, Jake and the others had joined them.

"Oh, he heard!" Marian breathed, flushing.

With Doctor Frank riding Gypsy and Jake driving the wagon, they were shortly ready to continue their journey.

"Wish you'd try to ride, Marian," Virginia pouted, guiding Rusty to her usual place beside the carriage. "It's lots of fun really!"

Crack!

Marian jumped and turned quickly around. Crack! Again Jake's long whip cut the air and whirled above the mules' twitching ears. White-nosed Baby and skittish Buck leaped in surprise, then sprang through the startled idlers, carrying the lurching wagon into the lead—West!

II

Sounds in the Dark

It was not until the travelers had reached Abilene that Marian became really afraid.

She sat in the rear seat of the carriage staring round-eyed at the strange scene about her. Cowboys wearing low-crowned Mexican hats, gay handkerchiefs, six-shooters and jingling spurs, rode past. Evil-appearing Mexican riders mingled with ox- and mule-drawn wagons along the crowded street. Rough looking plainsmen idled about the plank sidewalks in front of the stores. Hard-faced men swaggered into frame buildings from which came the sour smell of beer.

The crack of whips cut the sultry air above the rattle of wheels and the dust-muffled thud of Indian ponies. Cattle bellowed from the corrals along the railroad.

"Jiminy!" Marian gasped to Virginia who had suddenly crowded Rusty closer to the carriage to avoid two galloping riders. "Did you ever see so many guns? And such wicked looking Mexicans!" Marian shuddered.

"Looks like we're really getting West!" Virginia answered delightedly.

"I don't see Injuns!" Russell complained. "Where's the Injuns? Hidin'?"

"Thank goodness we don't see any Indians!" Marian cried. "I know I won't sleep a wink tonight anyway" She shivered and withdrew her eyes from a swarthy face leering from a doorway. She noticed that even Mother had drawn closer to Father.

Since leaving Junction City, two days before, the party had traveled up the Smoky Hill Fork of the Kansas River. The country was less rolling and the farms farther apart. All morning a hot dry wind had swept their faces. Marian hoped they'd find a nice cool place to camp, and far enough from Abilene.

Virginia galloped ahead to join Doctor Frank. In the late afternoon the two of them often rode in front of the wagons to keep a sharp lookout for desirable camp spots.

Marian, watching her, felt a wave of envy sweep over her. Virginia was so at home on Rusty, so sure of herself anywhere, for that matter. She wished that she wasn't such a ninny about Gypsy, but she had never forgotten that one time she had tried to ride her pony. She had been terror-stricken, when with only one foot in the stirrup, Gypsy had started off. She had dangled there, clinging wildly to her side-saddle and screaming, "Stop her! Stop her! She's running away!" Nor had she forgotten Virginia's amused remark after she had rescued Marian. "She wasn't running away, silly! Gypsy's used to a rider swinging up quickly and starting right off." Marian flushed at the memory of it.

Gradually she had grown rather fond of the frisky pony. Often she longed to pat her silky nose and talk to her as she did to Chase. But the restless shaggy hoofs and wiggling calico body kept her at a distance. However, her hand often strayed over the new leather of the side-saddle packed away in the wagon. It reminded her of those she had seen in Lincoln Park and of the lovely ladies in their trailing riding habits cantering beneath the trees.

Russell interrupted her thoughts. "Wish Virginia would come back!"

"I suppose you want some more wild stories Don't you ever get tired of them?"

"No! I like 'em better than *Rollo* books!"

"Well, then don't always be after me to read them to you. But I certainly don't like to hear such scary tales! Bloody scalps! Ugh! Such stories give me shivers."

"Let's play with Lily and John tonight an' have Injuns chase 'em an' my soldiers save 'em," her brother suggested eagerly.

"Let's," Marian agreed. After all it wasn't so much the dolls themselves, or amusing Russell, that led her occasionally to play secretly with them in the shelter of the wagon. It was for the fun of imagining. It made her forget where she was and how very far away was Chicago. But there was always the danger of being caught. Virginia would think her a terrible baby if she ever found her playing with dolls!

Just then Virginia raced her pony back to tell them there was no farm in sight, but that there was a shady camp spot up the road.

The carriage and wagons drew off the trail. Father helped Mother down, and Marian ran for her camp chair and set it up under a tree away from the bustling activity about the wagon.

Things moved like an army camp since Father had hired Jake. Now the tent was up in a jiffy and the mules and Gypsy were staked out to graze. Doctor Frank, who had mastered the sheet-iron stove so that it no longer burned biscuits but browned them, had dinner ready in no time. Marian set the tent to rights and made up Mother's and Russell's cots. Her own was still used for a dining table until bedtime. Then she unpacked the dish box, set the table and peeled the potatoes.

When supper was over, Marian hurried through the dishes and put the remaining quail, which Jake had shot the day before, with the apple sauce and cold biscuits, into the food box. Then she made up her cot and ran to the wagon and hopped in, calling impatiently, "Hurry up, Russie!"

SOUNDS IN THE DARK

"Let's play John's a cowboy," Russell said, clambering up and over the seat, carrying his box of soldiers.

"All right," Marian smiled, "but hurry. Virginia might come over any minute, so don't let's bother to get the feed boxes tonight."

When not in use, the mules' feed boxes became the dolls' house. Marian's imagination endowed them with all the elegance of a brownstone front.

Sitting cross-legged on the wagon floor, Marian pulled the dolls from their hiding place in the trunk.

Lily was a fair, china-headed doll with a waterfall of real hair caught up in a net like Mrs. Blane's own. Her Paisley dress had a train and she wore a tiny blue cashmere cape about her shoulders. Rosy-cheeked John was as dark as Lily was fair, and was dressed in black broadcloth with coat tails. It would take a great deal of imagination to pretend that John was a cowboy, Marian thought, smiling. He looked more like a fashion plate.

While Russell arranged his soldiers, Marian carefully laid out Lily's plaid silk and poplin dresses. Just as she lifted out the little set of upholstered bamboo furniture with its curved back chairs and low sofa, Virginia stuck an inquisitive head through the canvas opening.

"Forevermore! What are you doing?"

"Why—why——" began Marian, flushing.

Virginia swung into the wagon and dropped down beside Marian. "Aren't they the cunningest?" she cried, picking up John and examining his tucked white shirt, high cravat, and elegant long coat tails.

"I thought—I didn't suppose——" Marian continued.

"But I've never seen such teeny dolls or such pretty clothes!" Virginia cried, fingering Lily's dresses admiringly. "She looks just like the fine ladies in Godey's *'Lady Book.'* Why didn't you tell me about these dolls, you old meany?"

"Well, you see, I just brought them because they're little and there wasn't room for anything else. Lizzie, my best friend, and I used to have such fun with them in her beautiful doll house when we were—were small. I thought they might——" Marian broke off.

"I never liked dolls much except an old wax one I had. But then I never had a doll house. Tell me about Lizzie's."

Marian's face brightened. "Oh, Virginia, you ought to see it! It's the most wonderful house that's ever been made. Lizzie's father won it at the Fair for disabled Civil War soldiers. It has three floors and a real little bath in the attic. Lizzie and I used to stand on a hassock and pour water through a tiny funnel in the roof and then turn on the taps in the bathtub."

"Land sakes! A bathtub in a doll's house Why even most folks don't have them," Virginia exclaimed.

"Well, Aunt Lily does! And the Palmer House has lots of them! Father was going to put one in our house soon as times got better."

"Good land! I've never even seen one! We used wash-tubs!"

"And just think!" went on Marian, her eyes aglow with memories. "There were teeny dishes and real little leather books in the library with engravings and writing in them and . . ."

"Let's play!" Russell interrupted crossly. "You said . . ."

But at that moment, Doctor Frank stuck his head in and called, "Say, you three! Don't you know it's bed-time and blowing fit to take your hair off! Your mother has called you twice, Virginia."

It was not until Marian lay under her log cabin quilt, that she recalled those fierce looking Mexicans in Abilene. The wind shrieked outside and lashed the tent fly, like the crack of Jake's long black whip.

Fearfully she glanced up at the billowing canvas above her. Tents were flimsy houses when it blew.

Chase had stealthily crept up on her cot after her parents had fallen asleep. Marian hugged him hard. "You're so comfy!" she whispered into a long silky ear. In spite of her cramped position, she loved having him there.

My, how the wind moaned! It sounded alive—like a woman crying!

She closed her eyes tight to shut out the inky shadows and the flapping canvass above her head. Her longing thoughts drew pictures before her closed eyelids, pictures of her own little bed at home, cool with sheets and so comfortable and safe. If only she were there!

Lately the men had taken turns guarding the animals. It would soon be time for the men to change guard, she told herself. She listened anxiously for some comforting human noise outside the tent. However, only strange night sounds fluttering about in the dark, and the crying wind, answered her.

At length the wind died down. Just a murmur in the trees and the swish of prairie grass remained. Now she could hear her father's heavy breathing from where he lay rolled in a blanket near the threshold. From her mother came a sigh. The horses and mules stamped restlessly.

Something moved stealthily outside. A twig snapped. Marian held her breath. Was that Jake changing guard with Doctor Frank? However, there was no low talking, no fragrant odor of tobacco from the doctor's pipe. Silence followed. Even the murmuring in the trees was hushed as if they, too, were listening.

A stone rattled, followed by a stealthy footfall.

Suddenly there was an uneasy movement among the animals picketed some distance from the tent. Someone strange was out there. Someone was creeping up to the frightened animals. Marian felt Chase stiffen and a low growl rumbled in his throat.

Virginia's tales of horse thieves preying on helpless travelers swept through her mind.

SOUNDS IN THE DARK

She wanted to cry out, warn her father—awaken the camp. But she was too paralyzed with fear to make a sound.

At last she managed a hoarse whisper. "Father!" There was no answer from the dark form lying near the tent fly. Trembling, she tried again, "Father!"

At that moment, Chase leaped off the cot and flew like an angry black bear out into the night, barking furiously.

The roar of a gun shattered the air. The next instant, Mr. Blane leaped to his feet and snatched up his revolver.

"William!" screamed Mother, sitting up suddenly. "What's the matter?"

"Oh, Father!" Marian shrieked. "Don't go out there! Someone's . . ."

"Stay quiet! Don't make a sound!" Father commanded. He thrust back the flap and ran out after Chase.

Through the tent opening, Marian saw the dark figures of Doctor Frank and Jake rolling from under the ghostly outlines of the wagon. She hear Jake shouting as they ran. A revolver barked in the direction in which her father had disappeared, then another.

"Marian! What has happened?" came her mother's frightened whisper. Marian dived out of bed, and the next minute she was held tightly in her mother's arms.

"I—I don't know," Marian chattered against the comforting woolly wrapper. "Maybe it's horse thieves or—or Mexicans. Maybe it's Indians!"

"Horse thieves! Indians!" cried her mother. "Oh, what'll we do?"

"Marian!" came a scared little voice muffled in quilts. "Is it Injuns—honest?"

"I don't know," Marian shivered. "Listen!"

Just then Mr. Cooper with shirt tails out lumbered past, followed by Casper.

A moment later Virginia and her mother rushed into the tent and Virginia cried in a stage whisper, "Mrs. Blane . . . Marian! Are you all right? Isn't it awful? Aren't you scared out of your wits?"

Mrs. Cooper and Virginia sank breathlessly beside Marian. "Mercy-on-us!" cried Virginia's mother. "Who'd have thought folks would have such goings on this far East!"

They huddled close, listening. Now Chase could be heard barking above the crack of guns and the rat-tat of horses galloping toward Abilene.

"What do you suppose is happening?" cried Marian.

"Let's peek out and see," Virginia suggested, although her voice shook a little.

The girls crept to the tent opening. They could see several indistinct figures running down the road shooting at the fleeing horsemen.

"Oh, I hope Father is safe, and everybody," Marian whispered, clinging to Virignia.

"They will be," Virginia consoled her. "But I suppose we'll have to turn back if our mules are stolen."

SOUNDS IN THE DARK

"If we only would! I hate this awful life, this scary old country! And if—if Father's hurt, I'll hate it worse than ever!" Marian was sobbing now.

"Listen! The men are coming back!" cried Virginia. "Come on! Let's run to meet them."

Forgetting their stocking feet, the girls dashed toward the approaching men.

"Are you hurt, Father?" Marian called anxiously.

"None of us has a scratch!" Father answered. "Lucky old Chase woke us up! In another minute those robbers would've stolen the horses and mules."

"Then they didn't get Gypsy? Oh, I'm so glad!" For suddenly she realized that she would have cared a lot if Gypsy had been taken. After all, Gypsy was her pony. "I'm so thankful you're safe—and everybody!" she added, hugging Father about the waist, glad that the darkness hid her tear-stained face.

Then suddenly she had a dreadful thought. "But Chase! Where's Chase?"

"Chase!" her father repeated. "Why, I don't know. Frank, have you seen him?"

"Last I saw of him he was running the horse thieves home," the doctor answered, as he lit a lantern.

"Look!" cried Virginia, pointing to a large black shadow which limped within the circle of the lantern's glow.

"Chase! You're hurt!" Marian ran to the dog. She knelt and drew his panting body close. "They've shot you!" she sobbed. "Doctor Frank, come quick!"

41

"Don't cry! Don't feel so badly!" Father patted Marian's head. "Frank'll fix him up."

"Come, Virginia," Mr. Cooper urged. "We'd better be getting Mom back to bed."

Virginia, who was kneeling beside Marian stroking the dog's curly head, jumped to her feet. Over her shoulder she called, " 'Night. I'll be over first thing in the morning to see how he is, Marian."

In the meantime Doctor Frank had been gently examining the dog. The lantern light shone on the young man's rumpled hair and his pale, freckled face.

"A bullet just grazed his paw, Marian," he reassured her. "Nothing serious! I'll fix him in a jiffy."

It took but a few minutes to dress the paw. Then between them Doctor Frank and Marian half carried Chase back to the tent.

"Put him here on the end of my cot, Doctor Frank. He mustn't be on the cold ground."

"There you are, old fellow," the young man said. Chase wagged his tail and put out a paw as if to say, "Thank you."

"Better hop in bed now. We mustn't keep your mother awake. Are you all right, Mrs. Blane?" Doctor Frank turned toward Mother's cot.

"Yes, Frank." Mother's voice sounded tired and faint. Marian felt conscience-stricken. She was always forgetting to be thoughtful, to watch over Mother. Tonight she hadn't thought of anything but her own fear and Chase!

SOUNDS IN THE DARK

Gently she bent over Mother and kissed her. "Goodnight!" she murmured.

"Is Chase hurt bad?" A small head peeked out from under the covers, as Marian started to blow out the light. "I want to see."

"No, Russie. He'll be all right. Go to sleep."

But after several restless moments, Marian tiptoed outside. "Father!" she called softly to Mr. Blane who was taking a last look about camp. "May I say goodnight to Gypsy?"

"Well, I suppose so—but hurry! We must get some sleep. After what happened tonight I want to start early tomorrow and get away from this part of the country."

Marian stumbled nervously through the dim starlight to where the pony was staked. "I'm glad they didn't get you, that you're safe," she whispered to Gypsy. "I'm going to prove to you how glad by—by not being so afraid to ride you any more." Suddenly she reached up and timidly patted the pony's shaggy mane.

To her surprise, Gypsy nickered and rubbed her shoulder with a cold, gentle nose.

"Ain't ya 'fraid to be here with them horse thieves out thar somewhar?"

Startled, Marian whirled about. A huge shadow moved toward her. "Oh!" she gasped, and flew like a scared rabbit toward the safety of canvas walls. A harsh laugh followed her.

But as she dived under her quilt she realized that it

was only Jake. How silly of her to be so nervous, she thought. However, she lay trembling for long minutes. What sort of a life was this going to be? What would happen next, she wondered over and over, until sleep at last closed her eyes. But it was a restless sleep, peopled with evil-eyed Mexicans who crept about her cot.

III

A Hero!

The dishes were scarcely emptied the next morning before Marian snatched them from under her family's surprised faces and began scouring them vigorously in the soapy dish water. Chase did his part by licking eagerly at the remains of mush sticking to the plates which Marian set down for him when no one was looking.

"What's the hurry?" Doctor Frank laughed as he turned back to his half-finished breakfast only to discover that his plate had vanished.

"Oh, I'm sorry!" cried Marian, flushing. "I thought you were through. Shall I get you some more eggs or mush?"

"No, thanks! But why are you in such a hurry? Don't tell me you've actually fallen in love with dish-washing?" the young man teased. He winked at Father.

"Course not!" Marian retorted with a toss of her curls. "But Father said last night that he wanted to get an early start and—and goodness knows I do!'' For in spite of the sunny peaceful world about her, the terror of the night before was still vivid in her mind.

"I'd better get to work, if that's the case," the doctor grinned.

While the men packed up and Mother brought out her knitting, Marian scowled at the boiled-over rings on the mush pan. Well, the old pot would have to do, she decided. She hoped Doctor Frank wouldn't notice. He had a habit of running an inquiring finger around the inside of pans.

The dishes put away, Marian knelt above the food box, the frowning line still between her eyebrows. They carried their lunch now. It saved time, and, best of all, it saved dishes. But often Marian longed for Tillie and her delicious picnic lunches. In fact she was sick of camp food and most of all the queer wild taste of game with which Jake supplied them since he had joined the party. Now that the preserves were gone and they had no store bread, it would have to be cold biscuits, milk and hard cooked eggs again! Unless—Marian ransacked the box. Presently she found the tinned fruit and vegetables that Aunt Lily had insisted they bring. In spite of the fact that she knew her mother would shake a doubtful head over any but home canned food, Marian decided to try some tinned peaches.

At last both families were packed and ready. For a time the drivers urged the mules rapidly, in order to put

A HERE!

as many miles as possible between them and Abilene.
Chase was privileged to ride in the Blane wagon on account of his paw, and so Marian and Virginia rode with
him.

At length Marian put down *"Nelly's Dark Days."* It
was much too hard to read against the jolt-jolting and
the dim light within the wagon. She glanced at Virginia
who sat cross-legged near the canvas opening in the rear.
Virginia's mouth was screwed to one side as she
struggled to pick up a dropped stitch in the gray sock
she was knitting.

There was a warm little feeling in Marian's heart for
this strange new friend with the awkward clothes and
the blunt manner. She knew it was because Virginia had
not laughed at her last night when she had caught Marian
playing dolls with Russell.

However, she wished Virginia would talk. But Virginia
made a silent business of knitting. Mrs. Cooper demand-
ed perfection in Mr. Cooper's socks. "And, land knows,
I don't want to have to take this all out like I did yesterday," Virginia had warned Marian into silence already
that morning.

Through the back of the wagon Marian could see the
flat-topped carriage, her father's black hat above his
short dark beard, and Mother's round blue straw pulled
down in front to shade her eyes. Russell was stretched
out on the rear seat asleep. Gypsy, she knew, was tied
behind, though she could only see the whirls of dust made

47

by her shaggy white hoofs. A turn in the road revealed the largest Cooper wagon, with red-faced Casper nodding over the slackened reins.

After passing the town of Solomon, the heat in the wagon became stifling. Beads of perspiration trickled down Marian's straight nose. Impatiently she pushed back her moist curls and fastened them behind her ears with her long rounded comb.

In order to forget the heat, Marian leaned back against the trunk and thought of Lizzie and the Singletons' cool brownstone house. Perhaps that very minute Lizzie was taking her music lesson in the vine-shaded parlor. Grandmother had promised to let Marian take lessons that winter. She wondered if they had music teachers in Colorado.

Dreamily, she watched Doctor Frank and Jake swaying on the high seat in front.

"Thar's the ferry whar we cross the Smoky Hill Fork," said Jake suddenly. "The old stream's sure high today. High as ever I seen it."

Marian sat up quickly. Jake was pointing with his long whip. She scrambled to her knees, balancing herself against the dog's panting body and the heaped-up bedding.

Just ahead, the hurrying freshness of the river gleamed through low willows. "Look, Virginia!" she directed. "There's a log raft. Do you suppose we'll have to cross over on that thing?"

A HERO!

Virginia followed the direction of Marian's finger. "Course not! There must be a real ferry somewhere," she insisted.

"Git us across?" Jake asked as the wagon squeaked to a halt before two rough, bearded men who appeared from a sod house beside the river's edge.

"Waal, I guess maybe," answered the taller of the two as he spat a stream of tobacco juice through broken yellow teeth. "It's purty high. Have to haul ya over one at a time."

"All out, girls!" called Doctor Frank, leaping to the ground. He stuck his head back into the wagon and grinned. "Hurry! The ferry's about to shove off!"

Marian and Virginia, followed by Chase, scrambled over the boxes and bedding, and crawled over the seat. Quickly the girls slid to the ground beside the doctor, and gazed about them with interest. However, there was no boat in sight on the swollen river. Just the tippy-looking raft which rose and fell below them.

The carriage and the other wagons arrived in the meantime, and lined up waiting their turn. Marian watched Jake whip up the sturdy Buck and Baby, and the camp wagon lurched down to the water and the raft. Marian always flinched when Jake used his whip. She wondered if the sting of that whirling blacksnake skin didn't hurt the mules.

"I don't believe I'm going to like crossing on that raft," Virginia remarked. She was watching the Blane

49

wagon bob up and down on the water. Suddenly she clutched Marian's arm. "Look! The raft! It's being swept away!"

"Oh! Oh! What'll they do? How'll they ever stop it?" Marian cried, jumping up and down in her anxiety.

The two men were desperately poling the angry river. Jake leaned out of the wagon shouting orders. But the rushing water carried the raft further and further downstream. Those on shore watched breathlessly.

Just then Doctor Frank joined the children. Suddenly he shouted, "Look!"

The men had conquered the churning water, for gradually the raft swung about and slowly made for the shore with the men working frantically at their poles. Now the raft was almost across, and before the onlookers could do more than gasp their relief, the mules were straining every muscle to pull the swaying wagon up the bank.

The largest Cooper wagon left next with Doctor Frank and Casper. Strangely enough, this time the raft had no trouble in reaching the other side and was soon back for another load.

Father helped Mother into the small wagon with Mr. and Mrs. Cooper, and turned to the girls. "Virginia, you go along and Marian will come with me."

Soon Mother and the Coopers were safely across and from the opposite shore Virginia was waving her pancake hat. Mr. Cooper swung heavily to the ground and helped Mother and Mrs. Cooper descend from the wagon.

A HERO!

With Doctor Frank and Casper they watched the raft struggle across the stream once more.

After what seemed and interminable time the men arrived for the last load.

Toby and Dinah certainly were skittish. They shied at the water and at the raft. After three attempts Father finally succeeded in driving them aboard. Gingerly, Marian stepped on the uneven logs. Holding on to her brother with one hand and to Chase's collar with the other, she stood beside the carriage. She kept her eyes on her father who was holding the reins taut. Presently she relaxed somewhat. It was not as scary as she had expected. In fact, she rather liked the sound of the water slapping against the logs.

Marian waved gaily to the group watching them from across the river.

In the middle of the stream the current grew swifter. The raft tipped and Marian felt a flood of water splash across her feet. Suddenly Toby reared in fright and kicked Dinah. The carriage lunged and nearly slid overboard. Marian struggled to get out of the way, and, in doing so, she pulled at her brother. Russell stumbled back, lost his footing and went over the side and into the water.

Marian screamed, "Help! Russell!"

The next minute a black streak shot out from beside her and into the swirling water.

"Chase! Oh, Chase! Save him! Please!" she prayed to the black head bobbing up and down like a cork.

Russell disappeared!

"Father!" Marian shrieked.

Suddenly the boy's head appeared close to Chase. Russell's hands clawed the air.

In her fear for Russell, Marian was unconscious of the fact that her father had jumped to her side and, though he could not swim, was tearing his coat off. Her eyes never left Chase and her brother. Now the dog had hold of Russell's blouse and was swimming with him toward shore.

Like frozen images Marian and her father watched the dog struggle through the water. Once a huge wave washed over Chase and Russell. Marian shut her eyes tightly. When she opened them again Chase was swimming steadily with his limp burden, and she discovered that from the far bank Doctor Frank had leaped into the river. But, inspite of his frantic efforts to reach Russell, the doctor was swept down-stream. Marian lost sight of him. For what seemed hours, she stared at the curly black head of her dog and at the bit of blue blouse. Suddenly she gave a cry. Chase had made the shore!

"Oh, Father! He's saved Russie!"

Chase pulled himself out of the water and sank to the ground exhausted, while Mr. Cooper quickly lifted Russell and carried him up the bank and laid him down. Mother dropped to her knees beside the unconscious boy.

52

A HERO!

Mrs. Cooper hovered over them, silently wringing her hands.

The next minute Doctor Frank had reached the shore. Marian drew a long, shuddering breath.

"Hurry, men!" cried Father, watching the doctor work over Russell. "Hurry!"

Madly the men poled the river while Father went back to the now demure Toby and Dinah. The reins shook in his hands.

As soon as they reached the bank Marian rushed to her brother. "Is he . . . Is Russell all right?"

But Russell was sitting up! Water streamed down his funny snub nose. A scared, surprised look was in the eyes he turned toward the anxious group bending over him. "What you cryin' for, Mummy?" he asked in a queer little croak.

"Just because you're all right, I guess," Mother answered shakily, forcing a smile through her tears. She grabbed him, wet clothes and all, and hugged him close.

"Here, Mary," cried Father gently, "let him go. We must get those clothes off him right away!" He lifted the boy in his arms and strode toward the wagon followed by the dripping doctor.

"Mercy-on-us! What a scare!" Mrs. Cooper wiped her eyes on her apron. "Ezra Cooper," she nudged the big man, "start a fire going and I'll brew her some tea. I'm thinking she needs it!" Mrs. Cooper nodded toward Mother.

"Sure! You're plumb beat out, Mrs. Blane. And no wonder! I'll . . ." Mr. Cooper began.

"I should say not;" Mother was on her feet, her chin high. "We must move on! Why, you'd think I was a baby!" she exclaimed, smiling and forcing a gaiety which Marian was sure she did not feel. But then Mother was like that.

Mrs. Blane started to follow the Coopers. "Goodness!" she cried, stopping short. "Chase! We've forgotten all about our hero."

As if he had been waiting for some recognition, Chase bounded up and hurled himself toward them.

"Nice old fellow! I don't know what we'd do without you!" cried Mrs. Blane, caressing the dog's wet head.

Chase wiggled happily and ran to each one to be patted. Suddenly he shook himself, spraying them all with water.

"Go 'way! Shoo!" Mother cried, stepping back to avoid another shower bath.

Chase's head drooped; so did his tail.

"Beats all how he seems to know what you say to him," Mrs. Cooper said chuckling, and wiping the drops of water from her dress. "Land sakes! I don't know what we'd done without the rascal today, nor last night, when he woke the camp. We might none of us be going to Colorado now, 'cepting for Chase."

As Mother and Mr. and Mrs. Cooper turned away,

A HERO!

Marian hugged Chase and her eyes grew misty as she thought of what might have happened to Russell.

"Come on," Virginia urged, linking her arm through Marian's. They started toward the wagons. "I just knew that old raft would be dangerous. It was mighty lucky Chase was there, because Doctor Frank could never have reached Russell in time, and none of the rest of us can swim," she finished soberly.

"I'd 'a' saved him," Jake boasted, sauntering up, flipping his black whip against his boots. "But thar weren't no sense fer two of us gittin' wet."

"Oh, I'm sure you would have!" Virginia retorted, with a withering glance. "But it's lucky Chase didn't wait for you!"

Marian was watching Russell, who sat in the carriage wrapped in quilts, his eyes like burned holes in a scrap of white paper, and remained silent. Her hand tugged affectionately at the dog's thick ruff. Nor did she see the inscrutable smile on Jake's lips as she said, "So much has happened to us already, Virginia. I wonder if we will ever get to Colorado?"

IV

Gypsy Plays Her Part

That evening the Blanes and Coopers camped across from a lonely farm. A creek lost among the tall grass lay between them and the few acres of discouraged corn. Not far to the left was a deserted gypsum mine. The spring that bubbled near their camp had a hard bitter taste from its nearness to the mine. Even the soap refused to lather in its customary foamy whiteness when Marian did the supper dishes. But it was not the water that made her sigh.

"Jake told me they make plaster-of-paris out of that chalky stuff they used to take from the mine," Virginia commented at last, as she dried a plate for her friend.

But Marian barely heard her. Her worried eyes and thoughts were on the tent where her mother had retired to her cot. She shook her head doubtfully. Mechanically she tossed the greasy water from the dish-pan.

WAGON WHEELS TO DENVER

As she packed away the dishes which Virginia handed to her, she noticed her father leaning against the water barrel, cleaning the rifles and carbines. Every once in a while he would glance toward the tent. Once his hand dropped to his knee and he gazed off toward the west where the sky-line was beginning to blur into the grayness of the plains. A troubled line deepened between his dark brows. His eyes looked worried and abstracted,

"He's thinking today was too much for Mother and wondering what's going to happen next," she told Virginia.

Virginia darted a swift glance from Marian to Mr. Blane. But she remained silent, ill at ease.

The bottom just dropped out of everything when Father worried, Marian thought. He was usually so cheerful, so comforting.

From behind the Cooper tents came the hollow chop, chop of an ax and Russell's high-pitched voice following Jake as he fed the mules and Gypsy.

"You'd never believe Russell had such a wetting and such a narrow escape to hear him now," Virginia giggled.

"N-no! Oh, Virginia, I wish I'd know how to swim and had saved Russie! I never do anything but wash horrid old dishes, put up lunches and make beds and . . ." Marian broke off in disgust. She turned a determined chin to her friend. "Tomorrow I'm going to ride Gypsy if it kills me!" she boasted with a toss of her curls.

An amused smile played over Virginia's mouth. Marian knew what Virginia was thinking. She was remembering that one time she had tried to ride Gypsy. Flushing, Marian brushed the crumbs off the cot with an angry flap of the tea towel, and faced the Cooper tents.

The pungent odor of Doctor Frank's pipe floated over from the other camp where he was talking to Mr. Cooper. Doctor Frank leaned forward in his chair, talking earnestly. Mr. Cooper's leathery face was serious. He pulled thoughtfully at his great beard. Marian strained her ears to hear what they were saying, as she hung up the tea towels on a branch above her head.

"But, Doc, this route's the safest, bar none. We'll soon be hitting those Forts along the trail."

Marian grabbed Virginia's arm. "Listen!" she whispered.

"Yes, I know," came the doctor's reply, "and they promised us protection and an escort when we needed it. Gave us orders and everything. But, great guns, what good's a scrap of paper going to do us when we're miles from help? Take the other night when those horse thieves stole up on us! No, Cooper, I'm not so much afraid of Indians as I am of . . ."

The girls failed to catch what Doctor Frank was most afraid of. They gazed at each other silently. Marian slowly turned back to her work. Presently she stowed away the cold biscuits and a pan of stewed pigeon in the food box.

"There!" she said, as she pulled down her sleeves

with a jerk. "The work's done, thank goodness."

The girls made up Marian's cot with her blankets and quilt, and between them they pulled it into the tent, taking care not to awaken Marian's mother who was asleep. Silently they tiptoed outside.

"Let's play dominoes or something," suggested Virginia, when they were out of ear-shot of the tent.

"Oh, let's," Marian agreed. Perhaps if they played until bedtime she would forget Doctor Frank's unfinished words and her father's worried eyes.

But in spite of Marian's fear, especially at night, the next few days proved strangely monotonous, except for her several attempts to ride Gypsy. To city-bred Marian, danger lurked in every stomp of the pony's hoofs and in every jerk of the frisky calico body. Virginia insisted that Gypsy was as gentle as a lamb, but she found it hard to believe after two hard spills into the dusty trail.

Virginia taunted her with, "Gypsy knows you're afraid. She likes to tease you. Don't let her see you're scared!"

Now, on the third day, Marian managed to stick to the pony all that long, blistering afternoon. She tried to sit erect in the side-saddle, but every muscle in her body ached. Only the shame of Virginia's teasing laughter had kept her from crawling into the carriage.

Marian gazed wearily over the plains. The wild portulaca with deep red blossoms, and the trumpet flowers, had disappeared. Only the new blue-green buffalo grass crept along the flat sun-baked soil, broken occasionally by the purple bloodroot weed which perfumed the sultry air with a heady fragrance. The town of Salina lay far behind. Even the farms were so far apart that they often went without butter, eggs and milk now.

Suddenly she saw a great cloud of dust in the distance.

Forgetting her aching muscles she rode hurriedly up to Rusty. "Virginia!" she cried, "what's that? You don't suppose it's—Indians?"

Virginia grabbed for her father's glass which was slung from the saddle and peered through it.

"Is it Indians? Tell me, quick!" Marian pleaded, clutching at her friend's sleeve.

Then Virginia burst out laughing. "Land no! It's cattle! Hundreds of them! They must be from Texas bound for Abilene. Pa says they ship them to New York from there. They get six to ten dollars a head for them."

"Why do they only sell the cow's heads? Why, Virginia?" Russell asked.

The travelers had pulled to the roadside, and so intent were the girls in watching the dusty, long-horned cattle pass that they failed to hear him. Here and there a rough-looking rider in a wide hat and gay handkerchief rode by and called out, "Howdy, strangers!"

Russell followed them with admiring eyes until they dropped from sight over the eastern blue horizon. "I'm goin' to be a cowboy," he confided to the girls, "'stead a fightin' Injuns! I want a big hat and a red handkerchief, too!''

Toward evening the party halted for the night. Marian tumbled from the saddle. She stumbled painfully toward the men who were making camp on a knoll covered with buffalo grass.

''My goodness! You walk funny! Like somebody's spanked you,'' Virginia giggled as she followed Marian leading Rusty. ''Never mind, you'll be all right tomorrow if you ride again.''

''Ride again!'' Marian groaned. ''I'll never, never get on that old Gypsy again! Never!'' She sank dejectedly by the food box which Jake had just lifted from the wagon. She was sure Virginia thought her a baby. Well, perhaps she was! But she didn't care. She didn't care about anything but to be comfortable and at home where no one laughed at you.

She gazed about her with miserable eyes. Red sandstone bluffs surrounded them. Each bluff was crowned with queerly formed monuments of rocks. The valley before her was more than wide enough for the road they had traveled, the railroad and a stream of gleaming water. Presently there came the creak of the train rumbling past for the last time that day. The shrill whistle echoed among the bluffs. As usual, it comforted her. They didn't seem quite so far from civilization. She watched the belching black smoke until the train disappeared into the setting sun.

GYPSY PLAYS HER PART

Father looked at her silently — reproachfully. Then he turned on his heel and started setting up the cot they used for a table.

"All right, Father, all right! I'll help." Marian flushed, getting clumsily to her feet.

"You'll feel better standing up," Doctor Frank teased, looking up with a grin from the stove where he was building a fire. "Guess I'll have to serve your dinner from the wagon, then you won't have to sit down. Maybe I'd better get you that horse liniment we put on Toby. That'll fix you."

"No, thank you!" Marian retorted, hoping he hadn't seen the tears spring to her eyes.

Miserably Marian went about her evening tasks. Presently she overheard the word "Indians." Looking up quickly she saw that Doctor Frank and Father were gazing at the bluffs above them. The doctor was saying, "Jake tells me that those rock monuments up on the bluffs were put there by Indians. That's why this valley's called Rock Creek. Wonder when the redskins were here?"

Marian shivered and looked away. But shortly she forgot there were such creatures as Indians absorbed as she was by the nagging ache of her legs and muscles. As she stirred the sputtering potatoes in the skillet, she thought of Virginia's words, "You'll be all right tomorrow if you ride again." But she knew she wouldn't. It didn't make any difference how many resolutions she had made in the past few days, she was never going to ride Gypsy again. No, sir! Never!

In the morning Marian felt better, though it took determination and several suppressed "Ouches" to sit up on her cot and finally to swing her legs to the ground.

Virginia arrived promptly after the breakfast dishes were washed and packed away. She rode Rusty and led Gypsy by the bridle.

"I saddled her for you," she told Marian with a suspicion of a twinkle in her eyes.

"Oh—oh, thank you." Marian looked dismayed. "But I'm not ..."

"Of course you are. Don't be a ninny! Hurry up," Virginia interrupted. "The folks are ready to start and Pa said we could lead the way."

Marian knew she couldn't bear to have Virginia laugh at her. Before she realized what she was doing, she found herself walking toward Gypsy. She knew that she would have to ride, even if it killed her. Besides, there was that promise to her father way back in Leavenworth. She hadn't made the best of things—ever! Her feet dragged as she drew nearer the pony.

Carefully she avoided the white hoofs that could strike out so unexpectedly. Gypsy hadn't seen her and went on nibbling grass. Relieved, Marian reached for the bridle and the shaggy mane, and with an effort pulled herself up in the saddle. Before she had time to settle her skirts,

Gypsy reared. With a cry she clung to the pony's mane. For a fleeting second she remembered those other spills. It felt as if she was slipping now! She threw her arms around Gypsy's neck and hung on with all her strength, her eyes shut tight, her teeth clenched. She mustn't fall again! She mustn't! From a long way off, it seemed, Virginia was yelling to her. The next instant Gypsy settled to earth with a jolt.

Marian's eyes flew open. Why, she was still in the saddle and Gypsy was quietly grazing. Had those terrible moments been just a dream? Virginia was shaking her arm and speaking to her. "You certainly managed Gypsy like you'd ridden all your life. Why, when she reared up, I thought sure you'd slide right over her tail. Now you've showed her she can't tease you any more. You had a lot of spunk to try and ride today anyhow after being so lame." Virginia smiled her admiration.

At her praise, Marian felt a happy warmth steal over her, although, to be sure, she hadn't deserved it.

She had been dreadfully frightened for those few minutes, but after her pony was jog-trotting meekly along the trail beside Rusty, Marian felt a confidence in herself that she had never experienced before. When Virginia's head was turned, she leaned over and patted the pony's shaggy neck with a hand which still trembled a little and whispered in her ear, "Gypsy! Don't—don't tease me any more. Please be my friend now and always."

WAGON WHEELS TO DENVER

Gypsy tossed her head as if to say yes. Somehow Marian felt the pony understood. Suddenly she felt happier than she had since she left Chicago. She forgot her stiff muscles and everything but the thought that she would never be afraid of Gypsy again!

V

Buffalo!

"Look! Look, Russie," Marian cried the next day, after they had left the bluff country and were out on the rolling prairie once more. "See those funny fat squirrels."

"Where? Where, Marian?" queried Russell, jumping to his feet. "Oh, I see 'em!"

Virginia, who had joined Marian in the carriage, tossed her head scornfully. "Squirrels! Land, no, those are prairie dogs. Those dirt mounds are their houses. That's a prairie dog village. I've read, too, that rattlesnakes and owls live with the prairie dogs."

The bright-eyed, grayish-brown creatures sat stiffly at the entrance to their dirt homes and barked in shrill, squeaky voices as the wagons approached. Marian had to hold Chase firmly by the collar in order to keep him from leaping out. His ears cocked, his eyes as glassy as when he saw a cat, he watched the animals tumble back into their holes while the travelers passed. In the distance a few brave dogs stuck to their posts like tiny sentinels.

"I want a prairie dog. S'pose Jake'd catch one?" asked Russell eagerly.

"'Course not" Virginia answered.

"Well, he catched buffalo!" Russell returned.

The girls giggled.

The party drove miles over wind-swept country before they found water. The big water cask had to be filled whenever they were fortunate enough to reach some desolate farmhouse or small creek. The water was flat and hot as if poured from a teakettle. Trees became so scarce that they would soon have to pick up railroad ties for firewood.

At Fort Harker, which overlooked the two government warehouses on the railroad, a friendly settler gave them a dripping chunk of ice. In the days which followed, the campers often thought longingly of that ice.

For two days they plodded along under glaring sun, against hot winds that seared their faces and reddened their eyes. All day long the jolting wagons pounded on mind and body. The mules' long ears drooped. Gypsy, dripping with sweat, stumbled in the patch of shade made by the carriage. Chase, still limping on his sore paw, tagged faithfully behind, his eyes almost closed with dust and weariness.

BUFFALO!

The travelers passed through the town of Ellsworth, a depressingly flat place, and Fossil, which a colony from Wisconsin had settled just six weeks before.

Each evening since they had left Fort Harker the men and Virginia had been target practicing. Somehow, it relieved the tension of sitting a horse or riding in a jolting wagon for sweltering hours until one's muscles fairly rebeled.

"I don't see why you don't try it, Marian?" Virginia said after supper one evening. "It's more fun—really. And land knows we may all have to fire a gun some day."

"But I could never hold one of those heavy rifles!" she protested.

"Come on, Marian! I'll show you how," called Doctor Frank, breaking away from the group gathered before the Blane tent to watch the firing.

Marian backed away when the young man hurried up to her. "Oh, I couldn't!" she cried.

Doctor Frank laughed and grabbed her wrist. "No you don't! Might as well try. You can't learn younger, young lady!"

Timidly Marian took hold of her father's Winchester. She was conscious that Mother had put down her knitting and Mrs. Cooper the sock she was mending. She could see Mr. Cooper's enormous beard fluttering in the wind as he leaned on his gun watching, and Jake's narrow black eyes, below the jagged white scar.

"Come on, now! Aim at that tin can over there," the

doctor directed, "and pull this thing-a-ma-jig here. See, it's easy!"

With her teeth clenched, her eyes shut tightly, she fired aimlessly.

"Great guns! No fair closing your eyes!" Doctor Frank laughed. "Now; try it again."

Marian gritted her teeth and fired. Again she missed the mark.

Jake laughed—mockingly it seemed to Marian. She grew crimson.

"Never mind!" Mr. Cooper patted her shoulder heavily. "Not so bad for the first try! You'll have us all beat yet!"

"I should say you will! Even Jake!" Doctor Frank consoled her, with a blue flash of his eyes toward the hired man's sullen face.

Father had not said a word but his brown eyes were watching her. They twinkled a silent message of "Keep it up, little soldier! You'll win!"

How proud he would be if she really learned to shoot. With dogged determination she kept practicing though her arms ached dreadfully.

"It's no use, Virginia! Guess I'll never learn!" she admitted finally. "Come on, let's rest."

The girls sat down on the water barrel to watch the men practice. "I intend to learn to shoot as well as Jake," Virginia remarked. "Look at him, would you!"

Marian's glance followed that of her friend. Jake

hit the mark every time with an ease that drew gasps of admiration from the others.

"He's the best shot in the party," Virginia declared, watching the six-foot giant of a man give place to Mr. Blane.

"I suppose so," Marian said grudgingly as she folded and refolded tiny pleats in her skirt. She was remembering Jake's mocking laugh.

"Course he's always boasting about something or other and looks like he's swallowed something bad most of the time. But he certainly can fire a gun!" Virginia continued.

"Well, he is sort of queer. But he's nice to Russie; tells him stories and helps Father a lot," Marian admitted, watching Jake turn away from the firing with a shrug of his great shoulders.

They were camped at Walker's Station. The next morning before Marian was up, Russell came running into the tent and shook her awake. "Come on! Get up, Marian! There's somethin' on the plains. Animals with little white behinds!" he cried excitedly.

"Why, son!" Mother said in mock astonishment as she sat up in bed.

Russell dashed from the tent, calling over his shoulder, "Get up, Mummy! Come see!"

Marian tumbled out of bed, followed by her mother. As they never undressed at night it was an easy matter. Marian often smiled to herself at the thought of those

71

white nighties which Mother had insisted on bringing. They hadn't even been unfolded, and still lay, along with the discarded table-cloths, near the bottom of the trunk.

In the distance a herd of slender-legged animals stood poised for sudden flight.

"They're antelope, Marian!" cried Virginia.

"Wish they weren't so far. I'd like to get one!" Father remarked eagerly.

"Oh, Father—no!" Marian protested, watching the slender brown creatures leap away with lightning-like swiftness, as if they sensed what Father had in mind.

"Pshaw! We have to eat, Marian! We haven't had any fresh meat lately. Nothing but the fish we caught near Fort Harker."

"I know. It's only that—well, they're so pretty. I'd hate to see them killed even if they're good to eat. Besides, in the pictures I've seen the antelope had eyes just like Chase's."

Jake was building a fire in the stove. He looked up. "You'll like antelope, gal. Tastes like lamb."

Virginia hurried back to tell her parents about the slender animals on the plains. Mother called, "Russell! Come wash your face, son!"

"They did have white behinds, didn't they, Marian?" Russell insisted. He followed his mother into the tent with longing backward glances toward the antelope.

"Well," said Doctor Frank, "guess I'd better get

breakfast. What'll it be this morning, your Highness?" He turned to Marian.

"Oh, the usual corn-meal mush and apple sauce, I suppose. Don't you get sick of it?"

"Mush sticks to the ribs at that, little lady. But never mind. Soon we'll be having buffalo steaks," the young man remarked as he bent over the food box.

"Buffalo steaks!" Marian repeated, her blue eyes widening.

"Sure. We ought to be seeing some of the big fellows before long," the doctor answered as he measured coffee into the pot.

Marian hauled out her cot and started to set the table.

Presently she saw Jake ride away with his rifle slung from the saddle, and wondered what sort of game he would bring back this time. She hoped it wouldn't be one of those pretty antelope.

The wind which hung over them suddenly grew worse. It blew the dishes off the cot as fast as she could put them down. "Will you look at that!" she fumed, grabbed frantically at a cup.

The next instant the teakettle lid blew off the stove and rattled across the prairie, with Father in hot pursuit. Doctor Frank, who was making biscuits, was quickly enveloped in a white coat of flour.

"Jiminy!" cried Marian, laughing. "You look like a ghost! Will you look at Doctor Frank!" she called to

73

Mother emerging from under the flapping tent fly. Mrs. Blane had no sooner joined Marian than she clutched at her billowing skirts. The net that bound up her soft hair blew off, and away it went after the teakettle lid.

"Never mind, Marian!" Mother called disgustedly, clutching her flying hair with one hand and her skirts with the other. "You'll never catch it."

The doctor retired to the wagon with the flour, "raising powder" and bread board, and Father fastened the lids on the kettles with tiny sticks.

Mr. Cooper joined the Blanes as they were finishing their decidedly wind-blown meal.

"Holy mackeral!" He grabbed his hat. "Some wind we're having!" He tucked his fluttering beard inside his shirt. "What do you say, folks, to staying over a day. I got to rig up something to keep our small tent from blowing down and Mom wants to do our wash while we're near plenty of water. The station agent, yonder, promised us all we could use from the tank. What do you say, Blane?"

"Good idea!" Father rose and set his plate down on the cot. "That ridge-pole of ours is likely to break in this wind. Frank could strengthen it some while I do our wash." He turned to Mother with one of his twinkling smiles. "Might as well get into practice, Mary. We'll be getting further and further from towns and soon I'll be forced to do the washing."

Mother smiled in return but as Father turned away,

Marian caught the look of doubt she sent toward the wash-tubs under the wagon.

Marian hurried through her work before Father discovered her. She knew she would hate to wash dirty old clothes. She decided that wind or no wind she would get Virginia, and the two could take a walk. The further from wash-tubs the better!

"Virgina!" she called peeking into the tent where her friend lay sprawled on her cot reading.

"What?" Virginia asked, not taking her eyes from her book.

Marian plumped herself down beside her. "Let's do something! I'm tired of camp and sitting around. I'm sick of reading *'Nelly's Dark Days.'* Goodness knows, ours are bad enough without reading about hers! Come on, let's go down and see the water tank."

"All right. But what's there to see down there?"

The girls walked the track, one on each rail, holding hands to balance themselves.

"Let's see who falls off first," Marian suggested. "The one that does must pay a forfeit."

"What kind of a forfeit?" asked Virginia, giggling.

"Oh, I don't know. I can't think of anything silly. Can you?"

"I have it!" Virginia giggled. "If you fall off first, you'll have to promise not to complain about washing dishes the rest of the trip!"

"All right. But that won't be easy!" replied Marian reluctantly.

"Now, what'll mine be?"

"I know," Marian's eyes shone mischievously. "Virginia, you must promise not to be always telling such terribly scary tales. It's bad enough to be way out in this awful country without having to listen to Indian massacres and robberies. That last one about the Indians causing a buffalo stampede, and kidnapping the two little children, was terrible. I've felt creepy ever since."

"All right then. But they aren't much worse than what could happen to us."

"Will you hush!" Marian scolded, playfully shaking Virginia's arm.

For a time they walked the rails in silence with Chase romping ahead of them. Each was so intent on not falling off that they failed to notice how far they were from camp, nor did they hear a distant rumble like thunder.

Suddenly there came the sound of pounding hoofs. Startled, both girls stumbled off the tracks at the same time. They stood still watching a lone horseman gallop toward them.

"Wonder who it is?" Virginia asked, shading her eyes with her hand.

"Why it's Jake!" cried Marian, somewhat relieved. "And he's got something hanging across his saddle."

Sure enough, as the hired man drew closer, they dis-

76

covered that a shaggy brown hide lay across the bulging saddle-bags.

With one of his twisted smiles Jake pulled up beside them. "Did ya see 'em?" he asked, wiping the sweat from his face on his dark shirt sleeve.

"See what?" Marian asked, suppressing a shudder. She had caught sight of blood stains on Jake's bowie knife.

"Buffalo!" Jake slid to the ground and pointed to the northwest. "Ya can still see 'em, yonder."

Far off against the horizon galloped a herd of huge dark beasts with enormous heads. The sound they made was like the roll of distant thunder.

"I'm glad those terrible creatures aren't coming this way," Marian gasped. "They won't turn around, will they?" she asked, anxiously.

"Reckon not. My gun scared 'em plenty. They're miles off. Look here at the steaks I brung ya." Jake yanked off one of the saddle-bags and displayed a quantity of fresh meat. He set the bag on the ground while he dragged off the buffalo skin. "Ain't this here a beauty?"

Marian looked away. She felt a little sick.

"It would make a fine robe for sleigh riding," Virginia declared.

As Marian turned back for another look at the buffalo hide, she caught sight of Chase sniffing at the meat. Before Marian could make a sound, Jake kicked the dog brutally aside with his heavy boot. Chase yelped and slunk to her.

Startled Virginia whirled around. "Land sakes! What happened?"

An angry sob stifled the reply on Marian's lips. She dropped to her knees and hugged the crouching dog. Chase lifted bewildered eyes to hers. Over his curly head, she looked savagely at the giant shoulders bending over the saddle-bag. Jake had kicked Chase! Now she knew she disliked Jake. She hated him!

VI

A Soldier Must Be Brave

"Don't you like buffalo meat?" Virginia asked several days later as she watched Marian feed Chase her portion left from breakfast.

"Goodness, no!" Marian shuddered. "Besides, these steaks were as tough as shoe leather. That buffalo must have been a hundred!"

"The rest of the meat'll be better. They say jerking it helps." Virginia nodded toward the rack made of poles which had been placed above a bed of coals. Buffalo meat, cut into long strips, hung from the rack. The air smelled of smoking flesh and of the brine into which it had been dipped before being hung up to dry.

Marian made a wry face and bent over the food box.

"Well, it's better than nothing," Virginia insisted. "Pa says the supplies we bought back in Hays City won't last forever and it's the last town of any size for a hundred and forty miles. You'll be begging for buffalo meat yet!''

''No sir! Never! Marian replied as she packed the food away. She glanced toward the creek where Mr. Cooper was patiently casting his line into the water. ''Maybe your father'll catch some fish today,'' she added hopefully.

''Maybe! He's been down there long enough!'' Virginia remarked in disgust. ''How ever he thinks we're to keep fish in this heat without ice is more than I know!''

''Well, I'll eat it up fast enough! ''Marian laughed as she tied on her blue sunbonnet. ''Come on, let's wait in the carriage until they start. It's too hot out here in the sun.''

The girls curled up on the rear seat and watched the bustling activity about camp. Doctor Frank and Jake took down the smoking strips of meat and threw them into a tub. Russell trotted back and forth at Jake's heels. The girls could her his high-pitched voice rambling on and on. Mrs. Cooper, her hands on her broad hips, talked to Mrs. Blane who leaned back in her camp-chair smiling wearily over her mending. Mr. Blane had disappeared inside the tent.

From the Coopers' camp floated the words of *''Rosalie, the Prairie Flower.''* Red-faced Casper sang lustily although somewhat out of tune, as he hauled down the small tent.

A SOLDIER MUST BE BRAVE

"Fair as a lily, joyous and free,
Light of the prairie was she;
Everyone who knew her
Felt the gentle power of Rosalie,
The prairie flo-wer!"

Virginia giggled. "I suppose he'll start on '*Annie Laurie*' or '*I'd Be a Star*' next."

The girls watched Jake put out the fire with a flood of brine water. They held their noses as the stench of brine, meat dripping, and ashes mingled unpleasantly.

"Why can't we ride up and see what the fort looks like?" Virginia suggested pleasantly. "It isn't far. There ought to be time enough. The rest of the tents aren't down yet."

"Oh, let's do!" Marian replied gazing up at Fort Hays which was built on a hill overlooking Big Creek and its dark green foliage. "It looks rather pretty up there."

She jumped from the carriage and ran to meet her father who was carrying the cots outside the tent. "May Virginia and I go to the fort?" she asked eagerly.

"Why, yes. I guess there'll be time enough. Why not let Jake drive you up there in the carriage?" her father answered, stooping to fold one of the cots.

Marian hesitated. Her dislike of Jake had grown steadily since he had kicked Chase, Reluctantly she called to him, "Will you drive us up to the fort, Jake?"

Jake carefully packed the tub of meat into the wagon

and then turned a sullen face toward her for a moment. "Naw, I gotta fix Toby's leg, 'fore we start!"

"Why, I didn't know there was anything wrong with it." Marian looked surprised.

Jake slouched toward the staked mules before Marian finished speaking. Father had failed to hear Jake for he was inside the tent piling up the bedding.

"Well, I can drive!" she remarked angrily to Virginia.

With the aid of Doctor Frank, the girls hitched the demure Dinah and white-nosed Baby, the wagon mule, to the carriage.

"I'll drive," Virginia announced, climbing into the front seat.

"Oh, let me! I can—really, Virginia," Marian pleaded. Since she had overcome her fear of Gypsy, she felt competent to handle the mules.

"All right. You drive then," replied Virginia reluctantly.

"What you doin'? Where you goin'?" Russell ran to the carriage.

"Climb in, Russell, and you'll find out. You sit here between us," Marian said, as she took hold of the reins and clucked at the mules as she had heard her father do. The carriage creaked up the well-worn trail toward Fort Hays.

"I'm just as glad that Jake wouldn't take us," Marian

remarked. "I don't like him around since he kicked Chase!" Her eyes flashed.

"He didn't mean to hurt him!" Russell spoke up. "Chase was nosin' the meat. Jake said so!"

The girls eyed each other knowingly. There was no use arguing with Russell on that subject.

At the fort they drove slowly around the grassless square. Above them the red, white and blue flag whipped the sultry air. A row of officers' brown wooden quarters faced the square. There was not a flower or blade of grass in sight. Only a few straggling Madiera vines clung desperately to an occasional veranda.

"My, what ugly houses! It doesn't look a bit pretty now that we're up here," Marian cried.

"Land, no! But I don't see how anything can be pretty in such a dry country! Oh, look!" Virginia added, nudging Marian.

A young girl, about Marian's age, had run out from one of the doorways and was standing on the vine-covered porch watching them curiously. She wore a cool-looking sprigged calico, and a pink ribbon bound her long black hair. Marian gazed at her admiringly. She looked like the girls in Chicago.

"Hello!" the girl called. "Where are you going?"

"We're going to Colorado," Marian answered, pulling up the mules.

"Way out there! Mercy! Are you girls going there all alone?" she cried in amazement.

"Land, no!" exclaimed Virgina. "Our parents are with us. We're camping down by the creek."

"Oh, I see. Well, won't you come in and play? I haven't seen any girls my age for—oh, just months!" There was a wistfulness in her voice that Marian could understand perfectly.

"We'd love to! Come on, Virginia."

"We can't, Marian. We must get back to camp. They'll be waiting for us—ready to start."

"Oh, dear! I suppose we mustn't," Marian sighed. "I'm sorry we can't stop," she called to the girl. "We have to hurry back. Good-bye."

The girl on the veranda waved her handkerchief. "Good-bye!" she called sadly.

"Goodness, Virginia. It must be awful, poked out here in this barren old country. I hope Colorado doesn't look like this."

"I hope not. But I bet a button it will. That girl must get dreadfully lonesome if there isn't anyone here her age."

"Poor thing! I wish we could have gone in. She looked so nice. I'm sure they have a comfortable home and pretty things—like ours back in Chicago. She reminded me of Lizzie," Marian sighed.

Curious faces peered at the carriage from windows and doorways. The lone sentry again smiled at them as they left the square.

Marian turned the mules toward camp. Presently she

84

could see Father and the doctor rolling up the tent. Casper was hitching the mules to the largest Cooper wagon. Mr. Cooper was hurrying from the creek swinging a string of shiny fish.

"Oh, Virginia, I wish I was home! I wish . . ." Suddenly Baby shied at something white by the roadside. Dinah leaped high into the air and before Marian knew what was happening they were racing down the road as if pursued by savages. She screamed in terror.

"Hold on! I'll help!" Virgina shouted, helping Marian pull at the reins with all her strength.

"Stop 'em! Stop 'em!" Russell wailed, clinging wildly to his sister.

"I'm try-trying to!" Marian screamed. The wind blew the words from her mouth.

The carriage swayed and bumped crazily along the road. They flew past the camp. Dimly Marian heard shouts.

"Father! . . . Help!" she shrieked.

"Oh! We—we almost turned over!" Terrified, she strained harder. "Virginia!" she gasped. "Stop them! We'll be killed!" The lines were cutting into her hands.

Russell threw both arms tightly about her neck and clung screaming. The carriage hit a rut in the trail and they were thrown violently against each other. Marian lost her grip on one of the reins. Frantic, she grabbed for it only to have the other line torn from her fingers. Alone, Virginia was tugging fiercely at the runaway animals.

The next instant the carriage stopped with a jerk that shot them all forward. The traces snapped and the mules broke loose and clattered down the road. Marian pitched over the dashboard into the road and lay stunned.

Something was licking her face.

"Chase!" She sat up dizzily, her head pounding.

"Oh—Marian! Are you all right?" Virginia bent over her, white and shaking.

Then her father helped her to her feet, his face pale with anxiety. "Are you hurt?" he asked tenderly.

"I—I . . . No, I'm—I'm all right!" Marian gasped.

"Thank goodness you children weren't killed! That's a mean bump on your forehead, Marian. It'll be the size of a goose egg if we don't do something for it quickly. Here, let me brush you off and then you'd better ride Gypsy back to camp and have Mother fix you up."

"But where are the mules?" asked Marian anxiously, wiping the dust from her face with a hand which shook a little.

"They broke somepin' and—and ran away," volunteered Russell who still sat in the carriage white-faced and wide-eyed. Doctor Frank and Jake and Mr. Cooper went to catch 'em."

Suddenly, Virgina pointed to a cloud of dust far down the road. "Look!" she cried. "They're coming back."

Mr. Blane, who had been examining the carriage, turned around. He shaded his eyes with a hand which was none too steady. "Good work!" he exclaimed. "I guess

86

we'll have to get the carriage repaired in Hays now. They broke the shaft. We'll never put that rascal Baby with Dinah again. What was the matter with Toby?''

Marian didn't answer for she was thinking that Jake must have used that for an excuse not to go to Fort Hays. For there—emerging from the whirls of dust, rode Jake on Toby! And Toby did not limp!

Due to the delay, the party traveled late and made only twelve miles instead of their usual fifteen or more. The country was flat and blistering hot. Even the buffalo grass had turned a discouraged brown, relieved here and there by a green swale which looked like bright little oases in a desert. Their camp that night was a mile from a small Division settlement of Ellis. The wind shrieked and blew so violently that the men were unable to put up the tents. Consequently the women and children had to sleep as best they could in the wagons.

''Virginia was sick all night,'' Mrs. Cooper confided to Marian's mother when she bustled over for her morning visit. ''That runaway was too much for her. Funny how a scare turns her stomach.''

''Strange that Virginia should be the one. Now, if it had been Marian . . . ! But she hasn't complained once, not even about her head. I do believe she is becoming a bit reconciled to the ups and downs of this life on the plains,'' Mother added proudly.

Marian, who was standing within ear-shot, blushed. She had tried not to complain of her throbbing head. It did hurt—awfully—and her hands felt raw and burned. But a happy feeling fluttered in her heart. How glad she was now that she had tried to be brave. She met her father's twinkling eyes just as he emerged from the tent. Chuckling softly he threw back his shoulders and lifted his hand in salute. With head and shoulders up she solemnly saluted in return. Then they both laughed merrily. Marian hummed *"Rosalie, the Prairie Flower"* under her breath as she turned back to her hated task—dishwashing.

The next evening they camped at Parks Station with its three lonely houses and small dreary depot. Some distance from their tents was an old mud hut. This one was different from any they had seen in the past, for it was lined with gaping port-holes!

After supper Marian played dolls and soldiers with Russell in the wagon. But every once in a while she glanced toward the building with the sinister looking port-holes.

"Want to go up and see that thar fort?" Jake inquired, poking his head into the wagon.

Marian quickly shoved Lily out of sight in her pocket. "Why, ye-es."

Jake sauntered away with Russell, and Marian ran to the other camp for Virginia. Shortly the girls caught up with the others.

They were as silent as the building itself as they wandered about the low mud walls and peered curiously through the dark port-holes into the one room of the fort which was dirt-floored and empty.

Marian broke the silence at last. "I'd hate to have to stay in a dark earthly smelling place like that."

"We'll be seein' more like it from now on," Jake told them, holding Russell up to another port-hole.

"What's it for, Jake? Who lives here? Where'd they go?" Russell asked, as Jake set him down on the ground.

"Waal, Russie, this here fort was built by a fellow named Parks. He built it to protect his men agin' the Indians. He was a contractor on the railroad when they was a-buildin' it 'long here. Didn't help him none."

"Why not, Jake?" Russell asked eagerly.

" 'Cause the redskins got him 'fore long!"

Marian shuddered and turned away. "I don't believe I like to hear about such things. It always makes me think that we . . ." She turned to Virginia. "Come on Let's go back. It gives me the shivers here."

At the railroad station, the telegraph operator called to them. He had been leaning against the dreary building watching them as they wandered about the fort.

"Want to see a real Indian suit?" he asked when they drew near.

"Oh, let's see! Let's see!" cried Russell, racing ahead of them. Jake and the girls followed him into the station.

"This suit belonged to a chief in Red Cloud's band," the man explained when they had gathered about him.

89

He held up the elaborately beaded and fringed buckskin coat and trousers. "He was killed on the Republican River in 1866. These ornaments around the neck are made of antelope skins. The beads that trim the skins weigh thirteen and a half pounds. They're sewed on with linen. It must have taken some fat squaw six months or more to sew them on." He indicated with a broken thumb nail the tiny stitches which held the rows of bright beads in place.

"Oooh, isn't it lovely!" Marian admired. "I didn't know Indians wore such wonderful things. I thought they just dressed in paint and feathers."

"Land, no!" cried Virginia. "Why, I've read that they . . ."

"Here," interrupted the settler. "Here's his buckskin leggings and moccasins. Look at the bead work! This is his wampum belt. It's made of buffalo hide."

Marian stared at the belt with its trimming of brass buttons and at the huge buffalo robe which the man laid out for their inspection, and at the brightly painted bows and arrows.

"Handsome, aren't they?"

The bronze-faced man was holding the suit up in front of him. For a second Marian seemed to see the ghost of the dead Indian spring before her. Then Russell's high-pitched voice and the ticking telegraph instrument broke the spell.

"Wish I had a suit like that!" Russell said wistfully,

stroking the velvety surface. "I'm goin' to shoot an Injun out West!" he added boastfully. Russell had felt very grown up since starting for Colorado and all the more so because Jake, a man of thrilling adventures, was his hero and friend.

Virginia giggled.

"Don't," Marian whispered, drawing her toward the door. She had seen the hurt look in Russell's eyes.

On the way back to camp, Virginia and Jake discussed the Indian war on the Republican River. But Marian tried not to hear. Her hand sought her pocket where the soft silken body of tiny Lily lay hidden. As always the touch of her brought up the vision of those dear safe days in Chicago, far away from this dreadful country of horse theives, scary rafts, wild animals and runaways —and Indians (if only their ghosts) always somewhere around!

VII

The Buffalo Hunt

"This is the quietest Fourth of July I ever awakened to," Mrs. Blane announced laughingly the next morning as she made her daily entry in her journal.

"We'll give you some noise soon," Father returned. "The settler says there's a thousand head of buffalo not far from here. They're making for the Arkansas River. He saw them when he shot that antelope yesterday. We're going on a buffalo hunt." Father's eyes were boyishly eager. He paused as he noticed the look of anxiety shadowing Mother's face. "Now, don't look worried. There's no danger." He turned to Marian. "Want to come along?"

"Oh, Father—no! I hate buffalo! They scare me!" Marian protested. "Besides, I promised I'd read some of my *Juno* book to Virginia. She's still in bed with a little fever."

"All right. But I thought you could ride Gypsy and stay near the railroad so that you could find your way back and just look on from there. Ought to be a great sight!"

Marian turned away silently. However, she watched with interest as the men prepared for the hunt. Each man had his Winchester slung in a boot ahead of his right stirrup. On each hip hung an ugly-looking revolver and a bowie knife was sheathed from the belt near the back.

"Better come along, Miss!" Jake remarked, swinging into the saddle. A mocking smile twitched under his drooping mustache. Marian bit her lip angrily. He'd heard, then.

"Nothin'll hurt ya," he jeered.

Marian's blue eyes flashed. Suddenly she jumped down from where she had been sitting on the water barrel and ran to her father who had already mounted Gypsy. "May I go, after all?" she pleaded.

He looked at her in surprise. "Why, of course. Here, you take Gypsy. I'll ride Dinah."

"Be careful!" Mother cautioned. "Gracious, but you're armed to the very teeth! You look as dangerous as a posse!" she added delightedly, as she stood watching them ride away.

Marian followed the hunters on her pony, an important looking carbine slung from her saddle. Chase tagged

94

along beside Gypsy. At the station they were joined by the settler, who led the way.

Nervously, Marian listened to Jake telling her father about other buffalo hunts.

"Yes, sir, that was the time they almost got me. I was a-makin' a stand. That's gettin' off your horse and edgin' up near the buffalo you aim to hit, some fifty or sixty yards and shootin' as many as ya can 'fore they gits the smell of blood. The critters sure hate that smell. Makes 'em wild. Soon's they git wind of it they stampede, and ya can't tell whar they'll head. All ya can do then is git to your horse, if you're lucky

"This time my horse heard 'em first, and when they started thunderin' at me, he galloped away to camp. There I was. I'd been a goner in another minute but I knew they hated noise and I begun a-shootin' at 'em and a-dancin' and shoutin' and wavin' my arms and coat. I'll be hanged if the big bull in front didn't give me a fiery look and turned tail and led the bunch north just in the nick-a-time."

Jake shook his dark head in remembrance and spat a stream of amber at the prairie.

"I've heard tell of hunters ridin' one of them beasts out of danger, grabbin' 'em by the horns and swingin' up on their backs. But I ain't never done it."

Marian's eyes had grown wide as she listened. She repressed a frightened shudder.

"Waal, to go on," continued Jake, "the rest of the

hunters rode up expectin' to see me flat as a pancake. And were they took back! That's the way all the big hunters and skinners git buffalo. Shootin' from a stand. This here ridin' 'em the Indian way ain't no good. Ya miss too many. But with them guns ya got and them mules, ya can't do nothin' else and it's safer!''

Marian thought she detected a sneer in Jake's voice.

"Look!" he shouted suddenly. "No . . . over thar! See 'em? Thar's the herd!''

Marian followed the direction indicated by Jake's crooked finger. West of them the plains were dotted with great humps of brown. She thought they resembled dwarf trees, until here and there a huge body moved and she could see the fierce-looking curly heads.

"Come on, Blane!" yelled the settler. "Let's run 'em. We'll head 'em south. Don't waste any shots 'til you're near.''

"Now, Marian, you ride over near the railroad and watch from there,'' Father called over his shoulder. "If anything goes wrong and they stampede, make for camp. Gypsy'll get you there safely enough.''

Jake turned and looked at her a moment. "See here, gal. If them critters come your way, stand up in the saddle and yell at 'em and shoot. Them beasts hate horse-flesh and strange noises. They'll turn tail. Mark my words! Let's go!''

Marian watched the men gallop off toward the herd. The dust they raised soon hid them from view. She had hated to have Jake think she was afraid, but she wasn't quite sure now why she had come.

"Come on, Chase. Let's start back," she called to the dog.

At the rails she halted the pony and gazed over the plains. The very prairie seemed to be moving in giant muddy waves. She could hear the distant roar of guns. Suddenly the air hung lifelessly over the plains as if waiting—holding its breath—much the same as Marian was doing.

At that moment, she detected a rattling, bumping noise. Then came the shrill screaming whistle of the morning passenger train.

Marian quickly guided her horse off the tracks and watched the oncoming train. She forgot the buffalo in her interest in the faces that lined the windows. They were mostly men, bearded in the fashion of the day. Particularly she noticed a young man with interested eyes who leaned far out of a "palace car," a few well dressed women and a rosy-cheeked baby. She wondered where they were going and if any of them came from her dear Chicago.

"Oh, I wish I were on that train this minute!" she sighed to Gypsy.

She noticed that the train was slowing up—stopping. The last Pullman was just abreast of her. Suddenly she saw the reason. Hundreds of buffalo were thronging the tracks far ahead, racing madly toward the train.

She pulled in her reins tightly. What would happen if they kept on? Would they be crushed, train and all, under those deadly hoofs? She hesitated, not knowing whether to gallop back to camp or stay by the train—near to the protection of people.

Jake's words flashed back to her. Surely all that whistling and black smoke from the engine would scare them off!

"Gosh! Look at them come! Aren't you scared?" asked a nice boyish voice above her.

Startled, Marian looked up quickly into a pair of serious blue-gray eyes—the very nicest eyes she had ever noticed in a boy.

"But—but they may never get this far," she answered though her voice shook. She turned back and gazed fearfully at the thundering animals. "Jake says they're afraid of noises," she faltered. "That engine ought scare them to death . . . Listen to it! If—if they don't turn, you're supposed to ride at them and wave your arms and—and shoot!"

The young man was leaning far out of the car window, fascinated by the immense animals. At Marian's words he turned and looked curiously at her. "And you wouldn't be afraid to do that?" he asked admiringly.

"Why—why——" Marian blushed guiltily. She knew she would be—terribly, but somehow she couldn't tell this young stranger.

They held their breath for several seconds while hun-

THE BUFFALO HUNT

dreds of huge brown beasts with fierce-looking, shaggy heads roared toward them in great whirls of dust. Oh, why had she hesitated? Why hadn't she raced back to camp and safety! Any minute now those frightful creatures would reach the engine! The pounding hoofs grew deafening! She looked longingly at the window above her.

All at once the engine snorted like some great angry monster. The Pullman shivered and slowly creaked into motion. Marian stifled a scream. The train was going to plow them down—leave her—leave her— to be crushed by those dreadful hoofs. Her tortured eyes pleaded with the boy to save her. She hurried Gypsy abreast of his window.

Suddenly he leaned far out and grabbed her hands. "Quick—I'll pull you inside!" he cried.

Marian dropped the reins. She leaned toward the car window, ready to swing up beside the boy. For a fleeting second she saw Gypsy and Chase left on the prairie . . . She closed her eyes in horror.

"Look! They're turning!" shouted the young man, dropping her hands in his excitement.

Marian's eyes flew open. She grabbed at Gypsy's mane to keep from falling. Sure enough the herd of buffalo was wheeling and thundering after the huge beast in the lead!

"Thank heavens!" she breathed, clinging weakly to her pony.

"Gosh! That was a narrow one! That old engine certainly scared them plenty. This'll be something to write home!"

The train halted once more to let the giant brown creatures pass. They swarmed over the tracks as far as Marian could see.

They'd be gone soon. She breathed a sigh of relief. Then she thought of her father. "Oh, I hope Father and the rest are safe! They were on the hunt," she explained.

She put her hand up over her eyes and scanned the far horizon.

"Gosh! But I'd like a shot at one of those big fellows!" the youth exclaimed. "Sounds like the passengers are trying a hand at it now," he added, as here and there a gun barked at the retreating herd.

Marian looked up in surprise. Somehow the blue-gray eyes above her didn't look as if they belonged to anyone who would enjoy shooting things. But then men and boys were funny that way. Why, even Father and Doctor Frank liked the sport. She noticed for the first time the well-cut dark coat, the neat white shirt and string tie, the nose like Russell's, only a bit more grownup, and the good-natured mouth and determined chin. The youth's face had lost its eagerness now. He looked older, nearer twenty than the sixteen or seventeen she had first thought him. The eyes which followed the buffalo seemed lost in dreams. Marian knew that look. Mother often caught it on her face and called it "star gazing."

As the last of the thundering animals cleared the track,

the train gave a lurch and slowly creaked into motion.

The young man turned and grinned. "Good-bye! Sorry you're not going my way."

Marian rode beside the slowly moving cars. "Where are you going?" she asked timidly.

"Colorado," he replied.

"So am I. Are you going to live in Denver?"

"Not if I can help it! I'm going West for adventure, not city life! I want to get away from all that. Learn about wild life and Indians."

"Forevermore!" Marian's eyes widened.

"Well, good-bye—until we meet in Colorado!" He waved his broad-brimmed hat at her as the train gathered speed. Marian had a fleeting glimpse of tousled brown hair and twinkling blue-gray eyes, and then the train outdistanced her, carrying with it her newly-made friend.

Marian felt a little lonely as she watched the train until it became a dark snake-line in the distance.

"Adventure, not city life!" repeated Marian aloud. "Can you imagine that, Gypsy? My goodness, he ought to be with us!"

The buffalo had disappeared behind a far-off cloud of dust. Presently some figures rode toward her over the plains. Joyfully she discovered her father and Doctor Frank in the lead. Across her father's saddle hung a great buffalo hide.

WAGON WHEELS TO DENVER

"Come on, Chase!" Marian called as she galloped eagerly to meet the hunters. Now she had something to tell them that would rival even Virginia's tales.

VIII

Ominous Tracks

"Don't you wish you'd been along yesterday?" Marian asked the next morning as the girls jogged along on their ponies. She had been telling Virginia all over again about the boy on the train and the buffalo stampede.

"Land, no!" Virginia blurted out. "You can get into all the buffalo stampedes you want to, but none for me, thank you!"

"I didn't say I liked it, Virginia, silly! I was simply scared to death— really! But you know I'm beginning to think those old buffalo are more afraid of us than we are of them."

"Maybe. But I wouldn't want to sit out in a prairie in a stampede waiting to find out!" Virginia dropped the reins and pulled on the sunbonnet her mother had made to replace the pancake hat with streamers. In spite of the early start the travelers made, by eight-thirty in the morning the scorching rays of the sun beat down upon them unmercifully.

"You didn't tell me the name of the boy on the train," Virginia continued as she tied the limp bonnet strings under her chin.

"Name? Why I never thought to ask," Marian faltered.

"Why didn't you? Now you'll never be able to find **him again**."

"I didn't intend to. I don't like boys much. But he was rather nice," Marian answered, remembering the eyes which could dream as well as twinkle merrily, and the warm smile. Thoughtfully she fanned herself with her bonnet.

"Humph! You are funny!" Virginia exclaimed. "Now, if it had been me, I would . . ."

Marian broke in, flushing, "Yes, I suppose you would have heard his life history and told him yours all the time the buffalo were charging at you." Suddenly she knew what was the matter with Virginia! She was envious!

Virginia tossed her head and remained silent.

"Well, I did find out he's going to Colorado for adventure and to learn about Indians and everything," Marian admitted, presently.

"H'm! Well, he'll probably find it!" Virginia commented dryly.

"We've got a long ride today," Marian remarked, longing to change the subject. "I heard Father tell Doctor Frank that we must make twenty-six miles if possible. He's anxious to get over this lonely stretch to Fort Wallace."

"Lucky you've become a hardened rider then," Virginia giggled. "A few weeks ago you'd have had to have a pillow under you after the first ten miles."

Marian blushed but she ignored Virginia's thrust. In spite of the girl's blunt remarks, Marian had learned not to take them too seriously. She turned silently back to watching for possible game. The men had killed one animal on the hunt and had divided that with the station agent. The girls had been warned to keep a sharp lookout for some herd. Great barren patches burned by prairie fires stretched out on all sides. All along the route were dry remains and shrunken hides of buffalo.

"Wish folks on the trains would kill all the buffalo!" Virginia remarked after a time. "Then they wouldn't be dashing about scaring folks to death."

"But I think it's cruel to shoot them down just for the fun of it," Marian said as she tried not to see the bleached bones that were strewn along the railroad. "Father says that there won't be any buffalo left for the hunters and skinners if they keep it up."

The next few days proved uneventful, except for the

hordes of grasshoppers of all sizes and colors through which they rode. The same desolate stations with their mud forts raised slightly above the ground, the same port-holes through which to fire in case of an Indian attack. Underground passages led from the settlers' houses to these forlorn mud fortresses. Occasionally a few soldiers were stationed at these tiny forts.

The winds had become an enemy to be reckoned with. Some nights they had to find refuge in the wagons. The fifth day out from Parks Station, Marian and her mother and brother had slept crowded uncomfortably together in this manner.

"I feel numb, as if my arms and legs were still asleep," Marian grumbled to her mother as she lingered over the last breakfast pan. There was no need to hurry this morning. It was Sunday and the day the travelers usually remained in camp.

"That wind last night was enough to try men's souls!" Mother leaned back in her camp-chair and gazed at the plains with tired eyes. Unheeded, *"The Cyptogram,"* which she had been reading, dropped from her lap. It was a book on cypher writing which Mother usually found absorbing. "I don't wonder the men get cross. If I try to assist them in any way, down goes my hat over my nose—my precious net flies over the prairie and my hair blows down over my eyes. I can't help but think of Grandmother and Aunt Lily in their cool, comfortable homes drinking ice water and eating good dinners."

OMINOUS TRACKS

Marian looked up in amazement. The dish-towel dropped from her fingers. She hadn't dreamed that Mother felt this way. She had never complained before.

"Sometimes, Marian, I think it's a hard fate which sent me out here in this dreadful country. They can brag of their boundless prairies, their healthful frontier life, and boast of their crops, but give me dear New England where I was born, every time! There's no place like it. Not even your beloved Chicago. And as for their crops, I can't see they ever have any. One year they're killed by drought, the next by rain and the next by these ghastly grasshoppers!" Mother impatiently brushed a yellow grasshopper from her lap.

Impulsively, Marian reached over and patted her mother's frail hand. She wanted dreadfully to comfort her. But what could she say? She hated it all so much herself. For the first time she realized that she wasn't the only one in camp who dreaded this life and what lay before them.

"But—but it's different in Colorado," she managed. "Father says it isn't all prairie. The Rockies are cool and lovely. And—and Doctor Frank says you're better already. Soon you'll be able to ride Gypsy a little each day. And that's such fun, Mother—really!"

"I wonder . . ." Mother rose hurriedly and disappeared inside the tent. Marian looked after her with puzzled eyes.

Presently she was startled from her thoughts by the

shrill whistle of the train rattling along the tracks toward camp. There were two passenger trains and one freight train daily and each time they passed, it was an event.

"Virginia!" Marian called excitedly to her friend who was hunched over a book in the Blane carriage. "The train's slowing up. Looks like it's going to stop! Come on!"

"Me too! Me too!" cried Russell, tumbling *"The Toy Book"* of colored engravings from his lap and running after his sister as fast as his short legs could carry him.

Many faces peered curiously from the car window as the girls and Russell ran toward the train. The conductor swung off the platform opposite the children, calling, "Mail, folks! Letters and a bundle of papers! And I've got you a chunk of ice!"

Eagerly Marian grabbed the mail. "Virginia," she cried waving a creamy square envelope and jumping up and down happily. "Look! A letter from Lizzie! The first one!"

The rest of the party, including Mother gathered about her, their eyes alight with anticipation. It had been a long time since there had been mail for the lonely camp.

Father reached for the ice and heaved the dripping chunk to his shoulders. He smiled at the conductor. "Man, you're a life-saver! You can't imagine what ice means to us. We've had a time keeping meat fresh in this heat. Thanks a thousand times!"

"You're welcome," the man replied, leaping back on the platform. "See you again, folks!" He signaled to the engineer. The train jerked into motion. Several hands and a fluttering handkerchief waved from the windows, then disappeared. Silently the campers watched until the train vanished leaving a plume of inky smoke against the blue sky.

In the meantime Marian sorted the mail. "Here, Mr. Cooper, two more for you!" she cried, handing out the letters. "And one for you, Doctor Frank! Three for you, Mother, and all from Grandmother and Aunt Lily!"

Then she ran over to the food box and sat down to read her long-looked-for letter from Lizzie.

With downcast eyes, Virginia stood at her side, digging the toe of her shoe into the dust. If Marian had noticed she would have seen the look of envy and loneliness flash across her face for an instant.

"I just never can get used to having a train for a postman, can you?" Marian was saying. "To think that all Grandmother and Aunt Lily have to do is address their letters in care of the Kansas Pacific Railroad—then the conductor watches out for our camp and drops off the mail."

"I wish I'd had a letter," Virginia pouted.

"I'll share mine with you," Marian promised, looking up suddenly at a gay laugh from her mother, seated in the triangle of shade from the tent.

Mother seemed her cheerful self now. She was poring over the letters from home, reading aloud here and there. But Father and Doctor Frank scarcely heard her, so absorbed were they in the *Chicago Tribune* and *Times*.

"Good land!" Virginia cried impatiently. "I don't see how you can wait so long to read it!"

"But I want to make it last," Marian laughed. She tore open the envelope then, and slowly read aloud:

"Dear Marian: I've missed you dreadfully. I wish you hadn't gone away. But I know you are having a lovely time and interesting adventures. It's nice that you have Virginia to play with, but don't get so fond of her you forget me. Will you?"

At a queer little choked sound from her friend, Marian glanced up. Virginia's usually pale face was beet red. Marian poked her teasingly and smiled as she went on reading.

"We had a picnic down by the lake shore on the sand dunes. It was lots of fun. We built a fire and cooked our lunch—baked potatoes in the ashes, and your Aunt Lily sent us a pound cake. I thought of you having nice picnics every day. I'm taking music lessons still, but it's getting dreadfully hot to practice. I'm learning a piece called '*Night Bell Gallop*' and a duet. I wish you were here so you could learn to play the duet with me. I do wish you would write.

I haven't heard a word since you left Topeka. I don't
understand it as you must have lots of time on your
hands. Have you tried to ride the frisky pony yet?
I must stop now and get dressed. I am going to
Sarah's birthday party. Sarah said she would have
asked you if you had been here. I'm going to wear
my new pink silk poplin. It's a love and terribly
grown up. Lots of love to you and Chase. Your
faithful friend, Lizzie.''

"Oh, I wish I was the . . .'' The words broke off as
if they had been clipped with scissors. There was a tight
lump in Marian's throat. Somehow she wished she
hadn't received the letter now. She hid her face quickly.

Virginia squeezed her hand pityingly. ''Come, let's
play something. Shall we? Maybe Russell would like us
to play with him.''

Marian threw her a grateful look and a shaky smile
quivered on her lips.

Russell and the girls played dolls and soldiers in the
wagon until noon. Sunday the Blanes had their heavy
meal in the middle of the day. After the work was done,
the last dish put away and the dish-rag hung up on a
tent rope to dry, Marian and Russell curled up in the
back seat of the carriage and Marian read aloud from
her brother's "Rollo" book. She read until her voice
dragged with weariness and Russell's eyes drooped and
he flopped over asleep.

Marian gazed about the camp with a sigh. No breeze

111

ruffled the prairie grass, nor stirred the tent fly. The very plains slept. Mother was resting within the tent while Father and Doctor Frank leafed through the newspapers as they sprawled contentedly in their camp-chairs in the shade of the wagon. The Cooper camp was strangely still except for the regular whistling snores which came from the red-faced Casper who was stretched out beneath the large wagon near by.

Marian thought of the Sundays at home. There was the walk to church in the morning. Vividly she pictured herself in starched white muslin walking beside her father in his long coat tails and high hat and Mother in her best gray silk with the velvet Polonaise. Through the church service Marian heard little but the organ which always made her ache with longing to play herself, and set her dreams soaring with the music. When the family returned from the church they went in state to the rosewood furnished dining-room where Tillie had a piping hot dinner ready for them, finished off by vanilla ice-cream and marble cake. In the afternoon there were so many things to do: calls, a walk with Father, or visits with Lizzie. Later the family had a dainty tea served under the apple tree in the back yard.

Shuffling footsteps broke into her thoughts. Jake prowled restlessly about camp. Somehow he reminded Marian of Grandmother's tiger-striped tom-cat. The very set of his shoulders, the angle of his tattered hat, the restless eyes, hands and feet, spoke of action. Presently he sank to the ground, and leaning back against the wagon tongue, brought out his six-shooters. When Jake had nothing else to do, he always cleaned his guns.

He seemed to feel her stare, for he glanced up and the narrow eyes met hers. Marian looked away quickly. She took Lizzie's letter from her pocket. But somehow the rounded letters, so like Lizzie herself, failed to hold her attention long. Presently she picked up *"Nelly's Dark Days"* and tried to lose herself within its pages.

After a cold supper, the two families gathered in a circle about Father who read them a chapter from Mother's worn Bible. Presently they all joined in a hymn or two; Casper's voice was the loudest one of all. Jake remained in the background, ill at ease.

That was Sunday in camp. And, except for the weather, every Sunday was the same.

The next morning after the campers hit the trail once more, Marian saw a beautiful silvery lake, a town and many trees in the distance. She galloped back to the creaking carriage.

"Look, everybody— a town! Isn't it the loveliest one we've seen since we left Topeka?"

Father was looking up the road with a puzzled expression on his face. "I've been watching it. But for the life of me, I can't figure out what town it is."

"Let's see! Let's see!" shouted Russell, clambering to his feet.

Jake, who was driving the big wagon in front, turned

113

and smiled his twisted smile at them. "That ain't no town. That's a mirage. Ain't ya never heard tell of a mirage? It's what ya think ya see but don't. Travelers are always seein' 'lusions on the plains.''

Disappointed, Marian continued to watch the strange optical illusion.

Before long it faded away and there was nothing but dry treeless prairie rolling endlessly westward. Two buzzards, black against the sun, circled lazily above the place where the imaginary town had been.

About noon they came upon hundreds of horse tracks, plowing the trail into a veritable washboard.

"Land!" Virginia remarked. "Where did all these horses come from? Do you suppose it's a troop of cavalry?"

"Oh, I hope so! Maybe they're going to Colorado. Wouldn't we feel safe with a lot of soldiers traveling with us?" Marian cried in delight.

At the next forlorn station, Mr. Blane jumped down from the carriage to ask who had make those tracks and to find out why they were passing through the country.

"Them's Indians!" a gray-bearded settler told him. "Passed through here day before yesterday. We hid out in the mud fort there and they didn't bother us none. Went on through. Six hundred of 'em!"

"Good heavens!" Father cried, just as Marian rode up. "Do you think it's safe for us to go on?"

"Can't say, stranger. But they're two days ahead of ya."

"Jake," Father questioned, "you know this country. What do you say?"

"Waal," Jake drawled, as he swung from the wagon, "the rate you all go they'll be miles ahead of ya 'fore long. Sure, I'd go on."

After a brief consultation with Mr. Cooper, Father turned away saying, "We'll try it, I guess." However he shook his head doubtfully as he climbed silently into the carriage. He avoided Mother's eyes.

But the words of the settler had struck terror into Marian's heart. White-faced, she guided Gypsy back to her friend.

"What is it?" cried Virginia anxiously after one glimpse into Marian's stricken eyes.

"Indians! . . . Oh, Virginia, they've come at last! What'll we do? The man said there were six hundred of them."

"Six hundred!" Virginia echoed, paling. "Oh! . . . Well, I'm glad we've enough rifles and carbines to go around and that we can all shoot."

"Ye'es. But—what good will that do? We aren't all good shots. I'm not! Oh, Virginia, suppose—suppose they attack us! What could we do against so many?"

Virginia shook her head.

Marian tried to be glad that they were well armed— glad that Jake, at least, was a sure shot, but it was small comfort. Only too well she knew from Virginia's stories that even great wagon trains had failed to protect themselves against an Indian attack.

The others started on. Urging their ponies to a trot the girls were soon riding beside the carriage. But for a long time they remained silent, staring at the ominous tracks on every side.

IX

Chase

For two days the party followed the sinister horse tracks made by the Indians. Russell hoped that they would catch up with them, but Marian and the others hoped fervently that they never would. They were passing out of the flat prairie land and now there were low hillocks rolling away toward the sky-line.

Here and there were great gashes in the plains. Jake called them canyons or arroyos. The road which pitched headlong down their steep sides was so dangerous that all but the drivers climbed out while the wagons descended.

There had been no game. Grasshoppers, great hordes of them, seemed to be the only life on the prairie. And such funny ones! All black except for tiny, bright yellow spots.

At length the travelers reached Fort Wallace where

they stopped at the store for supplies. Here were the same wooden buildings as those Marian had seen at Fort Hays, drearily brown and ugly, relieved here and there by a cream-colored sandstone building.

"Did the Indians bother you at all?" inquired Father anxiously as he paid for the provisions.

"No, sir. They went right on. I guess they were afraid to stay around the fort. They seemed in a hurry."

"Thank heavens! But they may . . ." Father broke off at the sight of Marian's blanched face peering up into his.

The Indians continued ahead of them mile after mile. At intervals the travelers noticed the charred remains of a fire where the redskins had made a brief camp.

During the second day they met a train of nine wagons, each drawn by four huge oxen. Jake seemed to know some of the swarthy drivers.

"Them wagons have hauled freight to New Mexico and are returnin' fer another load," he explained.

When the campers stopped for the night, Marian climbed down from the saddle and looked about her with a sigh. "This is the worst camp spot we've had," she confided to Gypsy.

The dry ground broke through the thin coating of buffalo grass in great bald patches. The water near by looked white and horrid. Dust lay thick over her high buttoned shoes that were worn and scuffed at the toes.

Father, Doctor Frank and Jake were unloading the

wagon. Russell was tagging after Jake. Mother sat wearily in the carriage. Beyond, the Coopers were putting up their tents.

Marian pulled off her sunbonnet and started to un saddle Gypsy. Lately she had taken care of the pony herself because she didn't like the rough way Jake handled her. Once she thought he used his long black whip on the pony. Gypsy had never felt anything but kind hands since the Blanes had owned her, and Marian had never forgotten that Jake had kicked Chase.

At the thought of the dog, she dropped her saddle. Chase! Why, where was he?

"Chase! Here, boy!" she called.

The dog failed to answer.

"Where is Chase?" she called anxiously to her father who was busy with the tent ropes.

"I haven't seen him, Marian. He must be with the Coopers."

"But, Father, he never goes away. He always stays near, right behind Gypsy."

Marian ran toward the Coopers' outfit where the two drivers were picketing the horses and mules. "Jake! Is Chase there with you—have you seen him?"

"Naw, Miss, I ain't seen him," Jake answered sullenly.

Oh! What could have happened to him!

Marian called distractedly to Virginia, who was peeling the supper potatoes, "Is Chase with you?"

"Why, Marian, isn't he in your camp? I haven't seen

him since ———— Do you suppose he could have been left behind?"

"Virginia! Where? Oh, how awful!"

"Why, back there at Pond Creek Station. We haven't been near any towns or stations since. Maybe he's back at Fort Wallace."

"Oh no, Virginia! Not back there! I saw him just before we got to Pond Creek. He wanted to run after a prairie dog and I had to call him back. Oh, do you suppose . . . ?"

Marian sped back to the Blane camp. "Father! Father! I think we left him at Pond Creek Station. We must go back—we must find Chase!" she cried breathlessly.

"But that's seventeen miles! A whole day's journey. We can't do that, Marian. We——— Now, come on. Don't feel so badly." Mr. Blane patted her shaking shoulders. She pulled herself up. But tears filled her eyes in spite of herself.

Chase! Faithful old Chase—left behind in that lonely station—waiting with sorrowful expectant eyes. Her heart ached.

"Mother—can't we go back?" she pleaded desperately.

"No, dear, not if Father thinks it best not to. Don't grieve so. He was a fine loyal fellow, but we will find you another dog, Marian."

Another dog! How could they think that she would ever want another! No dog could take his place—never! She shook the tears away before anyone could see.

Virginia stole over and silently watched Marian set the table.

"Marian," Virginia wailed at length, "isn't it terrible? I'm so sorry he's gone. Oh, isn't there something we can do?"

Marian shook her head; she didn't trust herself to speak.

Mrs. Cooper's hearty call broke the stillness. "Virginia! Vir-ginia!! Supper!"

Reluctantly, Virginia wandered back to her camp. For the first time since she had known her, Marian saw her brush tears from her eyes.

Dimly Marian heard Russell pleading to go back for Chase. She could see Doctor Frank stop and gaze toward the east with anxious eyes. Several times Father peered down the road.

Suddenly she dropped the knife and fork she was carrying and ran to him. "Father! Please! I've got to find Chase! I'll ride back and look for him if you let Doctor go with me!" she begged.

"No, Marian. It's too far."

"Well, I think you ought to let me. Think what would have happened lots of times if Chase hadn't been with us. He—he saved Russell's life!"

"I know—I know—but . . ." Father turned away abruptly.

Marian turned on her heel and flounced off. She let the furious tears fall. She didn't care who saw them—now.

At supper she could not eat a mouthful. The fresh beef tasted like so much leather, and the biscuits choked her. Suddenly she pushed aside her plate and stumbled away from the little group around the table. Back of the tent she sank to the ground and buried her head in her arms.

Presently a desperate thought crept through her mind. Why couldn't she go back—alone? She could slip away when it was dark—ride to Pond Creek and back before morning! Gypsy could go like the wind. If only Gypsy understood the reason, she would try so hard. They were such friends, Chase and Gypsy.

"Oh, I've got to find him! I don't care if it's disobeying. I've just got to!" Marian moaned half aloud.

There was a defiant, determined angle to her chin when she walked back to the others. Father was putting Russell to bed and Mother had already disappeared inside the tent. Doctor Frank was meditatively puffing his pipe and gazing at the fading daylight. Jake mumbled as he scraped the plates with an angry clatter.

No one cared—no one, but herself! She bit her lip.

"Here, Jake. I'll do the dishes!" she said wretchedly.

Anything was better than idleness, waiting—waiting until dark. She watched Jake narrowly as he sauntered off with a shrug, and wondered if he had possibly been the cause of Chase's being left behind.

Would it ever get dark? Would they never go to bed?

She peered out where the mules were picketed. She could just see the spotted pony in the waning light.

A little later she crept, trembling, to her cot. Fervently she hoped that Jake wouldn't be on guard, that she would be able to slip away without being seen or heard. She shivered at the thought of what would happen if Father caught her. . . . Her heart beat so loudly that she feared her father would hear it from where he lay under the tent fly.

Finally, her parents' breathing told her they were asleep. Noiselessly she crept over the still figure at the threshold. Outside she stood listening. She could see Doctor Frank asleep under the carriage. Jake was nowhere to be seen. A murmur of voices floated over from the Cooper tents. Perhaps Jake was over there talking to Casper. She hoped so. She hadn't dared ask Virginia to go with her. Besides, two horses would make more noise. But now—for a moment she hesitated, looking toward the tent where she could see Virginia silhouetted against the lantern.

Stealthily, she stole out to Gypsy and untied the halter rope with cold nervous fingers. Her knees shook beneath her as she led the pony away.

"Oh, if I can only get started—far enough—so they can't hear!" she whispered to Gypsy.

She looked back. So far no one seemed to have heard her. Now, she must get away! Quickly! She scrambled astride Gypsy's slippery bare back. She hadn't dared get her side-saddle. She leaned over and whispered into Gypsy's ear. They were off, flying over the prairie toward Pond Creek. Marian clung wildly to the pony's mane to keep from sliding off. "Oh!" she moaned, "this is awful!" In desperation she put both arms about the pony's neck and clung there. Every now and then she glanced back. Her heart raced with the pony's beating hoofs.

There was no moon. It was dark with a thick blackness that hung over her like a smothering blanket. She wished she had brought a gun. Somehow, now that she was actually speeding back to Chase she was appalled by what she had done.

Suppose she met someone—horse thieves or outlaws. ... Marian shivered. How she wished now that Virginia was with her!

Suddenly, above the steady rhythm made by Gypsy, she heard the rat-tat-tat of other hoofs beating the hard road. As she strained her ears to listen, her heart turned mad flip-flops against her flannel basque. Was it something in front of her—or was it behind her? Could they have discovered that she was missing? Or was it someone else racing toward her—someone hostile? Limp with fright, Marian clung to Gypsy.

Then, pulling Gypsy up short, she listened, breathless. Yes, it was behind her! Rat-tat-tat! It was coming nearer—nearer!

She tugged at the halter rope and they were off again.

CHASE

The wind raced past her ears and her knees ached from holding to the pony's flanks. Once, she glanced back. She could see a shadow swiftly covering the distance between them. It was almost upon her!

What if it was someone not in their party—an outlaw! Panic-stricken, she urged Gypsy on. Oh, why had she ever left camp?

The pursuing horse was right behind her. Something white reached out and grabbed Gypsy's mane. The startled pony reared, then quivered to a halt.

Numb with fright, Marian raised her eyes. Why, the face was familiar! "Oh, Doctor Frank—you frightened me so! I thought—I wasn't sure who was following me." She laid a pleading hand on his arm. "Don't take me back! Please! I must find Chase!"

"But, Marian," the doctor argued, "it's miles to Pond Creek Station—even if he should be there—and you don't know for sure that he is. You've only gone a short way. Come now! I know it's hard,—I love Chase too. But there's your mother to think of. She doesn't know that you're missing. You mustn't frighten her! It might . . . Well, you can't tell what it might do to her!"

Mother! Yes, in her desolation over losing Chase she had forgotten her father's words, "Take care of Mother ———"

Sheepishly, she permitted Doctor Frank to turn Gypsy around and they started back toward camp. But her eyes blurred with tears, and her heart was as leaden as Russell's little soldiers.

Nothing would ever be the same again. Of course, Mother came first—always, but Marian knew that she would never be able to forget Chase's pleading eyes, sorrowful and accusing.

Doctor Frank reached over and patted her cold hands that clenched the halter rope so tightly. "Sorry, little lady."

She threw him a grateful look. But he was gazing straight ahead, his face hidden in the shadowy darkness. His presence comforted her somewhat. She hadn't realized until now how very much alone and afraid she had been.

"Is Father very angry?" she asked presently in a timid voice. "Is he going to punish me?"

"I don't know, Marian. He was very much upset!"

Oh, dear! He would be, no doubt. But she could stand the punishment. It was his stern eyes and his set white face, that she remembered on several occasions in the past, which left her weak. The look in his eyes cut deeply into her heart like the thrust of a knife. She had been twelve when last he looked at her in this fashion, and she never wanted to see his face like that again.

Doctor Frank was talking now. He was teasing her, trying to cheer her up—telling stories, trying hard to make her forget. But she barely heard him and soon he too fell silent. They let the tired Rusty and Gypsy carry them slowly back toward the light that flickered like a firefly in the distant darkness.

Marian awoke the next day and stretched out her hand to say a loving good-morning to Chase. Then she remembered. She bit her lip hard. Slowly she slid from under the quilt and joined the family. Father had not yet punished her, but he had been very silent the night before. Now Marian avoided his eyes.

The odor of frying salt pork and the stimulating fragrance of coffee drifted over as she sat down dejectedly on the dish box. She shook her head when Doctor Frank offered her a bowl of steaming mush. How could she eat with this nagging lump in her throat?

Silence hung over the camp, interrupted only by the chop-chop of Jake's ax, the rattle of a pan and the scraping of dishes from the other camp. It was evident that Chase's absence was uppermost in everyone's mind.

Far down the railroad track, the train bumped along toward them. Marian failed to raise her eyes when it jerked to a squeaking halt beside the camp. She had completely lost interest in trains.

Russell's excited scream brought her to her feet. "Look! Look!"

"Chase!" Marian cried. The dog leaped off the platform and in an instant he had hurled himself upon her. With great barks of gladness he danced around her, licking her hands and trying to flap his tongue over her face.

"That's your dog, isn't it, Miss?" inquired the blue-coated conductor, smiling at her from the platform.

"Oh, yes—yes! Where ever did you find him?"

"Back there at Pond Creek. We knew he belonged to you folks. He sure acted like he knew we were bringing him to you."

"Thank you—thank you so much," Marian said, hugging the dog close.

Chase greeted each member of the party as they crowded around him—wiggling his great body in joy.

"Did you run after a prairie dog and get left, you naughty rascal!" Marian scolded, shaking her finger at him.

Chase's head and tail drooped.

"Well then promise never to do it again and I'll forgive you!" Marian cried laughing.

The dog seemed to know by the laughter, if not the words, that he was forgiven. He eagerly nosed her hand.

The train slowly creaked on its way.

"Oh, Marian, isn't it great to have Chase back?" Russell cried.

"Oh, isn't it, Russie!" Marian answered happily as she threw her arms about the dog's shaggy neck. Then she caught the look of tenderness in Father's eyes. Her heart leaped hopefully.

"Please—I—I know I mutinied. . . . But please forgive me, Father," she pleaded.

"All right. But don't forget, soldiers obey! See that

128

you don't give us a scare like that again,'' Father answered seriously.

The six hundred Indians were still ahead of them. Their tracks stretched as far as the eye could reach. But for once Marian was too happy to pay much attention to them. She had Chase again and Father had forgiven her!

X

A Theft and Farewell

"Russie's been so funny ever since we crossed the Colorado line this morning," Marian laughed, as three days later the girls rode their ponies over the dusty wagon trail with its sinister horse tracks. He's been wondering where the line was. I guess he thought it should be drawn across the road."

Virginia giggled. "Well, it doesn't look like we were. Nothing has changed a single bit. Same old dry land and Mexican Bayonet, wild squash vine and sage-brush— everywhere."

"I rather like the smell of sage." Marian took a deep breath. "It smells like Grandmother's kitchen when she roasts a chicken. Father says we'll have to burn sagebrush if we don't find any larger wood for our fires."

Virginia wrinkled her nose and sniffed the pungent odor. "Un-huh. It does smell sort of nice. But I'll be glad when we see something else. Mountains and things. They say when we get to First View we'll have our first glimpse of Pike's Peak.''

"Oh, I hope so. I've never seen a mountain," Marian declared.

But the girls were doomed to be disappointed, for on arriving at First View where the travelers camped that evening they saw only a herd of antelope far off to the west—too far away to shoot.

"Pshaw! Too bad that it's so hazy we can't see the peak," Mr. Blane complained to the girls, putting his spy-glass down. "In 1806 Major Zebulon Pike made the first expedition to that mountain. He got the War Department at Washington to equip him for the trip. The peak is named for him."

They traveled fifteen miles the next day, and just as they were within three miles of the town of Kit Carson, Marian, who was in the lead with Virginia, cried out sharply, "Father! Doctor Frank! Look! The Indians have gone!''

The little party of travelers halted and gazed ahead. Sure enough, the wide plowed up trail made by their many animals had swerved away toward the south, leaving an unbroken stretch winding dustily westward.

"Thank heavens!" cried Father with relief. "The redskins must be heading for the Arkansas—hoping for better game, maybe.''

Marian turned to Virginia happily. "Isn't it wonderful? Now we won't have to worry about Indians creeping up in the night or ... Oh, Virginia, I just feel in my bones that now we're actually in Colorado, everything is going to be all right.''

"Well, I hope so," Virginia commented doubtfully.

Marian gazed ahead with anticipation as they rode toward the town of Kit Carson. Even the sky looked bluer, the sun-baked world less dreary. With the Indians gone, at last a sense of peace enfolded Marian.

Kit Carson proved to be a wild looking place of unpainted board houses and false-fronted stores, full of shaggy ponies and wicked-appearing Mexican greasers who drove the great wagon trains. From under dirty, broad-brimmed hats the Mexicans looked at the travelers out of narrow black eyes. Their clothes were tattered. Ugly-looking revolvers were slung carelessly from their wide belts and they took delight in cracking their long blacksnake whips at the mules as they passed.

The party drew up before the C. E. Musick & Company's store, "Grocers and Forwarding." Father and Doctor Frank went inside to stock up with provisions. Marian, watching them through the store window, saw a young man in a colored shirt and wide hat stride from a group at the back and greet Doctor Frank with a friendly slap on the back. She smiled. Doctor Frank had met a friend even in Kit Carson.

She looked about her. There were two hotels facing the wide street, "The American House" and "The

133

Perry.'' Numerous dance halls, freighters' and stock dealers' stores crowded each other along the plank walks. Farther on loomed a government warehouse. The windows and doors of some of the places were drearily boarded.

Jake noticed her interest in the place and spoke up: '' 'Fore they built the Kansas Pacific and fer a spell after, this here town of Carson was whar they transferred freight and passengers over the trail bound for southern Colorado and New and Old Mexico. Thar was lots of business and folks here then, but soon's they built the railroad to Denver, it ain't been so brisk an' folks 'a' been movin' away, though it's still a tradin' post for Mexico and some of this Territory.''

Presently Jake sauntered across the street to Snyder's Beer Hall. He seemed to be well known by the loungers sprawled about the doorway. Soon he was deep in conversation with a great hulk of a man, whose black-bearded head reminded Marian of a fierce buffalo. She noticed the men both glanced at their wagons. Once the big man nodded. Then Jake turned away and the words of the stranger floated over to her. "Sure, Jake. Meet ya the other side of the Arkansas.''

"Did you hear that? What do you suppose he meant, Virginia?'' she asked her friend who in the meantime had dismounted from Rusty to stretch her weary legs, and was gazing in admiration at the two brilliant cheeked girls who were sauntering by, swishing their gay ruffles carelessly over the dusty road.

"I didn't hear anything. What?" she remarked.

"Oh, nothing."

But Marian tried to puzzle it out as they rode silently along through the hot afternoon. When they finally camped for the night she was glad that they were two miles from those black-eyed Mexicans and that strange wild town. The Indians had disappeared, at least for a time, but a new uneasy fear gripped her heart. The feeling of peace which had pervaded everything that morning was gone. Even the fresh beef for supper and that luxury, new potatoes, failed to make her forget.

The next morning Marian was awakened by a commotion in the Cooper camp. She sat up sleepily. What had happened? She could hear Mr. Cooper shouting. She could hear her father's voice loud in argument. Mother and Russell had already left their beds. She swung her legs to the ground and groped for her shoes.

She had just reached the tent flap when Virginia came running up. "Marian! Guess what? Casper's gone!" Virginia paused to catch her breath and to let the significance of this remark penetrate into Marian's mind.

"Gone!" Marian replied in a daze.

"Yes! And he took the fresh meat and one of the revolvers and worst of all, Rusty! Isn't that awful? Pa is all for going back to Kit Carson and finding him, but

135

your father says it wouldn't do any good—not in that wild place. Mom thinks so, too.''

''Oh, how dreadful! Why, Casper was always singing —not a bit like a robber. Poor Rusty! How mean of Casper to take him!''

''Pa has just been telling your father that he thinks we'd better follow the railroad now that we've only one man.''

''The railroad! But, Virginia, we're going to follow the Arkansas. I heard Father say the camp spots were better along the river and that there was more water and game. Virginia, that means—we won't be together any more!''

''Yes, and I'll miss you so. There won't be anyone to play with. You have Russell and Chase and now I—I haven't even Rusty!'' And then, to Marian's amazement, Virginia burst into a flood of tears.

Marian threw her arms impulsively around the thin shaking shoulders. ''There, there,'' she comforted, just as she always did when Russell bumped his head. ''Don't feel so badly. We'll see each other soon in Denver. It's a place as nice as Chicago I'm sure and I know we'll have fun there together. It won't be long, just you see.''

A hard lump caught in Marian's throat. Until now she hadn't realized how fond she had become of Virginia. ''Come on! Let's find out for sure if we aren't going with you,'' she added hopefully.

But when they joined their parents it had been decided.

136

A THEFT AND FAREWELL

The Coopers were already packing their large wagon in spite of Jake's arguments that the Arkansas trail was safer.

"Father, can't we follow the railroad?" Marian pleaded.

"I'm afraid not. We must think of Mother. I think the southern trail will be the best for us. Mr. Cooper is in a hurry to get to Denver. We can't travel so swiftly with Mother. We must take our time."

Marian joined her friend and assisted her in packing her small brown satchel.

"Will you write to me, Marian?" Virginia asked as the last familiar garment was stowed away.

"Of course. Though I don't see where we'll mail letters now. Oh, Virginia ... !"

The girls stared at each other silently for a long moment.

"Come, Virginia!" called Mrs. Cooper. "Pa wants to fold the tent."

A half hour later the two outfits parted,—the Blanes to go south to the Arkansas River, the Coopers to follow the trail over the plains along the Kansas Pacific. There was a mist in Mrs. Blane's eyes as Mrs. Cooper, tears coursing down her round red cheeks, kissed her a hearty good-bye. Virginia clung to Marian, then dashed back to the wagon to hide her tears.

The Coopers were leaving. "Good luck! Good-bye! Good-bye!" they all called and waved.

WAGON WHEELS TO DENVER

Through the opening in the back of the wagon, Virginia's handkerchief fluttered—fluttered. Marian watched until their wagons were little black spots against the sky. Then she turned and gazed with lonely eyes across the bleak stretch of cracking ground that lay between them and the green-bordered Arkansas. Out of the corner of her eye she could see her father's thoughtful face, and on her mother's cheek, beneath the dark lashes, a tear glistened, then ran down and disappeared upon the golden enameled wings of the butterfly pin at her throat.

"I wonder if we will ever see them again?" she asked Gypsy.

Strange, she thought later, that it had been Casper and not Jake who had stolen the horse, revolver and meat. She might have expected it of Jake.

She watched his great shoulders swaying to the rhythm of the jolting wagon. There was a strange bulge under his left arm. For the first time she remembered what Russell had told her, "Jake 'totes' a gun under his arm for reasons." Reasons! Suddenly the words of the man that resembled a buffalo reverberated in her mind leaving her cold, frightened. "Sure, Jake, I'll meet ya on the other side of the Arkansas."

The Arkansas! What did he mean by that?

XI

In the Night

It was lonely without the Coopers' creaking wagons. Marian missed Mr. Cooper's hearty laugh, Mrs. Cooper's bustling visits between the two camps, and Virginia riding beside her over the dusty trail. Without them, the twelve miles they traveled the following day seemed endless.

In the late afternoon, Mr. Blane drew up the mules and thoughtfully surveyed the plains.

Presently he shook his head. "No likely camp spot here. I think we would best keep going until we hit some creek nearer the Arkansas. Nothing but these holes full of alkali water around here," he announced, turning to the occupants of the carriage. "How about building a fire and cooking supper—then riding as long as you are able to, Mary?"

"Of course, William. I'm not tired and we must get to

some better water. It's terrible, even with vinegar.''
Mother shivered and made a wry face. "I don't blame
the mules for turning up their noses!"

After an hour's rest and supper of salt pork and fried
potatoes, eaten picnic fashion around the sage-brush
camp-fire, the Blanes started on. Marian felt tired and
sleepy as she crawled into the back seat of the carriage
with Russell. It was the first time they had traveled at
night. Marian lazily watched the plains turn gold colored.
The world about her looked as unreal as a dream. It was
that hour of day which lent glamour to the most desolate
of waste lands. Presently the sun disappeared as suddenly as if a giant hand had plucked it from its bed of creamy
clouds. Gradually the gold blurred into gray. The glamour was gone.

Marian closed her eyes. When she opened them again
it was dark. Jake was calling from the wagon in front of
them, "Five more miles and we oughta hit water, folks."

She closed her eyes once more, but sleep would not
come. She could hear the jangle of the harness, the
creak, creak of wheels, and Russell's regular breathing
from where he lay curled up beside her. At her feet,
Chase's big warm body quivered with a sigh, then his
puffing snores told her that he too had fallen asleep.

How long they rode through the silent night, Marian
wasn't sure. She must have fallen asleep again for she
was awakened by something stinging her face. She sat
up bewildered. Another onslaught stung her cheeks be-

fore she realized what it was. Sand! The wind was blowing it furiously around them—at them—over them! Marian tried to see in front of her but even the mules were hidden in great clouds of fine whirling pebbles.

"Can't see a foot ahead of me!" her father cried. "We'd better stop."

Russell awakened suddenly and clung to Marian in fright. She pulled him down hurriedly to the floor of the carriage beside Chase, drawing her mother's shawl over their heads like a tent.

Once Marian dared to peek out from her covering. Jake had halted also, and he and Doctor Frank were staggering toward them through the furious, cutting storm.

"We'd better git under cover, folks. This here's goin' to be one o' them prairie squalls!" Jake shouted.

The next thing Marian knew she was swept up into the doctor's strong arms and they were battling their way to the wagon.

"Pull that blanket over you," Doctor Frank ordered, as he lifted her over the seat. "Jake," he cried, "hand Russell up. There you are, little fellow. Now—both of you move over and let your mother lie here where it's most sheltered. Great guns! This is the worst yet!"

Marian clung to Russell on one side and to the blanket on the other.

"Mercy!" cried Mother from under her quilt. "The wagon sways like a ship. I hope to goodness it doesn't blow over!"

"It's fun," Russell giggled. He was enjoying the storm now that he was under cover.

Marian wondered about Chase and Gypsy out there in the storm. "Chase!" she called. There was an answering whimper. The dog snuggled at her feet. He wriggled closer.

The sand beat the canvas top like hail, it pounded the driver's seat, it wrenched open the flap at the back and stung Marian's upturned face. She dived under the blanket again.

"Oh, I hope Father's all right," she whispered to Russell. "I wonder where they all are!"

It seemed hours before the whining of the wind and the fury of tiny stones had ceased. Marian peered cautiously from beneath her smothering covers. Everything was a pitchy blackness. After her eyes became accustomed to the dark she could see a figure in the carriage who looked like father, and the outlines of what must be Gypsy and the mules huddled close together for protection.

Her mother and brother were asleep. Marian lay back quietly and closed her eyes. What an awful country this was! She had heard of sand-storms on a desert obliterating the trail so that travelers lost their way. Fearfully she wondered if that would happen to them.

Suddenly from far across the plains there came a weird cry which grew in volume until it shattered the stillness. The mournful sound sent shivers up and down her spine.

Her mother stirred uneasily in her sleep. Chase stiffened, listening. More cries tore the air. Marian lay rigid and she wondered if it could be a wild animal—a pack of them. But the uncarthly howls did not come nearer; soon they died away and there was silence—silence broken occasionally by the stamping mules.

When Marian awoke the next morning, she jumped down from the wagon with a sense of dread. Suppose something had happened to Father and the others! That dreadful storm, those weird cries in the night! But the sight that met her eyes brought a merry laugh to her lips. Doctor Frank and Jake were great sandy mounds just breaking through their blankets under the wagon. Father was shaking sand from his clothes, and from his dark hair and beard. Sand covered everything; even the wagon wheels had disappeared up to the very hub.

"Oh, Father, I'm so glad you're all right! I was afraid —those scary howls in the night! Did you hear them?"

"Howls? No!" answered Father in surprise.

"Them was wolves," spoke up Jake stretching himself to his full six feet and yawning. "They was away off yonder," his arm swept out in a wide gesture. "I listened a spell to make sure they wasn't goin' to stalk the camp."

"Wolves!" Marian shuddered and turned away.

Breakfast was gritty from the sand that had sifted through into the food. The water in the canteen only added to their discomfort. It was lukewarm and bitter. What a relief it was to reach a small spring that afternoon—after plodding over twelve dreary miles of drifted sand. The water gurgling up through the tiny clean pebbles was cool and it eased their aching throats and furry tongues.

Mrs. Blane felt so much stronger the next day that the party was able to make thirty miles. The first sight of the Arkansas sent a glad shout to their lips.

"Look at those green cottonwoods and the nice cool shade, Russell!" cried Marian, her eyes lighting up at the sight of the lacy shadows along the shimmering water.

At Bent's old fort they forded the river. Marian rode beside the wagon and listened attentively to what Jake was telling Russell about the place. "See that mud house yonder?" he asked Marian and her brother, pointing his black whip toward the low sprawling buildings. "That's a cattle ranch now, but it used to be a fort. Built of adobe brick it was. Man by the name of William Bent and a Frenchy named Ceran St. Vrain built the fort fer a fur tradin' post on the Santa Fe Trail. It was started in 1828. Took 'em four years to build. It had towers and high adobe walls. Cannon was mounted in them towers. Must 'a' been a sight standin' thar five hundred miles from anywhar. Bent hauled them supplies clear from St. Louis and his other tradin' post at Taos. The old fellow had a couple of Indian wives, they say. Married the sister of the first one, when she up and died. He burned the place when the government wouldn't pay his price. Ya see, the fur trade had dwindled. Gold was the

144

big thing. They say it blew up when the fire reached the powder.''

Jake clucked at Baby and Buck. ''The old fort, what was left of it, was deserted fer a spell,'' he went on. ''Then it was fixed up some and used fer a stagecoach station. Now it's a ranch like I was a-tellin' ya. Ain't much left of the old fort.''

Marian looked curiously at the ranch. Several Mexican cowhands stared at them as they passed. A dark-skinned woman came to a door for a moment, her crimson dress a bit of color against the drab doorway.

It was not until they were safely on the other side of the river that Marian remembered the words which the rough man called to Jake, ''Meet ya on the other side of the Arkansas.'' Now, they were on the other side! She felt strangely fearful! And yet, why shouldn't the man say that? They would be on the other side of the river almost all the way to Denver. But what had Jake told the man? Why had they stared at the wagons?

There were moments when she felt she ought to tell her fears to someone. Yet she hated to worry her father. And it probably was just a foolish notion. As for Jake, she had nothing against him, really, but his sneers and his kicking Chase! Doctor would only tease her if she confided in him. How she wished that Virginia were there! She would know what to do.

At length she managed to shake off the spell of foreboding and give herself up to enjoying the green of the trees, the cloudless blue sky overhead—and the thought of the fish which she hoped they would catch for supper. Marian was getting very tired of their daily fare, salt pork.

Their camp under a huge cottonwood tree was so pleasant, and the shelter from the fierce rays of the sun so delightful, that the Blanes stayed over a day. Mr. Blane, with Marian's excited assistance, caught a large turtle and there was a promise of turtle soup. It was nearly lunch time when Marian and Russell, who were playing down by the water, heard the rattle of wheels along the road. Marian had just finished building a mud fort for Russell as near like Bent's as she could from Jake's description. Russell was about to stage an Indian attack on Lily and John who were occupying the fort when they heard the approaching wagon.

"Oh, Russell, it's a government ambulance. And an officer is getting out right in front of our camp! Come on! Let's see what he wants!"

With her brother tagging in the rear, Marian hurried up the bank. When they arrived at the camp, Doctor Frank was introducing the young officer to Father and Mother as Major Rayburn.

"Yes," Major Rayburn was saying, "I met the doctor back at one of the stations. Saw your camp over here and thought I'd run over and say, 'hello.' I'm stationed at Fort Lyon and am on my way to Fort Larnerd." Just then he turned and saw Russell and Marian. "Well! I didn't know you had some young folks with you.''

"These are my son and daughter, Russell and Marian, Major,'' answered Father.

"How do you do! Have either of you tasted antelope? I shot one yesterday—and I'd like to give you some.''

Russell was tongue-tied. His brown eyes were as big as saucers as he gazed in admiration at the well-built figure in army blue.

"Yes,'' cried Marian quickly, encouraged by the kind gray eyes, "we love antelope. We haven't had anything but salt pork and dried beef until last night when Doctor Frank and I caught some fish.''

"Well, antelope you shall have, and a big piece of ice also!''

Marian's and Russell's eyes glowed at the mention of ice—that rare luxury of the plains. While the major unloaded the meat, Father asked him questions.

"Haven't seen any Indians lately, have you, Major?''

"No. Not right around here, Mr. Blane. Most of the Indians are following the herds south. Quite a few of them are no doubt safe in Indian Territory by now.''

"Won't you stay and have lunch with us, Major?'' Mother invited. "Mr. Blane caught a terrapin the size of a platter this morning and we are going to have turtle soup.''

"Thank you, Mrs. Blane, but I'm afraid I must be off. I've a long stretch ahead of me. Perhaps some other time. Well, good-bye! Good luck! I'll surely meet you on the trail again!''

The little family watched until they could see the ambulance no longer, and the rattling wheels had died away in the distance.

"Left ya some ice, did he?" It was Jake, sauntering out from behind some cottonwoods.

Marian wondered why he had stayed in the background. Acquaintances on the plains were few and far between, but Jake always seemed to prefer solitude, except, of course, for little Russell's company. Since the Coopers had left them Jake had acted strangely—almost rudely at times.

As the campers moved farther west, living became higher, with butter at fifty cents a pound, potatoes at eight,—to say nothing of eggs at thirty-five, and milk, when you could get it, at the unheard-of price of ten cents a quart. These luxuries were as scarce as the ranches that supplied them. The Blanes had indeed been thankful for the large piece of antelope which the kind major had given them and for the plentiful fish in the stream.

Often Marian would see that familiar worried pucker between her father's eyebrows. She knew he was wondering how long the money would last. The money box hidden under her white night dresses seemed to grow lighter and lighter. Once she heard him tell Doctor Frank, "Pshaw! I sometimes wish, Frank, that we'd gone with the Coopers. It would have been a much shorter trip. I'm afraid there won't be much money left to start in business when we land in Denver."

But then again he would seem to forget his worry in his happiness over Mother's returning strength. She was riding Gypsy a few miles each day now. Her laugh had become light-hearted. She gloried in the green along the river and seemed to forget that there was dry hot desert just a mile back from the water.

Marian was restless the night before they left the Santa Fe Trail. The bugs had been worse than usual and she could hear the sizz-sizz of mosquitoes swarming above her. Even her mitts proved no protection against their sting until she thrust her arms impatiently under the hot covers. The smell of the sagebrush smudge outside the tent drifted in. For three nights, the men guarding the mules had kept up a fire of sage so that the rest of the party might get some sleep. But this night the smudge seemed to have very little effect on the insects.

Father had crawled into the tent some time before. Jake must be on guard. Far off she thought she heard a lone horseman, but she wasn't sure. She listened and hugged Chase closer. Yes, it was a horse! Chase had heard it too! His muscles were rigid. Now she distinctly heard the clop-clop of hoofs beating the trail.

Who could be traveling alone at that time of night?

The horseman was slowing up—stopping! Marian listened with straining ears.

Suppose it was an outlaw! Suppose it was that man

back at Kit Carson! Suppose ... Her frightened thoughts ran on and on.

Chase growled. There was a murmur of voices outside. Marian wanted to cry out, but before she could manage a sound she heard the sudden clatter of hoofs tearing down the road.

Marian had not regained her voice, but she had found the use of her legs. She crawled from under the quilt and crept to the tent opening. The sage fire was still burning and Jake was sprawled full length on the ground beside it. One arm upheld his dark head and he was looking down the trail—as if listening.

"Jake," she whispered, "who was it? What—what did he want?"

Jake sprang to his feet with a startled exclamation. "Oh—it's you! Go on to bed! That wasn't no one but a traveler—askin' his way."

Marian crept back to her cot but not to sleep for many long minutes. Why, she wondered, had Jake been so angry? He had scowled at her dreadfully. She shivered and buried her head in the dog's shaggy neck for comfort.

XII

The Attack

The next day Marian confided her fears of Jake to Doctor Frank.

"Jake! Why, he's all right," he scoffed. "He's just a rough plainsman! You're imagining things, little lady. However, I'll keep an eye on the fellow. Don't worry your curly head any more."

"But last night—and that man back at Kit Carson," Marian worried, in spite of Doctor Frank's reassuring words.

"Forget it, Marian, and enjoy what's ahead of you. Do you see them?" he asked mysteriously.

"See what? Oh!... Mountains!" Marian drew a sharp breath of awe and pulled up her pony. "Why, I thought they were clouds! Quick! Hand me Father's glass, please!" she cried. Through the spy-glass she could see a blue range of rugged mountains topped with snow.

"Those must be the Spanish Peaks that Jake told us about. Imagine, snow on them! And we're simply baking out here on the plains."

"That's the Huerfano range," said the doctor. "Hard to believe they are at least forty miles away."

"Forevermore! Well, I wish we'd see Pike's Peak!" Marian returned the glass to Doctor Frank. "When we see that mountain, I'll believe we're nearly there!"

For three days they plodded along, the purplish-blue mountains beckoning them to hurry—hurry to their refreshing coolness. One day they caught their first glimpse of Pike's Peak, some ninety miles away, coldly blue under a crown of snow. Another day, the Blanes forded the Huerfano stream and camped near the small adobe houses that lined the water's edge. They had their first visitor in many days, a dark-skinned woman in a faded sunbonnet, who timidly presented Mother with a loaf of homemade bread.

"Jiminy, how good it tastes!" cried Marian at lunch. "It's been weeks since we've had anything but corn bread and biscuits."

The third day they camped near Fort Reynolds. After pulling up stakes the next morning, they drove over to see the fort. Doctor Frank knew the government doctor and also one of the lieutenants stationed there.

Lieutenant Lamb, young and straight as an arrow, and fat, jolly Doctor Powers, led them to their quarters. The building was a one-story adobe affair with a broad ver-

152

anda across the front. The porch was strewn with wild animal skins. Comfortable chairs and couches invited one to rest, and here and there a potted red or pink geranium made a splash of color against the dull walls.

With a tired smile Mother sank gratefully into the first chair. "I don't see how you keep things so nice and home-like without a woman in the fort, Doctor Powers," she exclaimed as she looked about.

But Marian forgot the fort, the comfortable chairs, the wide veranda, these homey touches of civilization they had missed for so long, in her interest in the two strange animals which the lieutenant was bringing forward.

"These are our pets, Miss Marian," he explained, grinning.

"Oh! Look, Russie! A baby antelope! Isn't it a darling—and so gentle." Marian caressed the silky head. "See, she's letting me pet her! And look at her big brown eyes watching every move I make!"

But Russell was squealing with delight over a bright-eyed, grayish-brown animal clutched tightly in his arms.

"Why—it's a prairie dog! Lucky we left Chase down in the wagon. He always wants to run after them." Marian petted the tiny head. "My, but he's a smart looking little creature!"

The big doctor laughed. "Yes, he is smart. We couldn't keep house without Bill."

"Bill! What a funny name for a prairie dog! What do you call the beautiful antelope?"

"Diana! She was the goddess of the chase, if you know mythology. She was swift on her feet and certainly our Diana can outrun anything and anybody, if she wishes to," answered the doctor, patting the animal's head.

"Come, Marian!" Mother called. "The lieutenant is going to show us about the fort."

Marian turned away reluctantly, only to find that Diana was following at a timid distance and that Russell had a death-like grip on the fat Bill.

Lieutenant Lamb was in the commissary department, and he took them through the storehouse which was filled with shelf upon shelf of groceries. Enough for a whole year! Then they crossed the grassless square to the Quartermaster's warehouse where the clothing and uniforms were kept. At length they went through the immaculate kitchens filled with the odor of boiling meat and back through the barrack-like dining-room with its long tables and benches.

"Here, Miss Marian," the young officer said, as they were leaving, "here's a small present."

"Oh, thank you," Marian cried, accepting the basket. Her delighted eyes searched the contents. Two boxes of sardines, a can of currant jelly, several packages of raisins and some brown Mexican beans.

"Look, Mother, isn't this a welcome present? Tonight we can have a real party!"

"Yes indeed! And here's the doctor with a piece of ice!" smiled her mother.

"Thank you, Doctor Powers! Thank you both so much," they cried as they climbed into the carriage.

"You say it's about a two-day journey to Pueblo, Lieutenant?" asked Father as he picked up the reins.

"Yes, sir, if you take it slowly. And it's about a week's travel from there to Denver," replied the officer.

"Good-bye! . . . Good luck to you!" the men called.

Marian leaned out and waved. Her eyes lingered on Diana and she wished she had an antelope for a pet. Father flapped the reins and clucked at the mules. Marian settled back in the seat hugging her basket when she suddenly discovered that Russell was still holding Bill, the prairie dog.

"Father! Stop! Russell is running away with Bill!"

"The little scalawag! Here, Russie—give the lieutenant the prairie dog. You mustn't take him away."

"Oh, that's all right," the officer laughed. "Let the little fellow keep him. Here, son, he's yours!" The young man handed back the squirming Bill. "Good-bye!" he said smiling at the radiant little face upturned to his.

Mother and Father gazed doubtfully at the happy boy who clasped Bill tightly in his arms.

"Mercy!" Mother commented. "What will we ever do with the creature?"

"Oh, I'll take care of him," Russell volunteered eagerly, "and I'll sleep with him at night like Marian does with Chase."

After the carriage had joined Jake with the wagon,

155

Russell whispered to Marian, "He's mine, Marian, mine! You got Chase an' Gypsy, but Bill's mine! Don't you dare let your old dog hurt him, will you?"

"Course not. But you can take care of him yourself, feed him and everything. What in the world do you suppose he eats? Ouch! He dug his claws into me then! Move over, Russie! Keep him off me!"

The ride that day proved uneventful. At long intervals they passed an adobe ranch house, bare and lonesome, among a few scraggly acres of yellow-tasseled corn. However, most of the country was uncultivated prairie through which occasional cattle wandered.

Jake shot a jack-rabbit for supper and they had some of Marian's currant jelly and raisins for dessert. Over the supper table the Blanes talked of their plans for the future. Even Father breathed a sigh of relief now that the trip was nearly ended.

"Glad to get to Denver, Marian?" he questioned with a teasing smile, as he and Doctor Frank busied themselves later making Bill a rude sort of cage out of a feed box. Bill had indeed been a trial that day, hiding from Russell under Mother's skirts, upsetting the canteen and spilling their precious water over the prairie, and last, but not least, falling asleep in the food box!

"Oh, yes, Father. I can hardly wait to see Virginia. I hope it's nice there and looks like Chicago and that we have a pretty house with a garden! I'm so happy to think this old trip is nearly over that I could sing and dance

156

and shout for . . ." Her glance caught Jake's sullen eyes upon her. Marian looked away with a shudder. Jake had been positively rude that day. He had even been harsh with Russell over the little scamp, Bill Even Father had noticed his manner and commented on it. Marian knew she would be glad when Jake left the party. He had announced that morning that he would leave them at Pueblo.

It was growing late the following evening when the Blanes decided to make camp. The sun was blood-red over the distant gray-blue mountains. Mr. Blane had hoped to reach Pueblo that night but it was still three miles away. Everything had conspired to delay them that day. Jake had carelessly forgotten the food box and they wasted valuable hours retrieving it. Then Baby developed a sore leg.

"Better not try to make it, I guess," Father decided, noticing the violet shadows under Mother's eyes and patting her hand gently. "Marian, watch out for a likely camp spot."

"Why not right here, Father?" Marian answered. "It's close to the river and lots of trees and bushes. There's a nice level spot over there for the tent." She nodded toward a green clearing overhung with leafy branches, close by the river.

"Hold on!" Father shouted to Jake in the wagon. "We'll camp here."

Marian had just dismounted from Gypsy and had started unsaddling the pony when suddenly the air was rent with blood-curdling war-whoops. Five gaudy, painted horsemen dashed out from behind some shrubbery ahead, the feathered headgear of their leader trailing the ground.

"Indians!" Marian stood rooted to the ground in terror.

"Quick—the wagon!" her father yelled.

Marian ran madly for the wagon and pulled herself inside.

There was the whizz of a bullet close to the canvas, the bark of an answering gun, the fiendish yells of the Indians surrounding them.

They would be scalped—killed! Why didn't Doctor Frank or Jake do something, her heart cried out in agony?

Looking up she saw the reason. Jake was fighting to keep the doctor from reaching his holster. They swayed back and forth on the high seat, their arms locked. Jake swore and groped for his revolver. Doctor Frank fought desperately to free himself.

Marian screamed as Jake thrust the muzzle into the doctor's side. Unconsciously her fingers searched for one of the carbines. But before she could locate it a shot rang out, so close that the mules leaped into the air, the wagon lurched and the men were thrown over the side and disappeared.

The mules were running away!

THE ATTACK

The wagon careened drunkenly. "Father!" Marian shrieked. She was thrown on her face one minute, on her side another. Sobbing in terror she screamed at the frightened mules, "Stop! ... Dinah! Toby! Stop!"

Frantically she looked back. Doctor Frank was picking himself from the ground. Jake seized him and stripped him of his gun. One of the Indians held Father back at the point of his rifle while another yelling, feathered rider tore the Winchester from Mother's hands and snatched something at her throat. Mother cringed back against the carriage. Russell clung crying to her skirts.

Marian shut her eyes in horror. "Oh, what'll I do?" she sobbed. The next instant she was tumbled on her face once more. Crying hysterically, she struggled to her knees and looked for a ranch or for help of some kind. But the road was deserted nor was there a house in sight.

At the sound of more firing she glanced back again. Then her heart almost stopped beating. The Indians were following her!

XIII

Scar Face

Marian looked back in terror as the Indians gained on the swaying, bumping wagon. Any moment now the mules would get tangled in the dragging reins. They would stumble—fall, the wagon crash, and she would be thrown at the redskins' very feet.

"I've got to do something! I—I've got to!" she moaned.

Suddenly she knew there was only one thing she could do. Desperately she crawled over the bedding and prayed that the Indians would not see her. There! She was under the driver's seat. Blindly she groped for the reins. Her frantic fingers found but one. As she had feared, the other rein was dragging!

A bullet whizzed over her head. Panic-stricken, she dropped to the floor and lay there for a second.

Presently she edged slowly forward, hardly daring to breathe. She had to get that rein! She leaned perilously far out of the wagon. The swaying vehicle lurched. Marian clung wildly to the seat to keep from falling out. She tried again! Dizzily she leaned out once more. There! She had reached it! She had the rein at last!

Another bullet whistled close by. She heard the rip-rip of canvas.

Marian clutched the reins, praying that the frightened animals would keep on at this furious pace and would reach some ranch—safety and help!

The savages were coming closer! She was afraid even to look behind her. Those bullets had been meant for the mules,—for her! What would happen to her when they caught up with the wagon? They were so near, now! So near!

"Father . . . Mother!" she sobbed. Her tortured thoughts raced on and on with the clattering hoofs. Then something cold nosed her face. Chase! He had jumped into the wagon when she did. In her fright she hadn't noticed him. "Chase!" she cried. She and her faithful dog would die together!

She tried to pray. But her reeling senses could find no words. A great yawning blackness stretched before her. She was slipping! Falling! Suddenly she was jerked back! It felt like a huge wet hand clutching her shoulder. The Indians! She opened her eyes in terror. No, it was Chase! Chase holding her sleeve in his great black jaws.

162

What had happened? It was so strangely quiet! Then a short distance before her Marian saw the lights of a town blinking. Pueblo!

She glanced fearfully over her shoulder. The Indians had gone! They were afraid to go near the town! But the relief of this discovery was overshadowed by the thought of her family. She was safe, but what of them? Her heart sank. If the Indians had not already wiped out her family, they would return! She must get help! Save them!

She urged the mules on and on. They raced across a narrow bridge and into the town with the clatter of an artillery caisson. Frantically Marian looked around. The streets were deserted. The tired animals were slowing up when she saw a man and boy sauntering out of a building that resembled a hotel.

"Mister! Help!" she screamed, tugging at Toby and Dinah. "Indians! They're after my father and mother!" she finished breathlessly, as she pulled up in front of the building.

"Indians! Why, there ain't no Indians around here, gal!" the man answered, eyeing her curiously. But after seeing her white face and the dripping mules, he nudged his companion. "Looks like the gal's right, Tom. Maybe we better . . ."

"Oh, please—please save them!" Marian implored hysterically. "The Indians—they chased me—until we reached the town. Please help them! Please! I'll go with you! I'll . . ."

"All right, gal! We'll raise the town!" The man ran back into the hotel.

The boy started to follow, then stopped. "Here, you go on inside and let Ma take care of you. You look petered out." He turned toward a roughly dressed man just leaving the livery stable next door. "Hey, Swan, get some horses. Quick! Indian uprising! Whelan and me'll call the men. This girl got away, but her folks are out there needing help." He ran down the street to spread the alarm.

Shaking all over, Marian stumbled down from the wagon and sank to the porch steps. Four armed men ran from the hotel. Soon the street was alive with horses and men, who quickly gathered in front of the livery stable. Marian's heart cried out to these strangers to hurry—hurry before it was too late! Chase snuggled his nose in her cold hand. She bit her lip and blinked hard.

Then a motherly gray-haired woman with a fuzzy chin, who reminded her of Mrs. Cooper, folded Marian to her ample bosom. "Why, you poor dearie! Come inside. Ma Betts'll take care of you and give you a bite to eat after you've set a spell. Those miserable savages!" she added under her breath. As she muttered the word, "savages," a look of torturing hate came into her faded blue eyes.

"No! No, I can't! I must go with the men—show them

164

where. . . . Oh, I couldn't eat! I just couldn't! Thank you but—but I must go! See!'' she cried, springing to her feet. ''They're leaving!''

Tom Betts, the boy with the kind face, to whom she had first spoken, was swinging into the saddle.

''Wait!'' she screamed running toward him. ''Wait! Don't leave me! Take me—please!''

''Well, I don't like to,'' he hesitated. What he read in her eyes caused him to add gruffly, ''Come on, then!'' He swung her up behind him. ''Ma,'' he called over his shoulder, ''take care of her dog and see the mules get feed.''

Tom Betts spurred his horse and they galloped off. Marian clutched her arms around his waist to keep from falling. She glanced back. Twenty or thirty horsemen thundered after them, and before a turn in the road hid them from view, she saw Ma Betts on the hotel steps tugging at Chase's collar.

As they raced through the starlit darkness, horrible pictures painted the blackness before Marian's eyes, pictures that made her head reel and her heart like ice. She could see her father—a rifle pointed at his head—her mother cringing back against the carriage. . . . Marian closed her eyes to shut out the horror of her visions.

If only they were safe—her family and Doctor Frank! She thought of Jake and Doctor Frank—fighting—swaying back and forth on the driver's seat. Jake had drawn his gun! Jake was a traitor! He was in league with those

Indians! Oh, what could be happening to them? Her heart beats fairly screamed, "Hurry! Hurry!"

Presently, Tom Betts leaned forward and peered ahead.

"Do you see—Indians?" Marian faltered. But the boy made no answer.

Then she, too, saw something looming ahead of them in the road. What was it? She caught her breath sharply. She knew what it was—now. It was the carriage—the flat-topped carriage in which they had traveled so many miles. Her heart almost burst with glad relief.

"Look!" she cried. "There's the carriage!"

A gun barked in answer. The bullet cut through the tall youth's hat.

"The Indians! They're hiding in the carriage!" she gasped, her heart thumping over in terror.

A figure jumped to the ground before them, a figure in a wide-brimmed hat, a revolver shining in his hand.

"Father!" Marian shrieked. "Don't shoot! It's me—Marian!"

The next thing she knew they had reached the carriage and she was tumbling into her father's outstretched arms.

"Marian! Thank God, you're safe!" Father's voice shook. He held her close as though he could never let her go. "We were afraid they had . . . But come to Mother. She and Russell are safe here in the front seat."

Marian flew to her mother. Mrs. Blane was too deeply moved to speak but she held Marian very close and murmured little sounds of thankfulness into her tangled curls.

"Oh, Mother, I was so scared!"

Mother patted her heaving shoulders. "It's all right now. We're safe, thank God."

"But—where is Doctor Frank?" Marian asked.

"In back. He was wounded in the arm," her mother answered.

"Oh!" Marian looked around. She could see the doctor's white face, drawn with pain. He groaned.

Turning back, she noticed that the carriage shafts were uplifted—empty. That is, except for Baby who lay rigid on the ground. Buck was gone— and Gypsy! Where was her pony? With an anxious cry, she jumped down and ran to her father who was talking to the men gathered about him.

"Gypsy! What's happened to Gypsy? Did they kill her?" she cried.

"No, Marian. They stole Gypsy and Buck."

"Oh, Father!" Gypsy! Her own little pony! Gone! She would never see her again.

But she couldn't grieve long, for she was too interested in what Tom Betts was saying. "No, sir. Those weren't ary Indians. I'll bet it was that band of horse thieves and outlaws—Dan Wolf's gang. He and his brother, Scar Face, have been holding up travelers, usually south of here on the Santa Fe Trail."

"Scar Face! Dan Wolf!" Marian cried out. "Father!

WAGON WHEELS TO DENVER

Jake's name is Wolf! And he has an ugly scar. He was in that band of outlaws, then. Jake stole my Gypsy and Buck! He sent them word—perhaps that man at Kit Carson was ...''

"I'm afraid so. And I trusted the fellow," Father answered. "But we mustn't think of that. We must get Mother to safety and Frank to a doctor." He stroked her head. "Oh, little soldier," he added huskily, "you can never know how thankful I am to see you safe and sound."

Half the rescuers started back toward Pueblo to keep a sharp lookout for the outlaws. A pair of horses was hitched to the carriage and the remaining men waited to escort the Blanes to Pueblo. Marian cast a sorrowful glance at the silent Baby.

"Poor Baby has gone to her happy hunting ground," Marian told her brother as she boosted him over the carriage seat to make room for her father in front.

"Hope they don't hurt old Buck or Gypsy," Russell replied. "But I'm glad they didn't take my Bill."

"Oh, I hope they won't be mean to them but ... Anyway, I'm glad that Toby and Dinah are safe—that they were hitched to the wagon today. I—I guess I love them best—next to Gypsy."

Marian sat in front with her parents. Russell curled up on the floor in back. Doctor Frank lay on the back seat, weak with pain, but stubbornly insisting in response to their anxious queries, "I'm all right. Just a scratch!"

168

In spite of the comforting nearness of her father and mother and their escort of men and horses, Marian was nervous. At every thicket, behind every tree along the river bank, she expected to see those sinister figures dash out at them, or hear a gun bark from ambush. But the night remained serene except for the cloppity-clop of horses beating the road. The night had surely swallowed Scar Face and his outlaws.

Suddenly the men riding ahead of the carriage pulled up sharply. Marian caught her breath as they halted with the rest, and the Blanes peered nervously along the gleaming road, white under the stars. Ahead of them twinkled the lights of Pueblo.

"Shucks!" the big man, who had been riding on Marian's side of the carriage, chuckled.

"What is it?" cried Marian. Then she saw it, too. A big black shadow.

Why, it was an animal—a dog! Chase!

The next minute the big creature, a frayed rope hanging from his collar, bounded to the carriage and into her outstretched arms.

Shortly they were clattering into the town, and the welcoming lights of the Colorado House shone before their weary eyes.

The next thing Marian knew, Ma Betts was leading Mother, Russell and herself through a lamp-lit room and up the stairs to a low bedroom under the eaves. And then motherly hands were tucking her into a soft cool bed.

169

"There you are, child! Now don't worry. You're all safe and sound. I must hustle down and tend that poor wounded man and ladle out some coffee for the men. I made a boiler full. Nothing like something hot . . ."

Exhausted, Marian was asleep before Ma Betts had bustled from the room.

XIV

Pike's Peak!

Warm sunlight danced across Marian's face the next morning. She stared about the strange bare room in bewilderment. Then she remembered.

She sat up quickly. Across from her in the other bed, her mother lay asleep, her white face shadowed with weariness. Russell had disappeared.

Marian threw back the covers and pattered across the pine floor and peeked out the sunny window. A dusty black team with a rattling wagon was passing on the road below. Across the street were several adobe buildings,— beyond lay the river. Marian turned away. From somewhere in the hotel there came voices and the clatter of dishes.

Suddenly she realized she was hungry—starved, in fact. Hurriedly she dressed. She scrubbed her face and hands vigorously in the white bowl on the wash-stand before the splasher which proclaimed in bright red stitches that, "Cleanliness is next to Godliness." The face reflected in the cheap mirror over the dresser was shining and rosy when she ran her comb quickly through her curls.

Marian ran from the room and down the stairs in search of Russell and her father. At the foot of the steps she paused uncertainly. The enticing smell of frying meat, crisp corn bread and boiling coffee floated toward her from somewhere in the rear.

She glanced about. A fat-bellied stove met her eyes, and a red geranium-filled window with a low rocker beside it. Above a narrow counter, a long, gaily painted clock tick-ticked merrily. Suddenly someone straightened up back of the counter. It was an old man with a shriveled face and faded eyes, and he gave her a kindly smile.

Timidly she returned his smile.

"Go on in back, Miss. Ma Betts'll feed ya."

"Thank you." Marian turned and skipped lightly down the hall.

In the large sunny kitchen smelling of soap-suds and spices, Ma Betts was dishing breakfast. Father, Russell and Doctor Frank, with his arm in bandages, sat about the long pine table which was scrubbed to the whiteness of damask.

"Good-morning, my dear! Set right down here by your

pa. You look as fresh as a mountain rose this morning,'' greeted Ma Betts with a smile.

"Good-morning," Marian answered shyly, seating her-self at the table.

"You'd never think that outlaws had chased you last night!" beamed her father over his coffee cup.

Doctor Frank grinned. "It's a lucky thing those old mules ran away, Marian. It just saved my life. Jake was certainly aiming to get me and make off with the wagon and money box. He didn't count on you being in there."

"But how did you get wounded?" inquired Marian.

"Well, when the mules started running away, Jake had his gun in my ribs and as we both tumbled to the ground the revolver went off and got me in the arm. Lucky thing, Marian, you kept the mules going until the outlaws had been frightened away. When they'd stripped off our valuables, they tore after the real loot. Never thought our little lady, who was so afraid of Gypsy once upon a time, could manage a couple of runaways like that."

"Poor Gypsy!" Marian met her father's eyes. Unconsciously she straightened up, but her chin quivered. She looked away quickly.

"Marian," Russell spoke up importantly, "they stole Father's and Doctor Frank's purses and Mummy's butterfly pin an' a rifle. An' I s'pose we'll have to live here 'cause Buck and Gypsy are gone."

Marian glanced at her father in dismay.

"Oh, no. We'll push on," Father reassured her. "Tom

WAGON WHEELS TO DENVER

Betts has kindly offered to lend us a pair of mules to make the trip to Denver. However, Frank and I have decided to stay over a day and let Mother get a good rest. Besides, we must have the wagon top repaired.''

"Pueblo is a fine little town," Ma Betts remarked, passing another plate of corn bread. "I expect it'll be bigger than Denver. You'd better plan to live here," she insisted.

Father shook his head. "Sorry, Mrs. Betts. You're all so kind, but we must go on."

"Well, I've been all over the Territory but this country around here has the best grazing and farm land to my way of thinking. I came here when there wasn't more than three or four adobe houses. Now, we've got several hotels, stores, a bank and two churches," Ma Betts remarked proudly.

"Were you ever attacked by Indians?" asked Marian when she had finished her breakfast.

Before answering, Ma Betts poured herself a steaming cup of coffee and plumped down beside Marian.

"Yes," she haid. "My husband and I were ranching south of here in 1864. The Indians ran off our cattle and horses and killed . . ." Ma Bettes broke off, her mouth grim. Her faded eyes held that look of torturing memory which Marian had seen there the night before.

She shook her head and pushed back her chair. "Well, I must be getting your mother's breakfast and tidying up

174

a bit. Russell, bring me that prairie dog of yours first. He's back of the stove. He looks kinda poorly."

"Oh, is he sick?" cried Russell anxiously as he ran for the cage.

"He'll be all right!" Doctor Frank consoled, as he stood up. "With a nurse like Ma Betts, he'll be as fine as a fiddle. Look at me!"

Marian followed her father and the doctor onto the long front veranda where Tom Betts joined them.

Presently the four of them started out on a walk about the thriving, sun-baked town.

"See that giant cottonwood over yonder," Tom pointed out at length. "That's a landmark here. During the 'Pike's Peak or Bust' excitement that tree sheltered plenty of travelers. Gramp says the trappers used to camp there before the fort was built. Pike's exploring party camped under that tree on their way to the Peak. They threw up a log breastwork for defense against the Indians. Built it right over there where the Arkansas joins the Fountain qui Bouille, 'The Forks' it used to be called."

"Who settled this place first, son?" Father inquired as they walked on.

"Jim Beckwourth, they say, started the first permanent settlement," Tom answered. "He built an adobe here surrounded by cottonwood pickets. Fort Napeste, they called it. That's the Indian name for Arkansas. The fort was burned and seventeen folks killed by the Indians one Christmas in 1854."

"Tell us about it," Doctor Frank urged.

"Well, there isn't much to tell 'cause nobody was left to explain it. Gramp can tell you more maybe."

"Who's Gramp?" Marian broke in.

"Gramp takes care of things around the hotel for Ma. He's real old. Was a trapper years ago. He's grown a beard now but he says most of the trappers were clean shaven 'cause the Indians hated beards and of course they wanted to be friendly with the redskins."

"Oh, I think I spoke to him," said Marian. "But isn't he afraid to have a beard now?"

"No. He says all his Indian friends are gone and that it don't matter. His trapper days are over. He was a friend of Uncle Dick Wootton who had a buffalo ranch on this town site way back in the forties. Wootton caught the buffalo calves and raised 'em, then he sold 'em to zoos back in the states."

"We'd better turn back," said Father presently. "We should have had Virginia with us. She could have learned a lot of new stories from our young friend here."

"Just think! In a few days I'll be seeing her!" Marian cried, her eyes shining. "And, oh, I hope there'll be lots of letters from Lizzie there!" Marian began to count on her fingers, "One, two, three ——— Oh, Father, will it take us more than six days to reach Denver?"

"Not many more, I hope," her father replied, smiling at her eagerness.

The next morning in spite of her impatience to reach their new home, Marian was sorry to leave the bustling Ma Betts who had hovered over them all like a worried mother hen. She dreaded also to leave the safety of the Colorado House and face the dangers of the lonely trail once more.

"I know why Father wants to leave here," she confided to Russell as they sat in the carriage ready to start. "That awful night of the attack seems so close here. He wants to get Mother as far away as he can so she'll forget."

She watched her parents and Doctor Frank bidding good-bye to Ma and Tom Betts. Mother was smiling gratefully and thanking them all over again. Then Father was helping Mother into the back seat beside Russell and the doctor climbed up beside her.

Marian was to drive Dinah and Toby until Doctor Frank's arm was better, while Father drove the borrowed mules in the big wagon. Kind Ma Betts and Tom and a group of curious roomers gathered about them to see them off.

"Good-bye!—Good luck!" they all shouted. "Don't worry about the mules," called Tom. "No hurry about getting 'em back."

"Glad to 'a' met you folks. Come again." Ma Betts

177

smiled and waved her calico apron as the carriage and wagon started on.

The day was bright, not a cloud marred the blue sky for ten long miles as they drove through natural limestone quarries.

"Look, Russie," cried Marian, "did you ever see such cliffs?"

"Maybe they're mountains," Russell suggested.

"Oh, no. The mountains are ahead of us." Marian nodded toward the blue peaks in the distance.

They drove twenty-five miles up the Arkansas valley and reached Beaver Creek the second night. There the travelers made camp. On one of the surrounding bluffs they located a cattle ranch and store.

As usual when they met some lonely settler, the Blanes queried him about outlaws.

"I ain't never seen any of that gang 'round here, folks," the settler reassured them about Dan Wolf's band .

Somewhat relieved by now, the campers soon forgot the outlaws. All except Marian. At the thought of Dan Wolf's band her heart would grow unbearably heavy.

"I know I shouldn't feel so badly about Gypsy when we're safe and Doctor's arm is nearly well," she confided to Chase. But she had only to close her eyes and the vision of Jake lashing her beloved pony rose before her. At such times she would clench her teeth to keep from crying.

PIKES PEAK!

But shortly she, too, began to forget in her interest in the fragrant woods through which they drove and the sight of rugged mountains but a mile or so away.

Four days from Pueblo they reached the piñon wood forests. Their road wound among the sandstone foot-hills covered with these strangely formed low trees. Further on they rode through dense forests of pine. It was fun to get gum from the pine trees, and Mrs. Blane told the children how she had procured her gum in just that way when she was a child.

That night the party camped in a needle-carpeted clearing among some giant pines. They were preparing for bed when a peculiar odor stole out through the tent fly.

"What's that?" asked Marian, stopping suddenly before the canvas opening.

"Smells very like a polecat," Doctor announced sniffing the air. "And I think he's in the tent."

"Good gracious, William! What shall we do?" cried Mother, who was sitting before the dying embers of the camp-fire brushing her long hair. "Russell's in there! Hurry and get him out!" Mother broke off as Russell's shrill voice yelled:

"Come here. A pussy with a big white tail is tryin' to hurt Bill!"

"Marian, grab that stick," her father commanded. "We must shoo him out. Here—around back. Don't move, Russell! Now!" Father shouted. They poked under the tent with their long aspen sticks. A startled

179

scream came from Mother—a terrified howl from Chase. Marian and her father ran around the tent just in time to see a streak of brown and white and a yelping black dog flying for the creek. Then the splashing of water told them that Chase was wallowing in the stream.

"Poor Chase! I'll go get him," Marian announced, starting for the creek.

"Great guns! Don't!" Doctor Frank laughed. "Do you want us to smell for weeks? Chase got in that skunk's way. Poor fellow—let him alone until morning."

Chase remained away all night. When he did appear long after breakfast was over and they were packed ready to start, he hung his curly head and his pleading eyes seemed to say, "It isn't very pleasant. I'm ashamed —but please forgive me. I just got in the way of that terrible, smelly cat!"

But in spite of his begging eyes, no one cared to stay very close to Chase all day. And he tagged dejectedly behind the carriage for twenty long miles.

Pike's Peak drew closer. Soon it semed to tower direcly above them.

Marian amused Russell by telling him, "Pike's Peak looks like a giant with outstretched arms to welcome us. He's wearing a cap of snow on his rocky old head." But inwardly she was filled with awe. The peak was so vast and cold looking that it made her feel very small.

The last few miles were through sweet, spicy pine trees. Marian sniffed the air delightedly. The woods were beginning to deepen into shadows. At last they emerged from the gloom of the forest on to a plateau, or mesa, treeless and barren, but at the very foot, it seemed, of the giant mountain

There they camped for the night. Below them was a log cabin and two tents not far from a hidden stream.

Before Marian and Russell crawled into bed, they peeked out once more at the mountain. The bright moonlight was bathing it in soft fairy-like beams of white. A friendly peak, now, it seemed to Marian. Far away, near the mountain's base, they saw the few gleaming lights of Colorado City. "Looks like a necklace of diamonds," Marian murmured dreamily.

"Oh, Russie! Just think! We'll be in Denver in just three days!"

XV

Here They Drove the Stake!

"Just think, Father, it'll be two months tomorrow since we left Chicago," Marian said wistfully the next morning. "Today is the thirty-first of July."

She closed her mother's diary and laid it back on the trunk with a sigh. Father had failed to answer her. He was lost in contemplation of the giant peak stretching before them. Over in the warm sunlight, her mother lay back in her camp-chair, her eyes closed, her knitting idle on her lap. Marian could see Russell and Doctor Frank down by the creek wandering among the cottonwoods and low green bushes beside the tumbling water. Every now and then her brother stooped to pick a bright flower for the limp bouquet which he clutched in one hand.

Presently Father sauntered over to the mules and started hitching Dinah and Toby to the carriage.

"Aren't—aren't we going to start for Denver today,

Father?'' Marian voiced the question which she had been anxious to ask ever since she awakened.

Father turned toward her with a smile. ''Oh, there's no hurry. I think we'll stay over a day. I'd like to look around a bit.''

''But where are you going?'' Marian asked trying to hide her disappointment. ''Colorado City?''

Her father nodded, then looked up as the rattle of wagon wheels broke the stillness. ''Wonder why all those wagons are gathering over there? I thought this spot was deserted except for that cabin and couple of tents. Marian, run over and see what those men are doing. Ask them the best way over to Colorado City.''

Marian started off with Chase at her heels. There were quite a group of men, twenty-five or more. They were dressed in the accepted costume of the West, broad-brimmed hats, dark woolen shirts and trousers tucked down into sturdy boots. Several carts, wagons, mules and saddle ponies were standing in the background.

As Marian timidly drew nearer, she could see that one man, who was perched on a pile of new lumber, was busily writing. Several others had just completed driving a wooden stake into the ground. A man, who towered several inches above the others, was speaking. Marian tried to catch what he was saying. The big voice boomed mightily and he accompanied his words with dramatic flourishes of his arms.

Now she could hear his words. Wonderingly she drew

closer. No one noticed her for they were all listening with rapt attention.

"Here will rise grove and orchards and over these hills the luxurious vine will climb and yield its fruit in its season to delight the hearts of those who watch its growth beneath the fostering touch of civilization."

What did he mean? What was it all about? Then his words caught her attention again.

"We can, today, upon laying, as it were, the corner-stone of this new and to-be flourishing city and upon driving the first stake, prophesy a most successful growth and a glorious future."

They must be laying out a town! This was to be a city —this very soil on which she stood!

The crowd was breaking up. The men were laughing, talking, shaking hands. They seemed to gather especially around a slender, mustached man under forty who had the proud carriage of an officer. But his eyes seemed to be looking past the gathering there—far beyond the tree-less plateau—into the future.

The men gradually wandered off, some to their wagons and mounts, others to start surveying for future streets and lots. A short, slender youth remained talking to the man who had been writing.

Now this young man was coming toward her. Marian timidly started to meet him. She would ask him about this new town and the way to Colorado City.

"Well!—If it isn't the little buffalo girl!" the young

man exclaimed in surprise. His blue-gray eyes were merrily alive in his tanned face and there was a new youthful stubble on his chin.

"Forevermore! You're the boy on the train!" Marian cried.

"Who'd have thought we'd meet so soon! When did you get here? I suppose you are planning to be a first citizen."

"Oh, goodness, no! We're going to live in Denver. We just arrived last night. That's our camp over there." Marian nodded toward the white tent and wagon some distance away. "Come back with me and tell my family all about the new town, won't you? I'm Marian Blane from Chicago."

"And I'm Charles Barry from New York," he laughed, a nice chuckly sort of laugh.

Marian liked this boy. She felt she could be friends with him—could really talk to him. Most boys left her speechless.

"But what are you doing here?" she asked as they started walking toward the camp. "I thought you weren't going to have anything to do with cities."

"I wasn't," Charles Barry laughed. "But, you see, I had to eat and there is adventure in helping to lay a railroad. I've been surveying for the Denver and Rio Grande."

When they reached camp, Mr. Blane and the doctor

186

were sitting in the front seat of the carriage with Mrs. Blane and Russell in back.

"Father!" Marian cried, running ahead with Chase. "Guess what! There's going to be a new town here. Isn't that exciting? Charles Barry told me. And I heard the man making a speech and . . ."

"What's this you're saying, Marian?" her father asked in surprise. He turned to Charles Barry. "Tell us all about it, young man."

Charles lifted his hat to Mother and smiled broadly at the sight of the prairie dog clasped in Russell's arms.

"Well, sir, they have just driven the first stake of the Fountain Colony. That's General William Palmer, the founder of the colony," he nodded toward the slender, mustached man whom Marian had noticed at the stake driving. "He also originated the Colorado Springs Company which is building the Denver and Rio Grande Railroad here from Denver."

"Well! Well! This is a surprise! A new town! Seems to me I've heard of Palmer. He was a Union Cavalry General, I believe."

"Yes, sir. He supervised the building of the Kansas Pacific Railroad to Denver and conducted the survey to the Pacific for them." Charles Barry followed the General with admiring eyes. He turned back to Father. "The Denver and Rio Grande will be finished to this point this fall. General Cameron, who just talked to us over there, is from Greeley Colony. He's organizing this colony with

187

several others. There's to be a drawing of lots in a few days.''

''Well, this is a mighty fine location for a town!'' cried Father. ''You know, I wouldn't mind staying on here.''

''Oh, no!'' Marian broke in. Then she blushed furiously at the look of surprise on the young man's face.

''It might be a good thing for me,'' Doctor Frank mused. ''New towns need new doctors—sometimes.''

''Well, let's drive to Colorado City and look the place over,'' Father suggested.

''May I ride with you?'' asked Charles. ''My horse is just beyond that cabin.''

''Of course. Come along, son! You can show us the way,'' Father replied, gathering up the reins and clucking to the sleepy-looking mules.

Colorado City proved a disappointment to Marian. It was a miserable little place. With its one long business street, Colorado Avenue, and its rows of false-fronted stores it was like the prairie towns through which they had passed. There were about forty-five frame and log houses which were occupied, although at one time, Charles Barry told them, there had been nearly three hundred dwellings and stores. Many of the houses had been moved off to neighboring ranches.

''Believe I'll stop at the county clerk's office,'' said Father. ''Where is it, young man?''

''Right there, sir. That log building.''

As they drew up before the building which housed the

188

county clerk of El Paso County Charles remarked, "You know, Colorado City is where the territorial capital was for five days in 1861. Then they moved it back to Denver. They held some of their meetings in that building next to the one your father is entering."

"Oh, tell us some more," cried Marian.

Charles laughed. "All right. But while I do, wouldn't you all like to ride up and see the Boiling Springs?"

"Yes, indeed! We can return for Father later," said Mother.

As they started up the wagon road which led to the Boiling Springs, or Soda Springs, as some people called them, Marian tried not to notice that Charles Barry's spirited little pony made her think of her stolen Gypsy— the way he lifted his shaggy hoofs over the rutted road, the curve of his head, the same sort of silky mane. Her heart ached every time she looked at him. She mustn't think of Gypsy. She must listen to what Charles was saying, she scolded herself.

"Yes," Charles went on, "Colorado City was founded eleven years ago. They hoped to make it the source of supply for the recently discovered Tarryall gold diggings. There were only eight women and nearly three hundred men here that first year. They had to endure great hardships and were often attacked by Indians, though as a usual thing the redskins didn't molest the town but attacked some lonely ranch or solitary rider."

The four in the carriage listened to the young man

with interest. "See those large trees over there?" Charles asked presently. "There's where they hung several men for horse stealing.

"This road we are traveling is an old Indian trail which goes up Ute Pass," the young man went on. "The wagons going to South Park and Tarryall used to go this way. They still travel it some, but the town lost out when Denver built a good road up Platte Canyon."

The country was wild and beautiful. Choke cherry and currant bushes covered the slopes below the green of pine and spruce. Above, Pike's Peak lay under a blanket of soft white clouds.

"Here we are," said Charles at length. "There's the big spring for drinking, and over there the one for bathing."

Doctor Frank pulled up the mules and everyone descended from the carriage. Chase ran to the roaring stream and drank thirstily.

The nearest spring bubbled out of a great flat rock and fell into a shallow basin made by its incessant gushing.

"This tastes wonderful! Just like the water at Saratoga Springs," cried Mother delightedly, after dipping a tin cup into the sparkling water. "Here, Marian—Russell, try it."

Both Marian and her brother made wry faces after the first swallow.

"Goes up my nose!" cried Russell. "Don't like it!"

Across from the Fountain stream were several white

tents. "Those are invalids," Charles explained. "I wouldn't be surprised to see a hotel there some day. There's talk now of making a resort of the place."

They all sat down by the stream and rested their prairie-tired eyes on the green hills and trees about them and listened to the music of the water as it tumbled at their feet. Chase splashed out of the rocky coolness of the torrent and began sniff-sniffing the strange mountain odors. A bluejay scolded him roundly from his perch in a pine tree overhead.

"Do you know, Russell," Charles remarked presently, "that you'd like that spring water better if you knew the Indian stories they tell about it. The Indians believe that the Great Spirit lives there in the spring—the Great Manitou. They think the gas and bubbles are caused by his breathing. So, when the Arapahoes and Cheyennes go up Ute Pass to fight their enemies the Utes, or when they are going hunting, they stop here and give offerings to the Great Spirit by throwing presents into the spring. The Utes come here too."

"Do you suppose there are any beads here now?" Marian asked.

"Gosh, I don't know. I've never looked. But they tell me the children in Colorado City always come up here after any Indians have passed by to hunt for beads and ornaments."

"I'm goin' to find somepin', too," Russell shouted, jumping up. He looked so earnest and funny as he searched around among the leaves and brush that Marian had to laugh.

"Then, there's another tale which I like," went on Charles Barry.

"Once, many, many years ago two Indian warriors, a Comanche and a Shoshone, stopped here for a drink. The Comanche, tired after the hunt, threw himself upon the ground and drank thirstily from the stream. The Shoshone, before he had satisfied his thirst, raised some of the spring water in the hollow of his hand and lifted it toward the sun, then he reversed his hand and allowed the water to fall back upon the ground—a libation to the Great Spirit who had given him a successful hunt. Seeing this, the Comanche remembered that he had neglected the usual offering, and having been unsuccessful in the chase, grew jealous and angry when he noticed the fat deer the other Indian had dropped to the ground. In his rage he started to fight with the Shoshone.

"Well, to make a long story short, he finally plunged the Shoshone's face into the spring and held it there until the warrior was dead. Suddenly he was filled with remorse and dragged the dead Indian from the water. He had no sooner done so than great bubbles sprang up and escaped in hissing gas. All at once there arose from the spring an aged Indian holding a mighty club in his withered hand. The murderer recognized him as Wan-kan-aga, the great Father of the Comanche and Shoshone

192

tribes, who had been deified by his people for his bravery and good deeds while on earth.

" 'Accursed of thy tribe!' the old Indian cried. 'This day thou hast severed the link between the mightiest nations. The blood of the brave Shoshone cries to the Manitou for revenge. May the water of thy tribe be rank and bitter in their throats!'

"Then the old man swung his club and dashed out the brains of the Comanche, who fell headlong into the spring. And the water from that spring remained rank and bitter from that day to this.

"To perpetuate the memory of the Shoshone, the good Wan-kan-aga struck his club against a rock which overhung the stream. The rock opened at once into a basin of bubbling, sparkling water—the sweetest, coolest water ever found. So the two springs remained. But forever after that the two great tribes were bitter enemies."

"Forevermore!" Marian cried. "Is this the good spring?"

"It's supposed to be. But the other one must have dried up—unless it's that horrible tasting iron spring further on up the canyon," Charles laughed.

"You must tell all this to Mr. Blane, Charles. He will be so interested," said Mother. "Now, I think we'd better return. Father will wonder what has become of us."

On the way back to Colorado City, Marian recounted to Charles their adventures west across the plains and the loss of Gypsy. It seemed no time before they drew up

193

before the county clerk's office where Father waited impatiently for their return.

His face was beaming and he greeted them with boyish excitement. "Thought you'd never come. Well, I've news for you," he cried, climbing into the front seat. "We're going to live in El Paso County. I've taken up a claim on the Monument."

XVI

"All of This 1 Saw and Part of This I Was"

"Oh—Father!" Marian wailed. She stared incredulously at his smiling face. Her heart seemed to drop with a disappointed thud to her very shoes.

"Yes," said Father, "I believe a healthy outdoor life close to these grand old mountains will be just the thing for Mother. Won't it, Frank?"

"Indeed it will! I could start to practice in the new town and be near enough to watch over her, also," answered the doctor enthusiastically.

"You certainly could, for the claim is only ten miles up Monument Creek from the new colony. I've got it all planned. We'll build a comfortable log cabin there and raise sheep." Father turned toward Mother. "What do you say to this plan, Mary?" His eyes were boyishly eager for her approval.

"Why—why if you think best, William. The air here

is wonderful.'' But Marian caught the look of dismay in her mother's eyes as she gazed over the dry treeless plateau which some day would become a town. The slender hands clasped on her lap tightened until the knuckles turned white.

Father's face drooped into disappointed lines. ''Well, I must say no one is taking it the way I expected.''

''Of course it's the thing to do!'' cried Mother, smiling bravely. ''You just took our breath away for a minute. Now, how about buying our supplies? After all, homesteaders must eat.''

''Yes, we'd better. There's a store over there.'' Father nodded toward a building across the street whose sign read, ''Emile Gehrung, Groceries, Drugs.'' Then he added, ''What do you say about getting Marian that pair of shoes she needs so badly?'' Father's face had brightened and now he turned to Marian with a smile.

Marian barely heard him. With miserable unseeing eyes she stared at a mangy dog crossing the dusty street, at a man sauntering into a corner saloon, at a rumbling wagon containing a roughly dressed rancher and three tow-headed children.

''Well, are you coming?'' Father cried impatiently.

''Ye-es—yes, Father,'' Marian murmured, climbing out of the carriage. What did she care about new shoes now or about anything, she thought brokenly. The only thing that had been really bearable on this long dreadful journey had been the thought of Denver—a city as nice as Chicago perhaps, and of seeing Virginia, and now . . .

Charles Barry's pleasant voice broke into her thoughts. He was saying, "See that old-timer coming out of Gehrung's store? That's an old sheepherder called 'Judge' Baldwin around these parts. He was shot by the Indians in '68. He tried to fight them off with his boot when they came upon him unarmed guarding his flock. They shot him down, however, and then when they started to scalp him the Indians discovered that he had been scalped before. Being superstitious at this discovery they quickly rode away leaving him for dead. But he's far from dead, as you can see."

"Well!" cried Father. "I didn't know anyone once scalped lived to tell the tale."

"Oh, only a small part of his scalp had been taken the first time," Charles laughed.

Marian shuddered and looked away.

She and Father went into Gehrung's. It was the usual frontier place of business. But Marian was not interested in the shelves of groceries and drugs, the bolts of gay and drab calico which lined the walls or the display of farm implements, barrels of salt pork or shoes. Nor did she care that there were no girls' shoes, only boys', sturdy and copper-toed. At her father's suggestion that they were better suited for ranch life, she only turned away to hide the sudden mist in her eyes, although she sensed the tightening of his mouth as he counted out the change.

At the carriage once more she discovered that Charles had ridden away. Silently she climbed into the back seat beside her mother. She cast a grateful look at Mother when she made no mention of the awkward footgear, but patted Marian's brown hand as if she understood. Silently they rode back to camp. The two men in front talked and planned for this new life which would soon be theirs in the shadow of Pike's Peak.

Two days later the Blanes broke camp and started for their new home. Their road followed the winding, tree-lined Monument Creek north. To the left of them ran a wall of mountains.

"That's Teachouts over there," nodded Mr. Blane, after they had driven about six miles. The others saw a large wooden building and several barns, lost among swaying trees. "It's a boarding-house for travelers stranded in these parts. I guess the railroad'll use it, too, when it gets this far. They tell me that it once was a large ranch with herds of cattle and horses. But three years ago the Indians raided the place and drove off all the herds. That's where we'll get our mail from now on."

In spite of her dismay at becoming a homesteader, Marian was keenly interested in the scenery that spread before them. She had been so engrossed in the tales told by Charles Barry that now she caught herself glancing over the low bluffs on her right and across the rolling country beyond to the Pinery. The Pinery was a dense, black forest which three years before had been the hiding place for the marauding Indians of the plains. These Cheyennes and Arapahoes were supposed to have been disbanded following those days of terror, but the Utes lived close by. She glanced toward the mountains. The Utes lived back there in the hills.

When they reached the claim which was to be their home for six months and probably longer, they had to ford the noisily rushing creek. The carriage swayed and bumped as the mules climbed the bank. Low bluffs stretched above them. They seemed to follow Monument Creek for miles. Soon the carriage halted on a sheltered grassy slope dotted with pine trees.

"Come. Hop out, all of you!" Father shouted, as excited as a small boy over his new possession. Eagerly he turned to Mother. "Mary, don't you think this would be an ideal spot for our cabin? We could build it to face the mountains, and the bluffs would protect us from the winds off the plains."

"Yes, of course, William. The cabin would have a lovely view from here."

Marian noticed a slight tremor in her mother's voice. "Poor Mother!" she thought sympathetically.

Quickly she pulled out her mother's camp-chair from the wagon and made her comfortable beneath the shade of a tall pine. Russell had trudged after his father and the doctor as they went over the ground—poring over papers one minute, examining the claim for landmarks the other.

Mother leaned back and closed her eyes. Worriedly Marian watched her. How she hoped that this country would make her well!

In a short time Mrs. Blane fell asleep and Marian tiptoed over the fallen pine-needles on an exploring trip. Chase had been missing since the moment of their arrival. Now, she discovered the reason. Not far away he sat on his haunches gazing longingly at a chattering squirrel high on a branch above his head.

"Come on, Chase. Let that nice squirrel alone, you old rascal!" Marian scolded.

She ran toward the creek and dropped down at the water's edge with a cry of delight. The noisy creek tumbled and sang at her feet. She watched its foaming freshness and listened dreamily to the wind in the trees. The wind seemed to be singing,—singing a lullaby.

Absent-mindedly she threw little rocks into the splashing, gurgling water. Chase dashed in after each pebble only to flounder around in the creek without finding them.

She wished that Charles Barry had been able to accompany them; that he had been able to see this new home of theirs, or best of all, that he lived near by. It had been such fun to have someone near her own age to talk to. To be sure, Charles was nineteen, but he hadn't seemed a day older than Virginia. She wondered when she would see him again.

"I'll see you soon," Charles had promised the day before when he had taken the stage-coach back to the point where the railroad had been completed. "We'll be going through your claim before you can say 'Jack Robinson'!" Marian searched the country before her for a plume of smoke or some other sign of a cabin. But as far as her eye could see below the unfriendly wall of mountains there appeared to be nothing but pines, scrub oak, and here and there a mushroom-shaped rock. Her delight over the singing trees and musical lapping of the water vanished. She sighed. For a moment she remembered that lonely girl back at Fort Hays. It was going to be as lonely for her here on this mountain homestead.—even more so. She shook tears of self-pity from her eyes.

Just after supper that night a sudden rain sprang up. It beat and tore at the tent until Marian was afraid it would pound its way through to their very heads. A chill wind from the mountains blew its icy breath around them until the doctor hauled in the stove and built a fire. They huddled around its warmth until bedtime.

Marian had a difficult time falling asleep. The wind no longer sang through the pines. It moaned. It filled her with a strange feeling of dread. Everything seemed to be creeping about out there in the night. For once she longed for the silence of the plains or the usual, long-accustomed sounds that belonged only to the prairies. The rustlings and strange stirrings without disturbed her,— frightened her.

She thought of the terrible tales she had recently heard. She lived over again the attack of Dan Wolf's outlaws.

The face of Jake mocked her from every shadow. Then the loss of Gypsy would drive all other thoughts away—until the wind would moan and moan again.

Marian overslept the next morning. When she hurried outside the tent she found everyone had already had breakfast. Her mother was bending over the leather trunk.

"Where is everybody?" Marian asked.

Mrs. Blane looked up. "Father and Doctor Frank have gone to the new town. There's to be a sale of lots today."

"Oh, why didn't they take me? Is Father going to buy a lot?" Marian asked as she poured water into the wash basin.

"You were sleeping so soundly we didn't like to awaken you. No, I'm sure your father won't buy a lot." Mother gazed ruefully at the trunk which held their carefully hoarded store of money. "Doctor Frank is going to buy one, however. They are hoping to find someone to take the Betts' mules back to Pueblo—and see if they can get some Denver papers."

To hide her disappointment Marian busied herself after breakfast with putting the camp in order. After her work was done she pulled one of the cots out under the whispering pines for her mother. Russell played down by the creek and Marian explored that part of the claim which lay beneath the sheltering bluffs and down by the crystal clear spring which bubbled among some choke-cherry bushes. Marian tasted one of the little red berries only to spit it out quickly. "Ugh!" she cried, "how bitter!" Her mouth felt puckery and unpleasant the rest of the morning.

That afternoon she took her portfolio out under the trees and started a letter to Virginia.

"I know that I just mailed you a letter," she wrote, "but I'm so lonely I must talk to someone. We arrived at our claim yesterday. A claim looks just like any other stretch of land until you put a cabin on it, then it becomes a homestead, I guess. It's really pretty country, Virginia, and the mountains are such lovely shades of green and turn so blue in the late afternoon and early morning. But I'm going to hate living here just the same. If only you could come down and visit us! But perhaps you can when we get the cabin built. There are so many things to show you. First we'd explore the homestead and then I'd take you to the Boiling Soda Springs and tell you all the Indian stories that Charles Barry told us about them. Then, of course you must see the Garden of the Gods. The old-timers call it the Red Rocks. There was a terrific storm on the peak the day we rode over there. It was rather wonderful but scary to see the lightning dance across the mountain tops and hear the roars of thunder. Mother said it made a picture she'll never forget as we first saw the stormy peak through the giant red rocks which form a gateway to the Garden. And, oh, Virginia, the rocks among the dark pines are so queer. Some of them remind me of animals in a zoo. There's nothing in the new town yet but streets. They're going to call them strange foreign names. Father says a few of them are called after the early Spanish explorers and French trappers: 'St. Vrain, Huerfano, Vermijo, Moreno, Bijou and Cache la Poudre.' Don't they sound romantic? Father has been telling me about some of those old explorers. The street names make me think of glittering armor, clinking sabers and long-robed monks with swinging crucifixes. Father says I would like this country if I knew more of its history. But I know I wouldn't!

"I do wish Father would have to go to Denver for something and would take me along. Wouldn't it be wonderful to see each other? But I'm afraid it would make me feel worse to see the place I hoped to live in. Sometimes, Virginia, it's hard to keep your head and shoulders up and to be brave. It seems lots harder out here than it used to at home. Mother says we must find happiness in ourselves and not let outside things bother us. But, underneath, I know she hates it here and is as lonely as I am. Only she doesn't show it. She has Father believing that all her life she has wanted to live on a sheep ranch. Imagine! I wish I would be like . . ."

"Marian," Mother's anxious voice broke in, "it's getting late. What do you suppose has become of Father?"

"ALL OF THIS I SAW"

Marian dropped her portfolio and sprang to her feet. "Why—why I don't know."

She had been so absorbed in her letter that she had failed to notice the sun sinking beyond the purplish range in wide, rosy bands. There was a slight chill in the pine-scented air that told of the approach of night.

She glanced back at her mother's worried face. "Goodness, Mother, don't look like that!" she cried, forcing a gaiety that she did not feel. "Doctor Frank has probably bought out the town or maybe they drove over to Colorado City and up to the Boiling Springs for water. They'll be along soon. Hadn't we better start supper for them? They'll be as hungry as wolves." But Marian strained her eyes to see down the trail that wound along the stream.

"Let's set the table in the tent where it will be cozy and warm," suggested Mother, apparently over her fears and smiling gaily. "And here's our Russell with a bouquet of flowers. Thank you, son," she said, taking the orange-red flowers from his damp hand. "Here, we'll put them in the center of the table."

"What a funny shape they have!" Marian cried, as they stood back to admire the bright bouquet set in a tin cup. "They look like paint-brushes, only fatter."

Marian had a dreadful time with the fire without Doctor Frank's guiding hand. First it smoked, then smoldered, then it went out entirely. At length she was rewarded with a tiny blaze, and before long the sheet-iron stove was crackling and blushing rosily. Soon the dried beef was bubbling in a creamy sauce, the potatoes were boiling in their clean brown jackets, and the teakettle was steaming merrily.

But Father and Doctor Frank did not come.

Silently they ate their supper. Silently Marian washed the dishes. She w a t c h e d the trail and strained her ears for the rattle of wheels; nothing could be heard but water splashing over rocks, the sighing trees, and Russell mumbling his prayers at Mother's knees.

What if something terrible had happened? What if they never came back? What if . . . ?

Marian put away the dishes. She made up her cot. And still they did not arrive. She glanced nervously at her mother. She was reading by the flickering lantern and her face wore a white, strained look. Unable to bear the silence in the tent, Marian fled outside. There she sank upon the grassy slope, hugging her knees to keep them from trembling, and watched and watched.

It was pitchy dark when wheels rattled above the noisy creek and the splash-splash made by carriage and mules told her they had arrived at last.

Joyfully she ran down the slope to meet them. "Oh, Father!" she cried flinging her arms about his neck when he halted the carriage. "We thought . . . We were so worried!"

"Sorry, Marian. It took us longer than we expected. Where's Mother?"

At that moment Mrs. Blane hurried from the tent holding the lantern high above her head.

"Did you buy a lot, Doctor?" Marian asked, running beside the carriage.

Doctor Frank chuckled, "Wait and see!"

Then as Father jumped down at Mother's side, Marian saw the tall, gaunt, gray horse hitched in back. The horse had a surprised look in his long face and practically no tail at all.

"Why—why, where did you get that pony?"

"That's my business lot!" Doctor Frank laughed. "A queer old-timer begged me to buy him so that he would have money to buy a lot and I decided I needed a horse more than a lot, just now. Let me introduce you to a new friend, Marian,—old Iron Side."

"Here's a copy of the *Denver Tribune* of August first, Mary," cried Father waving the paper. "It tells all about the stake-driving Marian witnessed at the new town." He put his arm gently around her shoulders. "Sorry you worried, my dear," he added contritely.

"I hope supper's ready," Doctor Frank called as he led the mules away. "I'm so hungry I could eat shoe leather!"

"It will be in a jiffy! And it won't be shoe leather!" laughed Marian, hurrying to the food box.

After their warmed-over meal, Father read the article aloud by the dim light of the lantern.

"How queer to think I was there and heard it all,"

Marian remarked thoughtfully when he had finished.

The words at the end of the review clung to her thoughts long after she had gone to bed. Her father and Doctor Frank had joked a little about it—laughing at the possibility of such dreams coming true. But perhaps there would be a city there, and perhaps she, Marian Blane, would live there.

Marian went to sleep with the words ringing in her ears, "In a few years, as we look out from some magnificent temple yet to be built and see the wealth and beauty thus spread out at our feet, we shall look back to this day and at this simple but expressive ceremony and say, 'All of this I saw and part of this I was!'"

XVII

Lost!

The chop, chop of axes, the squeak of saws, the hollow thud of fresh pine logs—the echo of the activity and bustle about the Blanes' new home came to Marian as she sat on the bluff. She had gone up among the sweet-smelling pines to sew.

The days had been so full. Everyone, except Mother and perhaps Russell—although one didn't dare tell the little fellow so—had helped on the cabin. The few neighbors who lived within a day's driving distance had taken turns assisting in the erection of the Blanes' home. The cabin and barn must be finished before the first snow and all hands rushed the hauling of logs and the raising of walls. One never knew just when that first flurry of white would coat the hills and plains in the Pike's Peak region.

WAGON WHEELS TO DENVER

Marian put down her needle and gazed at the busy scene below. Tall powerful Hiram Gray, who lived on a homestead two miles up the Monument, was helping with the cabin. Doctor Frank, his face a sunburned brick color, was unloading logs from the wagon. He had just hauled a load from the sawmill over in the Pinery. Father was filling in the log walls with mud. Down near the tent, Mother, who was gaining new strength in the brisk mountain air, was roasting coffee on the sheet-iron stove. Russell, in his now worn and faded blue flannel trousers and blouse, was trudging back and forth from the roofless house to the wood-pile on mysterious errands of his own.

Only Marian, Chase, and the mules grazing lazily down by the choke-cherry spring, were idle today. Chase sat at her feet, his nose between his great paws, his eyes ever alert for some frisky chipmunk.

The trunks and boxes containing the extra blankets, dishes, a few pieces of silver and Marian's school books, had arrived from Denver three days before. Doctor Frank had driven to the city for them.

"It will cost too much to get them down here by stage," Father had stated when he and the doctor were discussing the method of transportation. "Why, even the travelers themselves have to pay twenty cents a mile for riding that rattle-bumping stage-coach."

So Doctor Frank had hitched the mules to the wagon and started off. And the news he had brought back had made them all very happy, especially Marian. The Coopers had bought a ranch near the Pinery and would soon be their neighbors.

"Mr. Cooper must be on his way down, now," Marian confided to Chase as she let her eyes wander off toward the mountains. "Won't it be wonderful to see Virginia again! I won't mind it a bit after she gets here!" She ran her fingers through the dog's curly hair. "Oh, Chase, what fun we're going to have! How much we have to show her. First thing we'll take her to see the new town, won't we, old boy?"

Already there were two frame houses in the Fountain Colony—one to be used as a hardware store. And there were more buildings to follow soon. The Company had sent out circulars even to far-off England, one man had told her father.

"Guess there'll be a flock of folks movin' in 'fore long. This here's goin' to be a model town like Greeley. No saloons allowed. Oughta draw a good class of folks. Colorado City ain't any too pleased to have us here,—crowdin' in on their business, so to speak," he had told Father laughingly.

Just then the rat-tat-tat of hoofs broke into Marian's thoughts. She turned and looked anxiously over her shoulder.

"Hey, you!" A stubby-nosed boy, riding bareback, yelled at her. "Is this the Blane homestead?"

"Yes. Do you want Father?" she asked curiously, noticing his dripping sorrel.

"Don't know. Is he Doctor Wright? If he is, he's wanted bad. A man by the name of Cooper took sick and is at
our ranch on Plum Creek. Wants the doctor to come
quick."

Marian raced down the steep bluff. The boy rode after
her. "Doctor Frank," she cried breathlessly, "this boy
wants you. He says Mr. Cooper's very sick at his ranch
and . . ."

"Yes, sir," the youth broke in, "he wants you to come
right away. We're up the Divide about thirty-five miles.
He's mighty sick!" he added soberly.

"Great guns! Here—help me saddle up, son." The
doctor turned a serious face to Marian. "Run tell your
father. I'll go at once."

Without waiting to answer, Marian rushed to the half-
built cabin to tell her father the news.

"Ill! You don't say! Wonder what's the trouble!"
Mr. Blane exclaimed anxiously, when she has gasped out
the message.

"I'll hurry back as soon as I can, Mr. Blane!" called
Doctor Frank, swinging into the saddle.

Marian and her father watched until the riders disappeared over the top of the bluffs in a whirl of dust. With
a grave face Father went in search of Mother. Slowly
Marian climbed the bluff to fetch her sewing.

The next morning Mr. Blane drove south to buy sheep.
"I hate to leave you alone," he told Marian when he had
led her out of Mother's hearing. "But I have already

sent word to Tom Betts to meet me at Beaver Creek Ranch where I'm to return his mules. They tell me the southern part of the Territory is the place to buy sheep. Tom can probably toll me where. You know, Marian, I must find something to support our homestead. Farming doesn't strike me as possible here, even with irrigation. This is grazing land.'' He smiled at her and pinched her cheek.

"It's just possible I might find you a saddle pony cheap. When Doctor Frank moves to town we'll need a horse. Do you think you can take care of Mother while I'm away?''

At the thought of a new pony all her own, Marian's face brightened. "Oh, please do, Father. And then I won't be thinking about poor Gypsy and can ride for the mail and . . .'' Marian broke off and playfully saluted him. "I'll take care of Mother. Don't you worry. I'll carry on!''

But when Father had driven away and Hiram Gray had been forced to return to his sheep, Marian found it very lonely in camp with only Mother and Russell.

Before her father had left she had helped him haul the tent across the creek into a cave. There they would be out of reach of cold winds. Mother had caught cold the night before and Marian had forced her to lie down. In the sheltered cave it was warm and cozy.

Marian amused herself in copying the drawing lessons in the old copies of Godey's *"Lady's Book"* which Aunt

Lily had sent them and in re-reading the Chicago letters which she had brought back from Teachouts the day before.

Suddenly Russell, who had been building mud forts down by the water, came scurrying breathlessly up the bank. "Marian! Somebody's comin'. See!" Russell pointed in excitement.

Marian looked up quickly. The magazines and letters tumbled from her lap.

"Anybody home?" a roughly-dressed, bearded man called out from the other side of the creek.

Marian stared at him. "Yes. What is it?"

"A Doctor Wright asked me to stop here. He's at Turner's ranch on Plumb Creek. Wants a Mr. Blane to come and bring a sick man down to his ranch near the Pinery. Wants him right away."

After a few hurried directions the man wheeled his horse and dashed up the slope, disappearing over the bluffs.

"Goodness, Marian, what shall we do?" cried Mother, sitting up suddenly on her cot. "Your father won't be back before day after tomorrow, at the earliest. Doctor's forgotten he was to meet Tom. No telling the reason for Frank's message. I—I think I'd better go. It may be a life and death matter. I can do it. I must! I'll drop you children off at the Grays'." While she was speaking Mother had risen hurriedly from her cot and was reaching for her hat and cape.

214

LOST!

"Oh no, you mustn't!" Marian cried, horrified. "Why, Father would never let you do that! It's thirty-five miles! Besides, you're not able to—you shouldn't think of it!"

"But this is urgent I must!" Mother's mouth became a determined line. "I'm able to go!"

"Mother, you're not, and you know it! Father would never forgive me if . . . if something . . . if I let you! Suppose you were taken sick! No, I'm going!"

"Marian! . . . Oh no! Not that long way—and alone! Why suppose . . ."

"I can take Chase and the Winchester," Marian broke in. "I'm not a bit scared. I'll be all right—honest!"

"Well . . ." Mother looked doubtfully toward the Divide country on the north. "It's way after noon, now. You can't make it before night. You must stay over at Warren's ranch—the one where Doctor Frank spent the night. Oh, Marian, I—I wish your Father were here! I feel you shouldn't do this!"

"But just think of poor Mr. Cooper. He needs help. You said yourself it was urgent. I'll tell you what, I'll dress up in Father's old hat and put his big coat around me. No one will guess I'm not a boy. I'll go harness Toby and Dinah. Why, this'll be like crossing the plains again!"

Before Mrs. Blane could voice another protest, Marian had run down to the creek and skipped across the rocks and was racing up the slope to where the mules were staked.

Mother quickly followed her and hung about Marian as she harnessed the mules to the camp wagon. Russell watched them both in puzzled silence.

"There's plenty of cooked food in the box, Mother," Marian announced when she was ready to start. "I'll stop at the Grays' and get Mrs. Gray to come over."

"But there isn't time. You must hurry to get to Warren's before dark. It's fifteen miles. And it's much out of your way to Grays'. I'll be all right. I have the revolver and my big son here," Mother's arm tightened around Russell's shoulders.

Marian looked back when she had forded the stream. Her mother waved and smiled but Marian knew that her eyes were clouded with worry. Presently the homestead lay far behind. She looked back once more. Her mother was still standing at the mouth of the cave—watching.

Marian had left in a spirit of adventure and anticipation. She had never been north of the claim. But now that she had left the trail along the Monument Creek and was on one of the roads to Denver, she became a bit frightened. There were no ranches in sight. Even the feel of Chase panting against her knees, and the well-known creak of the wagon failed to dispel the great loneliness that engulfed her.

She met no one. The rutted road was deserted on this cloudless September afternoon. Ever so often a trail, overgrown with weeds, branched off to some possible ranch. She found herself looking constantly toward the black snake-like ridge of the Pinery on her left. Suppose Indians were lurking there! She groped for the rifle on the seat beside her. The feel of the Winchester comforted her somewhat. Again she tried to feel brave and adventurous. She tried to interest herself in the strange new scenery.

"What a funny flat-topped mountain that is off there!" she told Chase. It was a comfort to hear her own voice. "It looks like a big table."

Chase looked at her with his great solemn eyes. His tail flop-flopped in answer. No matter what she said, he always seemed to be happy to answer in the only way he knew. Then a frisky gopher ran across the road and Chase became interested in things much more important than table mountains.

As Marian watched the scenery about her, the reins slackened in her hands. Unheeded the mules stumbled on. After a time she became conscious of how slowly they were going and impatiently flapped the reins over the mules' broad backs. "Come on, slow-pokes! We must hurry!"

She had failed to realize how late it was growing. Now she discovered that the wagon was nearing the Pinery. She could see the sharp outlines of towering trees, black against the fading daylight.

"How funny! Why—why we should have passed that stone building the man told us about and McShane's ranch!" she thought. But where were they?

217

WAGON WHEELS TO DENVER

Marian halted the wagon. She looked anxiously to right and left. The man had said that McShane's, where there was an Indian fort, was off the road toward the mountains and the house was surrounded by willows. But there was not a house to be seen over the miles of rolling country.

She urged the mules on and tried to console herself with the thought that the ranch was still ahead of her; that she had failed to get the directions correctly. She even tried to sing, *"Rosalie, the Prairie Flower,"* to keep up her courage.

Suddenly the words stuck in her throat. She was on a little-used trial leading straight to the Pinery! She could see it winding endlessly eastward through dark pines.

Somehow she had taken the wrong road! She was lost!

XVIII

"Could It Be Jake?"

Ahead of Marian was the ominous stretch of forest—the place where anything might lurk—and things did. The tales she had heard of previous happenings in the denseness of the shadows beat at her brain and froze her in terror to the wagon seat.

Indians! The Pinery! The Indians hid there and emerged to prey on lonely ranchers. Marian shivered. The trail she was on might lead to the stage road to Denver, but nothing could induce her to ride through those menacing dark trees.

"Besides," she told Chase, "if I did reach the stage road how would I ever find my way back to Warren's on Plum Creek? No sir, we'll turn around!"

Chase wagged his tail.

Suddenly, as she started to turn the mules about, she noticed a rough trail branching off from her left. It seemed to lead back toward the mountains and over to a flat-topped butte. She hesitated a moment. After all, any road was better than the one she was on. She decided to take it.

Somehow she felt better with the sweep of mountains once more before her. The sun was sinking behind the dark blue ridges and the sky was a rosy heliotrope. The chill of approaching night fanned her pale face.

If only this trail led to the right road, she prayed, searching the rolling country for some ranch house where she could inquire her way.

The mountains became sinister dark walls now. The pine trees along the trail reached forth their grotesque branches like great clutching fingers toward the bumping, swaying wagon. It grew darker and Marian felt numb with fright as she pulled her father's coat closer about her shoulders.

All at once the clop-clop of horses' hoofs crashed in on her alert ears. Anxiously she looked back through the canvas opening. She could see nothing but trees and the white winding trail. Then two horsemen, black against the road, galloped toward her. She grabbed the heavy rifle, her heart pounding.

The next minute two rough-looking men, shadowy in the waning light, were riding alongside of the wagon.

"Howdy, stranger. Put down that gun! We won't hurt ya!"

Chase let out a deep growl.

"COULD IT BE JAKE?"

A chill ran down to Marian's toes. There was something strangely familiar about that voice. Or had she only imagined it? A dark face—a livid white scar across one eyebrow, flashed before her. Jake! Scar Face! Could it be? Surely not away up here and yet . . . She clutched the rifle, terrified.

"Can't ya talk? Are ya dumb?" another voice growled.

She must say something. The last speaker was leaning forward, peering at her from below his wide slouched hat. His eyes shone evilly. Quickly, Marian ducked her head, shivering. The man was expecting an answer. She struggled to find her voice. Without realizing why, she managed to make her voice a deep, harsh croak. "Hello! This the road to Warren's on Plum Creek,"

"Waal, if it ain't a boy! Thought ya was an old deafy. What ya doin' out here, son? This ain't the road ya want. We'll be hittin' it 'fore long. We're goin' that way. Follow us."

The men started on.

"But—but McShane's ranch—where is it?" she called desperately.

The man who had first spoken turned his head. "That's south of ya on the Denver road," he answered, nodding toward her left. "If ya was aimin' to hit thar ya must 'a' got off the road on to the sawmill trail 'fore ya come to McShane's."

Her heart sank. For one hopeful moment she had thought that McShane's might still lie ahead of them,

Then she could have slipped away from these men—found safety there. Now—well, there seemed nothing else to do but follow them. But she kept her trembling hand on the rifle.

"Thank goodness for Father's hat!" she whispered to Chase.

The trail they were on presently joined the well-worn road to Denver, which led toward the mountains for a time, and then ran north along the base of the range.

To Marian it seemed that they rode up hill and down for mile after mile and hour after hour. It had long ago grown dark, a pitchy dark which gradually grew light from the twinkling carpet of stars overhead and brighter still when a shy moon slid from behind a cloud. The beauty of the night was lost upon Marian. She could see nothing but the two dark horsemen.

Her mind traveled on and on with the creaking wheels in a nightmare of questions. Where were they leading her? Could that really be Jake? Suppose they were taking her to some out-of-the-way place, and intended to rob her of the wagon and mules—her gun! Perhaps they might hold her for ransom. She had heard of such a thing. Virginia had read . . . She shuddered.

In desperation, she was about to turn around and make a dash for it—anywhere—anyhow—back over the road she had traveled, when she saw a glimmer of light and the dark outlines of a house in the valley below. Warren's ranch! Could it be? Or was it some place that belonged to these men!

Fearfully, she followed them down the long road winding like a narrow white ribbon under the stars. She was thankful that the men were in front, for she had them covered with her rifle. However, if she was forced to use her gun . . . Her heart pounded until it seemed to drown out the creaking wheels, the stumbling clack-clack of the mules.

It was a ranch! She could see the stake fence—an open gate swinging under two giant guarding pines. The riders drew up their horses.

"Thar ya are, son. This here's Warren's. We'll be gettin' 'long now," called the larger of the men, turning in the saddle and pointing toward the ranch house.

In her relief and gladness to be safe at last, Marian called out in her natural voice, "Oh, thank you! Thank you so much!"

There was a startled exclamation from the man who had just spoken. An oath of surprise!

It must be Jake! He'd recognized her! Frantically Marian urged the mules through the gateway. In a moment of frenzied fear she lashed furiously at Toby and Dinah with the reins. The mules clattered down the road leading to the log house. Low branches swished the wagon top, slapped the long-eared animals, knocked the broad-brimmed hat over Marian's eyes. The next minute they were abreast of the ranch house porch, and a man

WAGON WHEELS TO DENVER

was hurrying from the open doorway. Quickly Marian pulled up the mules and then she sagged back in the seat, limp and terrified.

"Howdy, stranger!" the man cried. "Why, 'Liza!" he called as he discovered her small huddled figure. "Come here! It's a girl!"

The man helped her down. "Come right in, child. Mrs. Warren'll take care of you. I'll tend your mules."

Marian glanced apprehensively over her shoulder. They hadn't followed her! The horsemen were gone! "Thank you," she replied in a relieved voice. "May I stay here tonight? I'm Marian Blane."

"That you may. And here's Mrs. Warren to look after you," answered the short, elderly man with bushy white eyebrows. He watched her curiously.

A shriveled little woman in dark calico stood on the top step holding a lamp. She smiled invitingly. Gratefully Marian followed her into the cabin. Chase came sniffing at her heels.

"You must be tuckered out, Miss. I'll fix you some supper. We're poor folks, but you're welcome to what we got." She busied herself about the crackling stove. "Now, don't you talk," she admonished as Marian started to speak. "Just you set. You can tell us about yourself over your victuals."

A palace would have been no more inviting to Marian than was the safety of this mountain ranch house. She sank wearily to a small rocker and looked about her. The

224

log walls were lined with coyote skins and yellowed pictures torn from magazines. Here and there a chink in the wall was stuffed with old newspaper. A rickety ladder led to a loft above. The furniture and a rag rug were home made. The usual geraniums at the two windows, without which no mountain home is complete, lent a rosy brightness to the room.

Over a supper of cold beef, fried potatoes, coarse home-made bread and fresh warm milk, Marian told the Warren family of her errand and of how she got lost. The elderly couple tried to reassure her about the two men who had led her to their ranch, but long after she was tucked into a great feather bed under the eaves, she kept thinking about the horsemen and something told her that one of them had been Jake!

The next morning Marian reluctantly bade good-bye to the kind, hospitable couple. Mrs. Warren placed a package of sliced beef and buttered bread on the wagon seat. '' 'Case you get hungry, Miss,'' she smiled.

The day was warm and sunny, the sky as blue as her Aunt Lily's turquoise ring. The Plum Creek road was deserted as far north as eye could see. However, at every turn, from around every choke-cherry bush or straggling scrub oak, she half expected to find Jake. She passed but two ranch houses in the long twenty miles.

As the third ranch came into view, Marian happily urged the mules to a faster gait. That must be the Turners'! She could see the house now! It was in a nest of willows at the entrance to a canyon. Eagerly she turned into the ranch yard. They rattled past a barefoot youngster whose freckle-peppered face stared curiously, past meek, vacant-eyed cows and scurrying, cackling hens, and presently drew up before the squalid cabin itself.

But Marian's gladness on reaching the ranch was short-lived. Virginia met her at the sagging porch, her eyes red-rimmed, her mouth trembling. Marian stifled her cry of greeting. Soberly she mounted the steps.

"Virginia! Why—why what's the matter?" she cried anxiously. Beyond in the crowded kitchen Marian could see Mrs. Cooper staring with unseeing eyes at the faces about her, her eyelids swollen from tears. "Is—is your . . ." Marian stopped, unable to voice the fear in her heart.

"Oh, Marian! It's—it's all—over! Pa's ———" Virginia burst into a flood of tears.

Marian put both arms around her and hugged her close. "How—how dreadful! Oh, Virginia, I'm so sorry—so sorry!"

Four barefoot little girls in ragged pinafores edged out of the house. They stared silently at Marian, at the sobbing Virginia, at the panting black dog at their feet.

"Marian!" It was Doctor Frank. He came up the steps quickly, his usually grinning face white and strained. "What in heaven's name are you doing here? Where's your father?"

"He's away, buying sheep. I came instead. Mother

wanted to, but I wouldn't let her," answered Marian miserably.

"Well," Doctor Frank looked at Virginia with compassionate eyes, "it's no use now. Mr. Cooper was better, and we thought if we could get him down to his new ranch house, away from this crowded place that he would improve more rapidly. But—well, he had a turn for the worse last night . . ." Doctor Frank leaned against a post, his face hidden. Marian thought she heard him groan, "The first—I've lost!"

Suddenly he straightened up. He turned to Marian. "You must go right back. Your mother mustn't be alone. You take Iron Side and I'll keep the wagon. There'll be things to do in Denver but I'll be back at the ranch as soon as I can."

Marian's heart sank. The thought of that long lonely ride brought a rush of tears to her eyes. She turned her face from the doctor and Virginia.

"Come on, Marian. Better leave at once," remarked Doctor Frank, starting down the steps toward the Blane wagon.

"Good-bye!" Virginia's voice shook.

"Oh, Virginia!" Marian hugged her friend. "Will—will you be down at your ranch soon? We'll—we'll have lots of fun together—honest," she added trying to bring a smile to Virginia's quivering lips.

"Ma says we're going back to Ohio—soon as we get rid of the ranch. We—we aren't going to live there."

WAGON WHEELS TO DENVER

"Oh!"

They looked at each other silently for a long moment. All Marian's happy plans faded as quickly as did the mirage on the plains.

A wall seemed to rise between them. The next minute they were saying good-bye, a strained good-bye as if those weeks across the plains had never been and they were strangers now. Her friend's sorrow had changed everything. Marian stumbled down the steps to Doctor Frank who stood waiting beside his gray mare.

In less than an hour from the time she had arrived, Marian was riding the gawky Iron Side toward home. Chase followed close behind. The Winchester was slung to the saddle. Even this much protection failed to reassure her or lessen her dread of that long, lonely stretch before her.

All through the afternoon, she rode in the creaking saddle. "I'd like riding without a saddle much better," she confided to Iron Side wearily. Since the loss of Gypsy and her side-saddle, Marian had been riding bareback when she went for the mail. "Your funny old bony back wouldn't be nearly so uncomfortable," she added, stroking the wiry gray mane.

The afternoon was sultry. Perspiration trickled down her straight little nose. Her hair felt damp and stringy under the heavy man's hat.

"Gid-ap, you slow-poke! That's the way. Don't you know that we must get out of this part of the country?

We mustn't meet Jake!" she told the mare presently.

Marian looked over her shoulder. Chase was having a hard time keeping up with her. "Come, boy!" She whistled the bird-like call which Doctor Frank had taught her.

When she reached Warren's ranch, Marian hesitated. Doctor Frank had cautioned her about riding after dark. He had told her to be sure to spend the night there. She drew rein, half inclined to stay. But the thought of her mother alone, perhaps needing her, sent her hurrying on.

Suppose something dreadful happened to her mother! She shuddered. For the first time in her life, she sensed what death might mean. And Mother—Mother was ill,— ill! Suppose . . . Her now thoroughly anxious mind drew pictures which made her heart thump achingly and urged her to ride straight on.

"We'll make it to McShane's," she told the mare as they jog-trotted out of sight of Warren's. They would be safe and home in a jiffy from there! She was making better time than with the wagon. It would be daylight for two hours yet and then there would be moonlight, she mused.

A bright moon had swung into the sky and flooded the countryside with a soft mist, when Marian first noticed the light glimmering among the willows. It was just as the man and Charles had described it. "That's Mc-Shane's!" she whispered to the mare.

As she drew nearer she could see the outlines of the Indian fort. It was a small building of stone. Marian could see four gaping port-holes. David McShane had built the fort right after the Indian raids of 1868. At that time their only protection and refuge had been their large log cabin. She remembered Charles had told her that twenty-one people gathered there for safety when the redskins stole out from the shelter of the Pinery seeking to kill the settlers and to run off their cattle and horses.

As she pulled her horse close to the wooden gate, she looked longingly at the lighted windows. She wanted dreadfully to stay there. Suddenly she remembered what Charles had told her about Mrs. McShane. Alone she had kept the Indians at bay for days, firing at them whenever they drew near. That was bravery!

Why, she was just a scaredy! She wasn't a bit brave! She was afraid of that lonely ride and Mother was alone down at the claim—ill!

That settled it! Marian started on. "We'll go home, old girl," she said firmly. "We've just got to! Mother needs me!"

She must have traveled several miles when she heard the rat-tat-tat of hoofs pounding the road at a furious pace. Marian's heart jumped up in her throat. Who could be traveling at that speed? Oh, why hadn't she stayed at McShane's?

A clump of scrub oak and low trailing bushes grew close to the roadside. She would hide, she decided desperately, before that horseman could see her. Suppose

"COULD IT BE JAKE?"

it was Jake! Terrified, she scrambled off her horse. She slid down the bank, pulling the stumbling mare after her.

There now, they were all three screened from the road! She only hoped whoever it was couldn't see the mare's rangy had. She tugged at her bridle. Iron Side tossed her head up, provokingly.

Chase was running about them. "Here, boy! Down! Be still, Chase!" she whispered as she crouched behind the sheltering bushes. One trembling hand grabbed the dog's collar.

Rat-tat- rat-tat-tat, rat-tat-tat came the oncoming horse. Nearer! Nearer!

Thump, thump, thump, went Marian's heart, keeping time to the hoof beats.

The sound grew louder. Horse and rider were visible now. They were coming straight down the open stretch toward them. Marian crouched lower. Would the man see her? Her cold hands clutched the horse and dog fiercely.

There! He was passing!

Marian peeked through the bushes.

Then she screamed. "Father! Father! Stop! I'm here!" She ran from behind the scrub oak waving her hands wildly. Frantically she clambered up the bank.

The horse and rider pulled up suddenly. The horse rose in the air with the sudden yank on his bit. The man was turning and coming back. Then a terrible thought whirled through her mind.

231

"Suppose it isn't Father . . ."

But the next instant the rider had slid from his saddle, and Marian, with a glad cry of relief, was held tightly in her father's arms.

XIX

Bad News and Doughnuts

"Mother!" cried Marian as she rushed into the warm little kitchen a month later, her arms full of sweet-smelling, newly-washed clothes. "Minnie is back! She's in the barn, and she had all four of her baby kittens with her! Russell's so happy he's crying. You know how broken-hearted he's been since Bill disappeared. Minnie had just about taken Bill's place. But he's found her, after searching in the most outlandish places!"

Marian stopped, out of breath. She dropped the clothes on the pine table and impatiently pushed back her mop of curls. She had broken her long round comb ages before. Her curls were a great trial, always flopping in her eyes. She often thought she would cut them off, like a boy's hair. It would be much less trouble.

Mrs. Blane had been writing letters home. From the

portfolio resting on her lap she raised preoccupied eyes
to Marian's rosy face. Little did Marian know that her
mother was seeing her just as she had been describing
her to Aunt Lily. A Marian whom Grandmother and
Auntie would hardly recognize. She had become so tall
and rounded—so grown-up and pretty, even in the outgrown flannel dress.

"Minnie?" her mother questioned. "You mean the old
gray mother cat?" Marian's words sank into her
thoughts. "Why, how in the world did she get her kittens here? It's two miles to the Grays'!"

"I don't know. But she did! I think she must have
carried them one by one in her mouth. Those two miles!
That's why she was gone all night. Now I know why Mrs.
Gray named her Minnie. It's short for Minerva—and
Minerva was the goddess of wisdom. Oh, Mother! Can't
we keep the baby kitties if Mrs. Gray will let us?"

"Why, I suppose so. But dear me," answered Mother
with a soft little laugh, "we'll soon have most of the
Grays' animals down here! We already have Blossom,
their Jersey cow, and Napoleon, the rooster, to say nothing of all those brown hens Mr. Gray insisted we take."

Mrs. Blane went back to her letters, and the kitchen
was quiet except for the scratch of her pen and the
crackle of aspenwood in the iron stove. Marian started
to smooth out and fold the clothes. They had learned to
iron only those that just must be ironed—the rest were
"mangled" as they wore them. A term that Doctor Frank

laughingly applied to the "rough-dry" clothing they wore after wash day.

It had been such a busy month. The cabin had been completed two weeks before, and it was lucky for them because one night an icy sleet blew down from the Peak and covered the mountains and plains with a brief coat of white. At first it had been stuffy in the cabin after the months in the open, although Father had left a good three inches open at the top of the log walls to give Mother plenty of air. But as the nights grew colder it felt good to be housed at last, even if their home contained but two rooms and a lean-to kitchen.

Marian glanced proudly through the doorway leading to the next room. She could see the neat front porch beyond the fluttering muslin curtains in the open windows, and the glorious mountains dressed in their gold and red of autumn.

My, but she had worked! Of course, they had to make the cabin as comfortable as possible with their few belongings. The rosewood and walnut furniture had been left for their tenants in the Blanes' home back in Chicago. The cabin floors were bare, but Marian had worked hard to make those dainty curtains out of Mother's summer wrapper and one of her own outgrown muslin dresses. There had to be one homelike touch! How she had labored over the tiny stitches! It would take Father's spyglass to see them. She admired them anew as they fluttered in the breeze. They looked very like the little

235

starched ruffled pantalettes the girls wore during the Civil War.

Father had purchased an iron stove, an easy rocker, a comfortable bed for Mother, and a Doty washing machine, which looked very much like a butter churn, and he had hauled them down from Denver. Doctor Frank had built the large pine table, sturdy and creamy white on top. He also put up a rude sink in the corner of the kitchen, although the water had to be hauled from the choke-cherry spring.

Marian glanced about the kitchen with pride, as she pulled the wrinkles out of Russell's underwear. Mother's few pretty dishes with their bright nosegays looked lonesome on the rude kitchen shelves, as if they missed their old home in the rosewood china cabinet.

She had worked hard on the barn, too. It had been finished the day before Doctor Frank moved to the Fountain Colony to set up his practice. Now Toby and Dinah and the fiery brown Kite, Father's new horse, were warm and comfortable in the clean barn with its sweet smelling straw. There were the chickens to feed and Blossom to milk and the cooking and washing to be done. It had taken Marian all month to master the art of milking, but now she felt as competent as Hiram Gray. No wonder Marian's hands had grown red and toil-worn below her outgrown blue sleeves.

"Mother," Marian said presently, "I forgot to tell you. Russie and I have decided what to call the ranch."

BAD NEWS AND DOUGHNUTS

Mother looked up from her letter and smiled. "I suppose you're going to give it one of these foreign names they like so well around here."

"No. We've decided on 'Crow's Nest!'"

"Crow's Nest! Mercy, there aren't any crows about here! What made you think of that name?" Mrs. Blane smiled faintly.

"Because a crow's nest means a lookout. We can see for miles and miles from here. I found out in my studies yesterday that it means a lookout near the masthead of a ship. I think it's a much nicer sounding name than 'Lookout' or 'The Pines' or 'Grand View.' They sound so uninteresting and Spanish names are so hard to pronounce. Don't you think it's a nice name?"

"Crow's Nest!" Mother repeated in amusement. "Well, I suppose it does as well as anything else. We might as well be on a ship at sea. It's lonesome enough." Mother went back to her writing.

The flush of pleasure drained from Marian's face. She had thought it such a grand idea. Mother was strange sometimes lately, especially when she wrote letters home. Other times . . . Meditatively she went on with the work of smoothing out the wash. Perhaps, she thought, Mother had discovered the cause of the ever-deepening pucker between Father's eyes. Ever since the night a month ago when he had ridden through the night to meet her, he had been worried over money matters, Marian knew. He had been unable to buy sheep at the price he could pay, and he had told her once, "Marian, I must do something to make this homestead pay. McLane, who bought the hardware store back home, can't pay up until November. The rent from the house won't be enough!"

Her father's anxiety had partly wiped out all other worries. The fear of Jake and the certainty that he was somewhere in the Divide country had lessened somewhat, and even Marian's disappointment over losing Virginia had faded in the midst of work and money worries.

Marian folded the last shirt and carried the wash into the room she shared with her mother. It was cold in there, so far from the heat of the crackling stove. Cold and bare. The room contained but two neat beds, a dry-goods box and the trunk that had crossed the plains with them. On top of the box among the toilet articles were arranged the doll's sofa, table and chairs. Blond Lily in her best tan and blue plaid with the long train, and rosy John sat stiffly upright—neglected and forlorn. Marian had been too busy to think much about them lately and even Russell hadn't asked her to play dolls and soldiers with him since they had left Pueblo. Marian stooped and kissed them tenderly.

Bang! Bang! Marian looked up, startled, as she heard the loud pounding at the front door. Who in the world could that be? she wondered nervously.

They were alone—she, Mother and Russell. Father had just left that morning for the southern part of the Territory to try to buy sheep again.

BAD NEWS AND DOUGHNUTS

Chase barked furiously as Marian ran into the next room. Her mother had already opened the door.

Two men whom she had noticed at Teachouts stood on the porch. One of them handed Mother a message which she tore open quickly.

"Oh! . . . How terrible!" she cried, leaning weakly against the wall. The paper fluttered from her fingers to the rough board floor.

"What's the matter, Mother? What is it?" Marian cried, picking up the message. And then she saw the fearful words staring up at her.

"Chicago burned! Your home—everything gone. That section burned to ground. All of us safe. Lily."

"Chicago burned! Our house! Everything!" Marian repeated in a daze.

She clutched her mother's arm, her unbelieving eyes on the two men before her. "Is it really true?" she asked. "When did it happen? When did this come?"

"Ted here got the news when he went to Colorado City this morning. That message was telegraphed to Denver. They have a wire down to the old town. It ain't used much 'cause the telegraph operator lives on a ranch and he only gets in on Saturdays. The county clerk can take a message though he can't send none—so he got it. They say in Denver that Chicago's been burning since Sunday, October eighth. . . . Sorry, ma'am." The man fumbled with his hat. "Well, I guess we better be going. Bet it cost a lot to send that message,'' he added in awe, as he slouched away.

For some moments after they left, Marian was unable to move. Vaguely she heard her mother cross the room to the window. Marian turned and watched her miserably. Mother was standing gazing silently across at the mountains.

Then the realization of their loss swept over Marian. ''Everything's gone! Our pretty house—the rosewood and walnut furniture—the clock with the little gilded cupids—all Mother's and Father's things—and Clytie— all gone!'' Unconsciously she spoke aloud. How poignantly she remembered telling Clytie and their dear home good-bye—wondering if she would ever see them again.

She bit her lip, hard.

Mother turned from the window. There was a faraway look in her eyes and her lips were set in a thin line. ''Where are the clothes to be ironed, Marian?'' she asked in a strained, unnatural voice. ''I think I'll get to work.''

Silently Marian brought out the three heavy irons and set them to heat. She blinked her eyes to keep back the tears. However, one escaped and fell with a sizzle upon the hot stove. Mother was like that, she thought. She always got out her sewing or baked a cake when she was broken-hearted over something.

Suddenly Marian could stand it no longer. She ran from the cabin, past the fluttering chickens, the barn, up on the bluffs among the pines where she flung herself on the needle-strewn ground. She buried her face in her hands. No tears would come, however, only a desolate sense of loss engulfed her.

Presently she sat up with a start. There would be no rent! Oh, what would they live on? What would they do—now?

With dragging feet, at length, she made her way back to the cabin. Inside, she tried not to notice the bare room which served as Father's and Russell's bedroom and their parlor, nor the one rocker and camp chair, the two cots, the two rude shelves for books and magazines, Great-grandmother Willard's wall clock, ticking above them—their only home now!

The burning of their Chicago home was not mentioned again. But it was uppermost in their minds in the days following,—days which dragged like years.

Several mornings later Marian had finished milking and was just returning to the cabin with the pail of warm, frothing milk when she saw figures on horseback galloping over the rolling ground across the creek. She stopped. Could the railroad be near enough to have their men in this vicinity?

Then her feet froze to the ground in helpless fear. Those figures wore blankets—some wore feathers on their heads—some were hatted like the white men!

Indians! And they were headed straight for the ranch!

Marian dropped the bucket in her fright. The milk slopped over her copper-toed shoes unnoticed. Frantically she grabbed Russell, who was playing on the porch, and rushed him inside the house. She slammed and bolted the flimsy door.

"What's the matter?" her brother cried, catching hold of her dress.

"Hush! Don't say a word!" she whispered.

"But why hush?" Russell's eyes were frightened.

"Don't stand there staring! Run and bolt the back door, quick! It's Indians! I'll try to find the revolver! We must protect Mother!"

At the word "Indians," Russell sped to the kitchen as fast as his legs would take him.

"Marian," he said in a quivery voice, when he returned, "will they hurt us?"

"Hush! I—I don't know."

She could hear the clop-clop of horses' hoofs drawing near—nearer! All the tales she had heard since coming West flashed through her mind. A vision of the Indians burning the cabin, killing and scalping them all, left her stricken.

The hoof beats grew louder—stopped. A horse neighed. There was a dead silence. Then a twig crackled and stealthy footsteps approached the porch. Someone was pounding on the door so violently that it shook the cabin.

That would wake her mother, she thought wildly. "Russell, run in to Mother! Don't let her know . . ."

The pounding continued. Her mother's voice could be faintly heard from the next room.

242

BAD NEWS AND DOUGHNUTS

She knew she should answer that insistent knocking. She must open the door!

Trembling, she slid the bolt. Then with a desperate prayer in her heart she threw open the door.

A fat squaw whose face was a network of wrinkles stood there in the doorway. Beyond her, the stony faces of Indian braves and their squaws stared back at Marian.

"Young paleface, heap 'fraid." The Indian was looking at the revolver. "Me hungry! Want heap biscuit!" A timid grin flitted across her brown face.

"Biscuit! . . . Biscuit!" stammered Marian unable to believe her ears.

"Me hungry," the squaw persisted. Then turning she pointed a dirty finger toward the group on horseback. "Hungry too."

"But—we haven't any . . ." Marian was sure she caught a gleam of anger in the beady eyes. What should she do? Suddenly she thought of the huge pan of doughnuts which she and her mother had made the day before. They hadn't been fit to eat because she had put in too much soda. But perhaps . . . "Wait!" she commanded, although her voice shook. "I'll get you some!"

In a second Marian was back, the pan shaking in her hands. "Here—take these!"

The squaw beamed as she eagerly grabbed the doughnuts. Then a rush of Indian gratitude tumbled from her thick lips and bobbing up and down she trotted off to her band. There she was met by a clamor of guttural sounds as the Indians swarmed about her.

Marian hurriedly closed the door and leaned limply against it. Her mother hastened into the room at that moment clutching her plaid shawl around her. Russell followed, his round face as white as paper.

"Marian, what is it? What is Russell trying to tell me? Who was that knocking?"

"It's all right, Mother. Don't be frightened. It's Indians. They were hungry. I gave them the doughnuts."

"Indians! Oh, Marian, where are they?"

"They're eating. You ... you don't think they'll be mad about the soda, do you?"

"Soda? Mercy, I don't know." Mrs. Blane hurried to the window and peeked out. "They're sitting on the wood-pile," she whispered to Marian, who had joined her. "Why, they are actually eating them! And they taste horrid!"

"Maybe it'll kill 'em," Russell suggested hopefully, pushing his small body between his mother and sister and peering out at the Indians.

"Of course not," Marian answered. "But it might make them sick. Oh, you don't think it will, do you, Mother?" she asked, fingering the curtains nervously.

Mrs. Blane smiled and shook her head.

"Mummy better give 'em some of those little pink pills of Doctor Frank's," Russell advised soberly.

Marian giggled. Somehow the idea of handing out a

lot of Russell's hated pills as a remedy for too much soda was such a funny one that she forgot her fear of the Indians or what they might do to them after the last doughnut had vanished.

Every so often one of the squaws would turn her fat squat body, and the broad, blank face would stare silently at the cabin. The Indian braves, however, attended strictly to the business of eating.

In their interest in the figures on the wood-pile, the Blanes failed to notice the snow clouds gathering. Now the oncoming mist was turning into wind-whipped sleet. The cold sting of snow blew down through the opening under the cabin roof. Down by the creek the trees tossed. The Indian ponies braced themselves against the wind. The air grew thick with flying snowflakes, like feathers tossed helter-skelter from a great feather bed.

With relief Mrs. Blane and Marian watched the Indians mount their horses and ride down the slope and wade the creek. Soon they disappeared behind a heavy veil of snow.

Suddenly Mother turned. Her eyes met Marian's and then they burst out laughing.

"What you laughin' at?" Russell asked.

"Thinking of their eating all those awful doughnuts and liking them!" Mrs. Blane managed at last, wiping tears of laughter from her eyes. "Fiddlesticks! Weren't we foolish to be so frightened?"

"Weren't we?" Marian cried. "Here we've been expecting something terrible to happen when we met some Indians, and when we do, all they want is food, not scalps!"

XX

Jake

The next morning, Marian awoke to a white, freezing cold world. Shivering, she hurried into her clothes and built a fire in the stove so that Mother and Russell could dress by its warmth. Every now and then she would stop in her preparations for breakfast and peer nervously from the front windows. Presently she must go outside and tend to the chickens and fetch water from the spring. The Indians had been amiable but they might return, and today there were no doughnuts to offer them.

She hastened with the milking and feeding the animals sometime later, and carried the sloshing bucket of spring water up the slope to the cabin.

However, the snowy, pine-blackened country on every side of the ranch seemed deserted and she laughed her fears away when she rode Toby for the mail. But somehow the road never had seemed so lonely, nor the three miles so long. She found no word from Father, nor any further news from Chicago.

The snow disappeared before night but the mountains remained under a cold white blanket for several days—days of expected visits from the Indians and nervous trips to Teachouts. But each time she came back empty handed. There were no papers—nor letters. As for the redskins, they failed to return, although Russell thought he saw their ponies and feathered heads in every strange dark shadow when night descended over Crow's Nest ranch.

They told Marian at Teachouts that the railroad reached almost to the Blane homestead. Nevertheless she was surprised to see men, whom she took to be surveyors, riding along the creek one sunny afternoon.

She watched the riders with interest. "I wonder if Charles Barry is down there," she said to Russell. "That looks like him—the one with the black hat like Father's. That pony certainly looks like his frisky Jim."

"Let's yell at him," her brother suggested excitedly.

"Oh, no!" Marian blushed. She shaded her eyes with her sunbonnet. "Surely," she added, watching the three men ride on, "if that's Charles he'll come up and pay us a visit."

But the men disappeared beyond some dark pines

and a feeling of disappointment swept over Marian. They did have so few visitors on the Monument!

"Wish he'd come! He would have if you'd let me yell to him," the boy grumbled, "He tells stories. I like 'em. You and Mummy don't. You're so busy and say, 'Don't bother me'!"

"Why, Russie!" cried Marian contritely. "I didn't know you got lonely, too! Here, come on, let's play. Run get Minnie and I'll tell you the story of how she fetched her kitties that night."

"Oh, will you?" Russell breathed happily. The boy ran to the barn.

In the afternoon Marian gathered together her school books. She drew up the rocker beside a window and settled herself for an hour of study. Mrs. Blane had been a teacher in her girlhood and every day when the work was done Mother and daughter "played school" as Russell called it.

It proved a difficult task for Marian to keep her eyes and thoughts on the pages before her. Every few minutes she would glance out of the window and hopefully search the rolling country for a familiar figure on horseback. Presently she closed Ollendorff's *"Method of Learning French"* with a sigh. In spite of the fact that the book promised to teach you French in six months, Marian was sure it would take her six years. She hated those old irregular verbs! And what good was French going to do her, stuck away out West on a homestead? Impatiently she leafed through her *"Latin for Beginners"* until she found the lesson for tomorrow.

The sudden splash-splash of a horse through the creek startled her from her lesson. A young man in a wide black hat was riding his horse up the bank and straight up the straggling path to the cabin! It was Charles and his frisky Jim!

"Hello! Anybody home?" he shouted.

The French and Latin grammars tumbled to the floor followed by the *History of the States,* and *English Composition.* The next minute Marian dashed to the front door and threw it open.

"Hello," she called back. "Come in!"

"Thanks, I'll do that." Charles smiled at her and leaped from the saddle, tossing the reins over a near-by scrub oak.

"Mother's resting," Marian announced, as he joined her on the porch. "But come on in," she urged.

"You certainly are all settled," said the young man, looking around with admiring eyes. "Looks good to me after bunking in a tent for so long."

"Oh, but it's so bare!" Marian apologized. "We—we hope to get some tables and rugs and things soon. And Father plans to build a fireplace."

"Hello," Russell said, looking up from his soldiers. "Are you goin' to tell us stories?"

JAKE

"Why, hello, boy! How are you?" Charles picked him up in his strong arms and tossed him high in the air. Russell squealed delightedly. "No, I don't think I have any more stories. But haven't you?"

"Yes, Injuns! And my Bill ran away and we got a kitty and a new horse . . .our house burned an' . . ."

"Gosh! Did all that happen? Here, you'd better tell me about it, Marian." Charles' amused blue-gray eyes twinkled at her.

"All right," she laughed. "But come out to the kitchen. It's warmer there."

"You know," she added, as Charles followed her, Russell tagging at his heels, "I used to think it was backwoodsy to sit in kitchens but it's really cozier. Mother says all we need to be regular ranchers are geranium-filled windows. Have you noticed how nearly every cabin, no matter how small, has its geraniums? I never thought them a bit pretty before, but I rather like them now."

"Well, suppose I send you some from Denver on my next visit? What color, lady, red or pink?"

"How nice!" cried Marian. "Why, red, of course. They'd look so pretty and warm against the snow this winter. But sit down."

Shadows crept out from the corners of the kitchen before Marian had finished telling Charles all the news. When she wound up with their experience with the Indians, the young man broke in with a laugh, "I'm sure

251

those were Utes. And they're supposed to be friendly enough. I wouldn't worry about them.''

"I know it's silly after they were only hungry. But the thought of them around gives me shivers sometimes.''

"You know, I rather like them," Charles mused, gazing dreamily at the crackling stove which threw a rosy glow over his thoughtful face.

"You do?" cried Marian, her eyes wide.

"Gosh, I know well enough all the terrible things they've done to white people," Charles went on, "but just the same, they interest me. Next summer I'd like to go up among the Utes and learn how they live and everything.''

"Live with them! Jiminy!" Marian shuddered. "Why anyone would want to learn about them I can't see.''

"Oh, some day people will. They'll have forgotten all about the scalpings and bloodshed, then. They'll be interested in them as a race, as human beings. I am right now.''

Somehow Marian had a feeling that Charles had forgotten she was there. His eyes had a far-away look. Star gazing! Marian could understand that look if not its cause. She smiled sympathetically.

The next minute Mother was stirring about in the next room and Marian was surprised to discover it was nearly supper time. When Mrs. Blane came in she urged Charles to stay and join them.

"Will I! Mrs. Blane, you can't imagine what being in

JAKE

a real home means to me. As for a home-cooked meal!
Well, I warn you I'll do dreadful things to your larder.
I've been living on side meat and potatoes swimming in
grease, and coffee so strong it would hold up Russell.
One-armed Pete, our cook, can make flapjacks, but every-
thing else tastes just alike, only greasier.''

While Charles talked to her mother, Marian scurried
about the kitchen preparing supper. She made biscuits
according to the way Doctor Frank had taught her, and
creamed the salt codfish as her mother had learned to
make it back in New England. When the table was ready
and the big platter of rich creamy fish and boiled potatoes
set before them, Marian dropped flushed and nervous to
her chair. She hoped it would be good. There were so
few things she really knew how to cook, for supplies at
Crow's Nest were limited. However, her eyes shone at
the number of flaky biscuits Charles made away with as
she counted up to ten!

"Gosh, but that was a great supper! Haven't had anything like it since I left home!'' Charles announced as
he helped Marian with the dishes. Mother sat in her rocker, smiling and laughing with them. How good it was to
have company! Mother hadn't looked so young and happy since they had left their home in Chicago.

"Glad you liked it. But it really wasn't much,'' Marian apologized. "I would have tried to kill one of our
sacred chickens, though I hate to hurt them, if I'd known
you were coming.''

253

"Won't you save that for another time?" Charles laughed.

"Of course!" Marian replied as she hung up the dishpan outside the kitchen door.

"You know, Charles," spoke up Mother, "the Blanes have done nothing but talk about themselves. We've never given you a chance to tell us a thing about yourself, that is, of course if you care to."

"Well, there isn't much to tell. I've three sisters and a stepfather who wants me to work in a bank and—well, I don't like banking and I do like engineering, so—here I am!"

"Oh, tell me about your sisters?" Marian asked eagerly.

Charles grinned. "They're quite grown-up, at least they think so since they've been going to the Academy for Young Ladies. Such airs as they put on! Gosh!"

Mother suppressed a smile. "We had planned to send Marian to an academy in Chicago before we had to come West," she remarked.

"Gosh! Don't ever! It would . . ." Charles broke off, flushing.

Marian laughed gaily.

"I suppose," Charles announced regretfully after they had sat about the warm little stove laughing and talking for a while, "that I'd better be getting back to camp. We have to start early tomorrow. We're to survey south to Pueblo now. By the way, the graders will start work through your ranch tomorrow. It won't be long before the road'll be at the Fountain Colony, or Colorado Springs, as most everyone calls the town now. The Company promised me a job in the new hotel when it's completed. Have you been to town lately, Marian?''

''No, we haven't. We've been so busy and Father's away so much.''

''Well, you just ought to see it! You wouldn't know the place. Houses are springing up like mushrooms. Most of them are just one and two-room shacks but they hope to have several hundred stores and houses by Christmas. They're working on the hotel now and it'll be finished by January first.''

At the door Charles lingered. He turned and smiled at the Blanes gathered to bid him good-bye. ''Now, don't worry about Indians! Anyhow, you'll have plenty of company with the railroad so close by. Hope you get into town soon.'' He smiled at Marian. ''Won't the men be sore when I tell them what a good supper I had! Thank you lots. Good-bye!''

Marian listened at the door until the last hoof beat receded into the distance. He was gone. A lone star winked at her far above Pike's Peak. She closed the door to shut out the night and the wind swishing through the pines. Mother and Russell had started to undress before the kitchen fire. It seemed to Marian that Charles' chuckling laugh still lingered in the cabin. She felt happier than she had for a long time. It was nice to have found a friend, she thought, as she stooped and blew out the lamp.

The next day the slope on the opposite side of Monument Creek swarmed with rough-looking workmen. For two days Marian watched them from her perch high up in the limbs of a tall pine—"Grandfather Pine," Russell called it. Every day she climbed that tree, looking far down the trail for her father. From this lookout she could see farther than from the cabin, see for miles and miles over the rolling plains to the Pinery and the sweeping length of the mountains.

Late the next day, Marian suddenly realized that it was past time to feed the chickens and milk Blossom. She scrambled down from the tree.

Hastening through her chores, she carried the milk pail into the house. The kitchen had grown cold. She looked anxiously toward the stove and saw that the fire had gone out so she rattled and shook the stove and started a new fire. How careless of her to have forgotten! Mother must have fallen asleep and hadn't noticed. Marian stuffed in some paper, carefully laid the tiny twigs of pine and threw in a few sharp cones.

Then above the noise she was making Marian heard a startled exclamation from the next room.

She stood still, listening.

"Mother! What is it?" she cried, running in to Mrs. Blane.

"Look!" cried her mother, peering out the window.

"See them. Those men! They're coming up here! I don't like their looks. What do you suppose they want? Come away before they see us." She pulled at Marian's sleeve. "I think we'd better lock up."

Marian gave one look at the men climbing the slope and dropped the wood she had been gathering and rushed to bolt the doors. "Thank goodness you hadn't lit the lamp, Mother, and that the fire's out," she called over her shoulder. "I'll pull the curtains and they'll think we're out." Her fingers tugged at the shades as she spoke.

Russell came running from the bedroom. "What is it?" he asked. "What's all the dark for, Mummy? Injuns?"

"No—hush, Russell," his mother whispered.

They stood in the center of the darkened room nervously gripping each other. Marian's breath shook in the silence. Chase lay at their feet, tense, his ears listening as if he sensed that something sinister moved outside. Once he growled.

The crunch of boots—of trampled dry brush, the rattle of a stone came to them. Then heavy, stumbling footsteps on the porch and muttering voices. Bang! Bang! It sounded like a dozen determined fists beating on the door!

"They'll break it down!" whispered Marian. "Oh!" she added clutching her mother tightly. "If Father would only come—or Charles!"

Chase barked furiously. He rushed against the flimsy

door. Presently the knocking stopped. There was a noise on the porch, harsh voices above the angry bark of the dog. Then one by one, fumbling fingers tried and rattled each window. Marian suppressed a scream and ran into the bedroom in search of the gun. As the men rounded the cabin she could hear Chase following them within, growling menacingly.

With the revolver clutched tightly, Marian tore back to her mother and brother. After what seemed hours, the kitchen door was shaken roughly.

"Break her in!" a gruff voice ordered.

Marian raised the revolver. The next instant her mother snatched it from her shaking fingers and fired. A tiny round of light appeared in the wood above the growling dog. Silence followed, more breath-taking than the noise. Then voices loud in argument broke the stillness. "Don't ya think it! I ain't goin' to face no bullets, nor a hound like that a one!" . . . "I ain't either! Come on!" came from another man.

Grumbling voices passed the cabin. Chase stopped growling and stood listening with the others. They heard the crunch, crunch of boots. Then silence. The men must have gone!

Mother sank into her rocker as Marian tiptoed to one of the front windows and peeked out. In the waning light she could see the men disappearing down the slope below the cabin. A tall, beefy man in a tattered hat lagged in the rear striking a match on his pants leg. As the match flared up for a second Marian caught a glimpse of his features above the pipe. It was Jake!

"Have they gone?" cried her mother anxiously.

"Yes. . . . They've gone." Slowly Marian turned from the window. She took the revolver from her mother's limp fingers, glad that the darkness hid her eyes. Mother mustn't guess who was out there. Slowly Marian laid the gun within reach on the table.

She started a fire in the stove and cooked their supper. But often she stopped her work and listened. Now that Marian knew without a doubt that Jake Wolf was among them, she was sure they would return.

At bedtime Marian secretly took the revolver and carefully placed it near her pillow. She fairly held her breath until Mother and her brother had fallen asleep. They mustn't think her awake or frightened. But long into the night she lay tense—listening for the returning footsteps of Jake. His face flashed before her constantly as she stared into the shadows of the small log room.

"What was that!" Marian shot up in bed. A cold, gray dawn streaked the pine floor. Why, it was morning! Chase was barking to get out. Marian sprang from her bed. But before she freed the begging dog she peered cautiously out the window. What a welcome sight met her eyes! Far below, crossing the new railroad grade, swarmed droves of gray-white sheep, and in the rear rode a man on horseback. Father!

XXI

A Baby Railroad and a Birthday

Marian grabbed up her mother's shawl from the rocker and raced outside the cabin and down the slope to meet her father. He waved his hat when he saw her and spurred Kite past the swarming sheep.

"Thank goodness, you've come, Father!" Marian cried happily when he pulled the horse up beside her. "I'm so glad—so glad! It's been dreadfully lonely without you and we've been worried—not hearing a word," she said, flinging herself into her father's arms as he swung to the ground.

"Glad to be home, I can tell you!" said Father, giving her a hug. "It's been a long, hard trip. What do you think of our flock?"

"I never saw so many! But where'll we keep them? Won't they run away?" cried Marian, as she watched the sheep flounder through the creek.

Father chuckled. "I think not. We'll keep them up on the mesa above us until I get pens built. Come on, Marian, help me drive them up on the bluff," he said, swinging into the saddle once more. His voice sounded tired and strangely hopeless.

Marian studied his weary, travel-stained face. Just then Chase, who had been quivering nervously at her feet, made a sudden rush for the nearest sheep, barking and nipping at their heels. The startled animals ran in confusion toward the creek.

Quickly Father wheeled Kite and started after them.

"Here, Chase! Here, boy!" cried Marian anxiously. "Stop scaring them, you bad thing!" she scolded, as the dog reluctantly crept back at her call.

It proved a difficult task to herd the flock up on the mesa above the cabin in spite of the fact that, given rein, Kite was as dexterous as any sheep dog in herding a flock. Sheep-herding had been his life until Father had purchased him. The Newfoundland dog enjoyed the chase, and ran here and there barking happily at the thrill of this strange new game. But Marian was red in the face and ready to drop by the time the last stumbling sheep had cleared the bluff.

"Rather a hard job for greenhorns," Father remarked as he joined her. "We should have a sheepherder and a Shepherd dog, though Kite's pretty good. Seems to know just what to do. There's an old Mex in Colorado City who offered to come, but . . .'' Father sighed and leading Kite by the bridle, he and Marian descended the hill.

Marian looked up anxiously. She'd better get it over with before they joined her mother.

"Father . . . did you know about the Chicago fire and—and about our home burning?"

"Yes. Poor Mother! How did she take it?"

"Like a soldier. I—I'm afraid I didn't!" Marian averted her face.

Father squeezed her hand.

As they neared the cabin, he put his hand on her shoulder.

"Marian, can you be brave? Can you help?"

"Of course. What is it?" It had come. That something that she had been dreading since that first hopeless tone in his voice, that something that had made Father—of all people—cross to Chase when the frolicking dog had bothered the sheep up on the mesa.

"Well, the hardware store went too. I got word through to McLane, asking him. You know, the final payment was due next month. A letter was waiting for me at Teachouts. He won't be able to pay up now! There'll be no more rent with the old home gone! And here I have the rest to pay on all these sheep!"

"Oh, Father! . . . But don't worry. We'll get along. Why, we've Blossom and the chickens. Now, we'll have mutton. There'll be plenty of firewood—mountains of it!

It'll turn out all right. And we'll save every single penny for the sheep. Mother mustn't know, though."

"No, Marian, Mother mustn't know. That's my brave girl! But—there aren't any pennies left for the sheep!" At the look of concern shadowing her eyes, he patted Marian's head. "Sorry! I seem to be always loading cares on your young shoulders. I never dreamed when we started for Colorado that things would turn out like this...." Father looked across to the wall of mountains. His mouth and jaw had a new hard look and it seemed to Marian as if he hated that rugged wall now. Abruptly he started to walk on. "Pshaw!" he said, as if to himself. "Perhaps, when the time's up here, I can find work in the town."

Marian squeezed his roughened hand comfortingly, as they entered the kitchen. But the troubled look still lingered in his eyes long after he had greeted Mother and had tossed Russell to his shoulder.

The following days, however, were filled with watching the building of a railroad and this new fear, poverty, was overshadowed for a time.

When her work was done and her lessons recited, Marian would climb up in her favorite tree and watch the noisy construction gang to the north as they laid the new, shiny rails on this "Baby Railroad," as it was laughingly called. It was the first narrow gauge in the West.

She was timid about drawing near to these rough men. Their recent experience with the graders, the night she had seen Jake, was far from forgotten. But Russell in his curious little-boy way had made friends with them at once.

The day the tents and wagon, loaded with ties hauled from the Pinery, moved up the Monument and across from Crow's Nest, Russell hailed her. "Come down, Marian. Mike says they're goin' to lay rails 'cross from us today. Mike's nice," he added by way of inducement. "He's got a boy as big as me. Aw, come on!" he urged, peering up into her hide-out in the big pine.

Marian glanced uncertainly toward the busy scene opposite. Men were working along the right of way. On the slope above them tents had been pitched. A long, low wagon, with a large cook stove resting in the sagging center, had just driven into camp. A little man who limped was directing the placing of the cook tent above the stove.

"Hurry up!" shouted Russell impatiently.

"All right." Marian scrambled down from her perch. Hand in hand the brother and sister ran down the straggling path to the creek.

"Hello!" yelled Russell to the group of men across the stream. The men looked up. "Hello, there!" they shouted back. One of them, a heavy, red-faced man with a button nose, grinned broadly.

"Come on over an' drive a spike, big fellow!" he called.

"Sure, Mike." Russell tugged at Marian's restraining hand. "Come on!" he urged her.

Skipping from rock to rock across the splashing water, Marian followed her brother to the opposite bank.

"Howdy, Miss," greeted the man called Mike.

Marian smiled shyly in return, and then watched the men as they wielded their heavy sledge-hammers.

"Here, son. Have a try," Mike urged, offering him the hammer. But Russell was powerless to hold it. The heavy tool fell to the ground from his small, clutching fingers. The men guffawed loudly, all but Mike.

"I'll help you, big fellow," he said noticing the tears springing to Russell's eyes. "Wind your fingers 'round mine. See! Now, one, two, three, four! There, Russie, you've driven the first spike on your ranch!" Mike winked at Marian. "Come on, Miss. Want to try?"

"Oh, but I couldn't! Never!" cried Marian, drawing back.

"Sure you can," big Mike launghed.

Conscious of the staring men, Marian timidly put both hands on the handle of the sledge-hammer.

"Get ready! Go!" cried Mike. With the aid of the man's muscular right arm, Marian gradually drove the spike down, down into the wooden tie.

"Can't say you haven't helped build a railroad, Miss." Mike grinned at her flushed face.

Just then the little shriveled man in a big soiled apron limped from the cook tent above them. With one hand cupped at his mouth, he yelled, "Grub-pile! . . . Grub-pile! Come-an'-git-it!"

With a clankity-clank, bang, the tools dropped to the rails and road-bed, and the men mopped their sweating foreheads upon their coarse sleeves as they climbed the slope to camp. The bitter smell of over-boiled coffee, of scorched potatoes, and the smoky odor of grease floated down the hill.

"That's Pete!" Russell volunteered, nodding toward the aproned figure disappearing into the cook tent.

"One armed Pete? Charles' Pete?" asked Marian.

"Sure. He's great. You know somepin? He killed a man once who didn't like his grub-pile."

"Russell!"

"Well, he said he did!"

Besides the railroad there were now the sheep to watch, and the building of pens, interrupted by rides to Teachouts for the mail. Marian had not told her father about Jake. He had enough to worry him. But she never forgot the chill that had crept over her when she saw that scarred face in the flare of the match. The men in the construction gang were a cheery lot, not a bit frightening now that she had become acquainted with them. However, she always rode to Teachouts well armed. There were so many turns and projecting rocks along the trail! Even if Jake apparently had left the neighborhood, she took no chances. She never ventured far without Chase and her gun.

Birthdays and Christmas were made much of in the Blane household. But Marian knew better than to expect any sort of celebration or any presents this year. As her fourteenth birthday drew near, a wave of homesickness for Chicago swept over her. The remembrances of past birthdays, of gay parties and towering, frosted cakes glittering with little pink candles, of heaping bowls of vanilla ice cream, of the girls in starched muslin and bright sashes, was more than she could bear. She had but to close her eyes and she could see the last party; she could fairly smell the four cake layers baking to a golden brown in the shiny Stewart range, and hear the creak, crank, creak, of the big freezer turning under Tillie's capable hands on the shady back stoop. There would be nothing like that this year—nothing.

However, she resolutely made no comment. Even the last night that she was ever to be thirteen she made no mention of her birthday on the morrow. But something way down deep inside of her hurt cruelly. For no one else mentioned it, either.

The next morning she opened her eyes expectantly, then she closed them tightly. There would be nothing to see, no pretty things set invitingly at her bedside—this year.

"Wake up!" came an excited stage whisper from Russell. Marian looked at him miserably. "Mummy said not to bother you. But I got somepin'."

Marian set up in bed. "What, Russie? What?"

A BABY RAILROAD AND A BIRTHDAY

"See it. I made it. A pine pillow an' I filled it full of needles. When you go to bed you'll think Grandfather Pine's here." Russell, beaming proudly, stretched out a lumpy little pink pillow.

"Thank you, Russie! It's—it's beautiful!! Did you sew it all yourself?" Marian tried not to smile at the great, raggedy stitches closing one end of the pillow.

"Uh-uh!" the boy grinned.

Marian reached over and hugged him. "You're a dear not to forget." Russell wiggled uncomfortably. He jerked away. "Come on. Wait 'til you see breakfast!" he cried, running from the room.

Marian hurried into her clothes and out to the kitchen. Her mother, already dressed, was bending over the stove.

"Why, Mother! You shouldn't!" Marian cried in dismay.

"And why not? Birthdays come only once a year. You aren't to do a bit of work today, young lady!" Mother smiled. "Now, run outside and wash, and then sit down and eat. Russell, you'll have to wait. Sister's first today."

A few minutes later, Marian rushed back, her face still rosy and damp from a hurried splashing in the tin basin outside the kitchen door.

"I made some burned sugar syrup," said her mother setting a heaping plate of golden cakes and a pitcher before her.

Marian cast a horrified glance at the brown crock on

269

the shelf. She had hoarded sugar so carefully—so carefully! But she smiled at her mother's flushed face when she looked toward her once more.

"Oh, but they're good!" Marian mumbled, forgetting that her mouth was full of a large bite.

Just then Father flung open the door and stomped in carrying the milk pails ."Happy birthday!" he called. "Here! Fish in my pocket, Marian. I think there's something in there for you."

Eagerly Marian jumped up and ran to him. With exploring hands she searched his pockets. At length her fingers closed over something soft and leathery and she pulled out—a pair of Indian moccasins.

"Father!" she breathed. "Oh, how lovely!" Marian gazed in delight at the soft buckskin and at the bright beaded trimmings. Quickly she pulled off her copper-toed shoes and tried on the moccasins. "Why, they fit perfectly!" she cried.

"I traded a mirror and some tobacco for them. Met some Indians on my way to Colorado City with the sheep the other day," said Father. "I remembered there was a birthday about due at our house. Thought you'd like some real Indian moccasins."

Marian plumped down in her chair and stretched her slippered feet out before her admiring eyes. "And—and I thought everyone had forgotten! I thought . . . Oh, Father, this is a lovely birthday, and I didn't dream it would be!" Marian cried happily, jumping up and running to hug her father and then her mother.

Later she rode Kite down for the mail. Perhaps, in spite of the fire, there would be something there from Chicago. But there was not even a letter. Disappointed, Marian turned on her heel. Slowly she descended the wooden steps and started toward Kite who was tied to a near-by pine tree.

"Hey, Miss. Wait a minute!" called the man who had brought the telegram to Crow's Nest. "Wait! I forgot. Here's a box for you."

Marian turned back and raced excitedly up the porch steps. "Here you are," the man said, handing her an oblong cardboard box. As she took it from him, Marian saw her name scrawled in an unknown handwriting and below in great printed letters, "Rush—Fragile."

Aunt Lily must have remembered after all. Her heart fluttered joyfully. "Oh!" she cried. "I can't wait. May I open it here?"

"Sure," the man replied, lingering curiously.

Marian knelt on the porch floor. Hurriedly she wrestled with the cord which tied the box and then lifted the lid. Layers of newspaper met her eye.

"Well, what you suppose it is?" the man ejaculated, peering over her sunbonnet.

Marian's impatient fingers pulled off layer after layer of newspaper. "Oh!" she breathed at last. She sat back on her heels and stared, dumbfounded. For underneath there were six red geraniums, their earth-covered roots wrapped in still more paper. "Who in the world . . . ?" she gasped.

"Shucks!" The man turned away. "Nothin' but geraniums," he called to a male head disappearing through the doorway.

And then Marian saw the card tied to one red blossom. "Happy Birthday to the Buffalo Girl." It was from Charles! The geraniums he promised!

But how in the world had he known it was her birthday? Marian wondered as she tied up the box again and hurried down to Kite.

She puzzled over it all the way home. When she reached there, Russell's face gave the secret away. He had told Charles that Marian would have a birthday soon, and the very day. Charles had not forgotten!

After all, Marian's birthday was one to remember with the rest. There was no birthday cake or ice cream, nor a gay party. But she was happy! She had not been forgotten!

It was Doctor Frank who brought them big news several days later. The Denver and Rio Grande had been finally completed to Colorado Springs. Passenger service would start in a few days.

"Yes sir! It was a big day for the colony!" Doctor Frank grinned. "No one will ever forget the twenty-third of October, when the Baby Railroad laid the last rail to its doors. Great guns! You all should have been there!

A BABY RAILROAD AND A BIRTHDAY

Such cheering! Even Colorado City put on a smile!'' he added laughing.

Crow's Nest was elated. It would not be so lonely now with the cheery whistle from the little black engine, and the comforting rattle of the train past their cabin.

A week or so later the shrill screech of a special train from Denver tore the cold November air. It sent Marian flying from the barn where she had been feeding Kite and the mules.

"Hurry up, everybody!" she called. "The train's coming!" She danced up and down in her excitement.

Mr. Blane came running from the sheep pens, Russell trotting after him. Mrs. Blane appeared in the cabin doorway, a scrap of dark mending in her white hands. The family gathered on the porch steps and watched the little engine puffing and snorting like a fiery little Mustang around the bend to the north.

"Hurrah! Hurrah!" they shouted. Marian waved her apron, Mother her mending and Father his hat. Russell just stood spellbound as the miniature train with its passengers, composed of newspaper men and important railroad officials, creaked by.

From the cab of the tiny engine, proudly flaunting its name, "Montezuma," the engineer waved his hand, and jangled the bell in salute.

"Why, it is a baby train!" Marian cried.

And indeed it was, from the small coaches and miniature windows to the baggage car on wheels like a wagon, and the toy black engine.

"Wish I had a train," Russell said wistfully.

"What in the world would you do with it?" Marian laughed. "But, Father, why did they build it so small?"

"Well, you see the company didn't have enough money to build it full gauge, and besides, they expect the road to go through mountains and difficult passes. It wouldn't be practical to have it wider than three feet. They tell me it has but two seats on one side of the aisles and a single one on the other. That's all there's room for," Father answered.

The train had gone. Only a cloud, black against the clear November sky, told of its passing. Civilization had come to Crow's Nest at last!

XXII

Christmas at Crow's Nest

November and a turkey-less Thanksgiving had come and gone. For weeks the Crow's Nest had lain under a fleecy blanket of snow. Giant drifts closed in about the brown dot of a cabin like swaddling clothes. The new fence posts, which William Blane with the assistance of Hiram Gray had put up before the storm, were topped with little white mounds—looking for all the world like the frosted cup-cakes that Marian's grandmother made in her spicy-smelling Eastern kitchen. Even the trees had taken on all sorts of queer shapes.

How cold it was! How lonely! Visitors were few. Occasional bands of cold, hungry Utes stopped for the pans of doughnuts and biscuits which they seemed to know would always be waiting for them at the cabin. Word had passed by some system known only to the Indians themselves, that the ranch on the Monument never turned away a hungry Ute. Marian was in despair over the amount they ate, and the dirty slush which they tracked over her carefully scrubbed kitchen. But she dared not refuse them.

She worried, too, over her mother, who sat so very still for hours at a time, her eyes closed, and also over the vanishing store of supplies on the kitchen shelves. The brown sugar crock was empty now! The proverbial wolf seemed very close—howling at the doors, and blowing his breath through the three-inch crack under the snow-burdened roof.

Father's shoulders sagged, and the gray salting his dark hair became more pronounced as the days wore on. At length Marian decided to take matters into her own hands. She wrote to Aunt Lily without consulting either her father or mother.

"Dear Auntie," she wrote, "I'm so worried over Mother. She isn't as well as she should be. It's so cold here at the Crow's Nest, we can't begin to keep warm. Right now I can scarcely see out the windows because of the drifts outside. Two more sheep died yesterday. That makes fifteen! I'm afraid the supplies won't last much longer. And worst of all, the money box is empty! I peeked in this morning just to make sure. Do you suppose the Ladies Aid would send us a barrel? They're always sending barrels to someone. I remember when Mother made me put in my Scotch plaid for the Eskimos, and I didn't want to a bit.

"Mother needs a good warm cloak. She has only her black velvet one with the fringe and soutache braid. Goodness, how I wish she hadn't given away her old sealskin sacque! There'd be no one out here to see the moth holes except perhaps the Indians. Russell has grown so he just needs everything, especially a warm coat and hat. He looks like a little goose with one of Mother's shawls wrapped about his head. That blue sailor hat he had last winter is of no use against these storms.

"If the Ladies' Aid has any old trousers, I know Father needs them. He says he's soon going to have to patch his with his cardigan jacket. I've outgrown everything, even the blue flannels which the seamstress made for the trip across the plains.

"With love to all and to Lizzie when you see her,
              "Your worried niece, Marian.

"P. S. Father and Mother don't know that I'm writing. Oh, Aunt Lily, I just had to!"

When the letter was tucked into an envelope, Marian crept into her room and searched in the old pink candy box for her one remaining stamp hidden carefully under her clean white handkerchiefs. Then she rode Kite through the blinding snow with the letter clutched in a red-mittened hand. "How angry Father would be if he knew!" she told Kite, when the smudgy, snow-frosted

277

outlines of Teachouts loomed ahead. "But I don't care. Something had to be done!"

However, the long dreary days wore on and no answer came. Marian was forced to the conclusion that the Ladies' Aid preferred helping the missionaries, the Eskimos, or the Chinese, and that Aunt Lily must have lost everything in the big fire.

Father tried to sell some of the sheep, but no one cared to buy them, nor had the money if he did. He succeeded, however, in trading one lamb at Gehrung's store in Colorado City in exchange for some provisions.

Then Mother had a severe sick spell. Marian never forgot that terrible night when Father rode through the snow for Doctor Frank, while she sat huddled and afraid, holding tightly to her mother's frail hand. Nor the tense hours of waiting—waiting—and watching the lunging black shadows on the bare walls.

Mother was so ill for a time that Father decided to send them all to Colorado Springs after Christmas so that they might be near Doctor Frank. Luckily Job Greer, a new colonist, with whom the doctor had been living, offered them the use of his four-room house while he went East to get his family.

As her mother improved, Marian thrilled to the thought of moving to the new town. It would be less lonely there. If only there was some way that she could help her father —something she could do to earn money. But what?

The day before Christmas found Marian busy with

plans. Somehow they must make a celebration of the day in spite of the lack of money and presents, and the now nearly empty shelves in the kitchen. Russell, most of all, must not be disappointed.

Early that morning, Marian and her father had chopped down a lovely fir tree by the spring, its branches stiff and icy from the cold. Now, in the warmth of the front room the branches had lost their rigidity, and the spicy smell of evergreen filled the entire cabin. While Russell helped Father in the barn, Marian set to work cutting pictures from Godey's *"Lady's Book."* She even sacrificed the few copies of *Harper's Weekly* which she had been saving. A new story, "Poor Miss Finch," by the popular author, Wilkie Collins, had been running in the magazine since September, and though it was a grown-up tale Marian hungrily read every word. Stories of any sort were scarce at Crow's Nest.

Among her mother's things Marian found some red paper. From the pictures and paper she fashioned little ornaments, baskets and cornucopias, pasting them carefully with flour and water. While her hands were busy, her mind worked over the menu for the Christmas dinner. Napoleon, that strutting, red king of the lonely barnyard, would have to go. Marian loved the cocky little rooster. But the remaining two hens must be kept to supply Mother's morning eggs.

Marian sighed. She would miss Napoleon's joyous "cock-a-doodle-do" each morning.

They would have baked chicken and biscuits, and a deep bowl of rich, brown gravy. She would make custard for desert, "running custard," as Russell called it, with little islands of egg white floating on top. To be sure, it wouldn't be very good without sugar, but it would have to do.

There! The last ornament was finished. She hung them here and there on the tree, and then stood off to admire her work. It was a strange tree and just a little pitiful, but it added color to the room. She festooned the geranium-filled windows with pine boughs and draped some more boughs, heavy with pine cones, above Great-grandmother Willard's clock.

"It doesn't look like any tree I ever saw before," Marian sighed to her mother when she returned to the kitchen.

Mrs. Blane, who was bundled in shawls and blankets near the warmth of the crackling stove, looked up—her eyes too large for her thin white face. She smiled.

"Never mind! I'm sure Russie will love it. It isn't everyone who can chop down his Christmas tree on his own grounds. May I see it now, Marian?"

"Of course," said Marian eagerly, running to help her from the blankets and assist her into the front room.

"How pretty!" Mother admired. "It's really lovely, Marian," she added softly. Then she turned away quickly, but not before Marian caught a mist of tears gathering in her eyes.

Russell's shouts of delight and Father's astonished

admiration over the tree sent a glad little glow to Marian's heart when they returned from the barn. But later her heart became leaden when she overheard her brother remark, "Supposin' Santa Claus can't come, 'cause of the Chicago stores burnin'. S'pose he will, Mummy?"

"I'm afraid he may not, son," her mother replied slowly.

"I'm goin' to hang up my stockin'," Russell said. "He might."

"Poor Russie!" Marian thought, as she continued crumbling bread in a big yellow bowl for the dressing tomorrow. How glad she was that she had made him that little dog out of pine cones.

Late that afternoon, a smudge of flour on her nose, and her sleeves rolled up above her elbows, Marian was stuffing the late Napoleon for Christmas dinner, when the answer to her desperate letter arrived.

A man from Colorado Springs brought it. "Thought I'd bring it out as I was going to the Grays'," he remarked as Marian opened the kitchen door.

"Well, Merry Christmas to you," he said as he let fall the barrel from his broad shoulders. "Looks like you might be going to have one here," he added, as he shuffled to the door.

"Merry Christmas," called Marian, "and thank you!"

A draft of cold air blew through the kitchen and he was gone.

"Mother! Mother! It's come! Oh, hurry, hurry!" cried Marian joyfully.

A barrel it most certainly was! But not from the Ladies' Aid! Aunt Lily had more than answered her letter. As Marian pried off the top she gave a squeal of delight. It looked as though her aunt had ransacked every closet and trunk in the family for warm clothes and underthings.

"And look!" cried Marian to her mother who had joined her and was sitting beside the overflowing barrel. "Look, will you, at all the food! Everything we need! Flour, beans, coffee, tea, sugar—and home canned goods!" One by one Marian set the provisions on the table. "Oh, isn't it wonderful! Just like an answer to a prayer!" Marian danced gleefully around the barrel, her eyes shining like great blue stars.

"I should say it is!" Mother smiled happily. "But why do you suppose Auntie sent food? We could buy it here."

"No, we couldn't—that is—she probably can get it all so much cheaper in a big city," Marian replied hastily.

"Mother! Will you look at these!" Marian held up an armful of white packages tied with red ribbon. "Really, truly Christmas presents!" She hugged them close. "Yummy! They smell of violets and mignonette, just like Aunt Lily herself." Marian wrinkled her nose delightedly. "Santa Claus has certainly come to Crow's Nest even though Russie didn't think he would. I'd better hide them under the tree before he and Father come back. I'm glad they were up with the sheep. Won't they be surprised?''

Suddenly Marian dropped the packages on the table and whirled over to her mother and hugged her tightly. She rained kisses on her upturned, smiling face. ''Oh, Mother!'' she cried at last, ''I'm so happy I could shout and dance for joy!''

The next minute, her arms laden with parcels, she skipped into the next room. Even the pitiful little green tree with its strange ornaments looked more festive now. After she had laid the heap of bright presents under the tree, Marian stood off and admired the room. ''It does look Christmasy!'' she breathed aloud.

And what a happy time it was after all! Even the day shone warm and sunny for them. The cabin smelled enticingly of pine and roasting chicken. Mother looked so much better and so happy, dressed in her best gray poplin trimmed in crimson velvet ruches and adorned with bell-shaped sleeves.

Doctor Frank succeeded in riding out from town, for the snow was melting fast. He arrived looking like a merry red-headed Santa Claus; his pockets were bulging with gifts, and he had a round, dark fruit cake tucked under his coat, a present from Mrs. Kappus, his first patient. For once Father's eyes forgot to cloud with worry, and Russell beamed all day with his arms full of new toys. Even Chase looked blissful, panting by the stove with the red ribbon about his neck slipping rakishly under one silky ear.

But to Marian, Christmas was the dress!

"Oh, Mother!" she cried joyfully when she unwrapped its shiny folds. "Look! A dress—and new! Why, it's as long as yours—and its so grown-up looking! The most grown-up dress I've ever owned!" She held it at arm's length for her mother to admire, her sparkling eyes matching the blue sheen of the silk itself.

"It's beautiful, Marian!" said Mother, smiling at her happiness.

"Oh, I'm going to try it on this minute!" Marian cried, dashing into the bedroom. In a few minutes she was back, pirouetting the length of the room.

"Don't I look young-ladified?" Marian questioned over her shoulder. Her admiring fingers caressed the tight basque, the real lace collar, and the bell-shaped open sleeves. "And don't you adore the overskirt bunched up in the back this way and all the cunning ruffles and puffs that trim it?" she added, squirming about to catch a better look.

"Lovely! Simply lovely!" Mother admired. "And very becoming, too. But it does make you look old."

"Oh, but I'm fourteen now! Lizzie had a dress almost as old looking—" Marian stopped abruptly in her preening. "But where—where in the world will I ever wear it?" she asked plaintively.

CHRISTMAS AT CROW'S NEST

Mother shook her head. "Not at Crow's Nest, I'm afraid."

Dinner proved to be all Marian had hoped it would be and more, much more. For now they had cups of fragrant coffee, there was sugar in the custard, and Doctor Frank's dark, moist fruit cake to go with it. The meal was finished off with dainty bonbons from the beribboned box which Lizzie had sent along in Aunt Lily's barrel.

When the evening shadows darkened the front room, Father lit the tallow candles on the Christmas tree. Silently they stood before it, admiring the flickering lights among the green branches. And then Mother started singing an old Christmas carol:

"Silent Night! Holy Night!
All is calm! All is bright!"

Presently they all joined in the song, as one by one Father blew out the candles:

"Sleep in Heavenly Peace!"

It was very still in the darkened cabin as the carol died away. It was quiet outside, too. Calm and bright! As if, thought Marian, the pines had stopped their endless whispering for a moment, and had been listening breathlessly to their song.

XXIII

A Soldier to the Rescue

The following day Mother, Russell and Marian drove in to Colorado Springs. Kite was tied behind the carriage, as Father was to help them get settled and then return to the ranch.

As the lonely cabin receded into the distance, Marian turned her head for a last look. She wasn't sorry to leave Crow's Nest, and yet . . . Mentally she waved good-bye to the straggling ranch buildings, to Grandfather Pine, towering darkly and grotesquely against the wintry sky. They passed the choke-cherry spring, the last fence post.

Ten miles ahead of them lay the new town and a new life. But her anticipation over their move was clouded by the old worries. The excitement of Christmas and their happy day vanished with the last familiar landmark on Crow's Nest ranch.

WAGON WHEELS TO DENVER

She found herself asking the same question that had haunted her mind when she crossed the plains. "What will happen next?" However, it was a different anxiety she felt now. If only there were something she could do in Colorado Springs—some way to help!

Marian liked the newly-painted cottage that became their home. Home meant neighbors here. There were few painted houses and most of the buildings were mere shacks, rudely and hurriedly built. They looked like cardboard houses thrown down upon a wind-swept prairie, along the wide, muddy streets which formed the town.

"I like it here, Russie," Marian confided to her brother, as late that afternoon they watched their father ride Kite down Pike's Peak Avenue on his way back to the ranch. Chase followed at a reluctant distance, his tail between his legs.

"Like Crow's Nest better," said Russell wistfully, flattening his small nose against the window pane for a last glimpse of the tall, slender figure turning his horse north on Cascade.

"But, Russie, there's always something to watch here," Marian insisted. "A new house, or a store, or the men building the church, and down the street there, the hotel." Marian nodded to where, at the corner of Pike's Peak and Cascade, the square mansard-roofed hotel was nearing completion. "And there's the baby train this minute!" she added. Both listened to the cheery whistle of the little engine puffing up in front of the station.

A SOLDIER TO THE RESCUE

Marian turned away from the window and inspected the small room with appraising eyes. It was a pine-walled, doll house of a room, heated by a center stove and furnished with two hard, wooden chairs and an oval, marble-topped table with a lamp. The two bedrooms opened off the sitting-room on the right, and the dark little kitchen on the left were no bigger than Kite's stall back at Crow's Nest.

"Not room enough to swing a cat!" Father had laughed.

Marian turned back to the window. It was the town that interested her, the people. She could see down Pike's Peak Avenue to the very spot where they had camped that first night which seemed so long ago. Beyond, loomed the Cheyenne mountains and the giant peak, which brooded darkly above the toy-like towns.

The week passed quickly. Marian had seen nothing of Charles Barry, though Doctor Frank said he was busy getting the hotel ready to open on January first.

The day before New Year's, she was scrubbing the kitchen floor when Russell came scurrying breathlessly through the doorway. "Marian!" he cried, "come quick! Charles is comin'."

"You mean he's here, young fellow!" said a laughing voice from the door.

"Oh! . . . Hello!" Marian faltered, scrambling to her feet, conscious for the first time of her outgrown sleeves. She yanked at them, blushing furiously.

289

"This is the first time I've had a chance to run in to see you since you moved to town. I know you'll like it here. It's grown a lot, hasn't it?" Charles said, leaning against the door and watching her.

"I should say so! I counted over a hundred and fifty houses the other day," cried Marian. "But don't let's stay out in this dark place. Come on into the sitting-room," she invited, skipping over the swirl of soapy water on the floor.

In the parlor they sat down, facing each other. Funny, thought Marian, how the room or something made her feel awkward and stiff—shy, even. She hadn't felt that way a bit at the ranch the last time Charles was there.

"Did—did you get my letter thanking you for the lovely geraniums?" she ventured.

"I certainly did. Glad you liked them. I stayed with your friend Ma Betts in Pueblo, and when I asked her where I could get some flowers like hers, she gave me a few to send to you."

"They're beautiful! You ought to see how they've grown."

Silence again. Russell broke it with, "Sister's got a new blue dress. She got it Christmas an' it came in a barrel."

With the gale of laughter which followed this announcement, Marian's composure was restored.

"That's great!" Charles' eyes were sparkling. "Now you can wear it to our party."

290

A SOLDIER TO THE RESCUE

"Party? When?" cried Marian.

"Tonight! We're going to have a dance at the hotel. I hope you'll come."

"How lovely!"

"Here's the invitation," said Charles handing her a square envelope.

Eagerly Marian tore open the note. "Jiminy, but I hope I can go!" she breathed, as she finished reading. The envelope fell to her lap. Her eyes were starry with excitement.

"Gosh, I hope so!" Charles returned. He stood up. "Guess I'd better go. I've got lots to do before night. We're importing the music and most of the food from Denver, but I've all the decorating and cleaning up to do. Good-bye. See you later."

After the door closed on Charles, Marian dashed into the bedroom where her mother was resting, waving the invitation.

"Mother! Look! An invitation to a party!" Marian cried, dancing over to the bed and dropping down beside her mother. "It's tonight—at the Colorado Springs Hotel and it's going to be a dance!"

"A dance! My, but they're ambitious!"

Mother reached for the envelope. She read the contents, then laid the note on the bed. "Too bad we can't go. I suppose it will be quite an event for a frontier town," she remarked.

"Oh! . . . Can't I go?" Marian pleaded.

WAGON WHEELS TO DENVER

"I think you're a little young. Besides you can't go alone, Marian." Mother patted her rough little hand.

"Oh!" Marian turned away. Slowly she walked from the room.

She finished scrubbing the floor and then she borrowed old Iron Side from Doctor Frank. Perhaps if she rode out along the Fountain Creek and over to Colorado City it might help ease her disappointment.

She supposed she really shouldn't go over to the old town. Mother thought it a rough place—too many beer halls and the like. But Marian loved the ride along the frozen creek. Best of all, she loved to call on Mrs. Kappus, Doctor Frank's patient, and play with her cunning rosy-cheeked baby in the funny prim parlor. Besides, hot gingerbread had a way of appearing mysteriously from nowhere. And it was always so spicy and moist and altogether yummy!

Colorado Springs was far behind her. Furtively she looked around, then tossed her skirts to the other side and settled her copper-toed shoe in the stirrup. She was glad there was no one to notice her. Mother thought it unladylike to ride astride now that she was such a big girl, but no stretch of the imagination could make Marian pretend that the doctor's was a side-saddle.

On the way home from Colorado City, Marian felt better about the party. In fact, she forgot it completely. Hadn't Mrs. Kappus promised to give her music lessons on her square piano if Marian would come over once a week and take care of the youngest Kappus while she put out the wash? Often she had longed to play the ivory keys of this old piano. It had a real history, for Mrs. Kappus had brought it across the plains in a covered wagon, and for several years the piano graced the one dirt-floored room of a prairie dugout. And now Marian was actually going to learn to play it. Music lessons at last! Dreamily she hugged this new happiness to her heart as Iron Side loped homeward in the late afternoon.

Suddenly Marian jumped—or thought she did. But no, it was Iron Side who had jumped. From behind the snow-laden bushes that screened the creek at her left came the sound of harsh voices. Men's voices. Who could be talking so angrily? She pulled the horse to a stop and listened.

"Yeah! You're yellow, that's what ya are! Savvy? Just 'cause I made that slip a-gettin' the graders' pay-roll ain't no reason I won't make this deal. Ain't I been in this here business fer years? Ain't I heard that Barry brat tell 'em that the money would come from Denver today over the railroad? He's gonna keep it in the hotel safe. That Laurence guy's to take it by stage to Pueblo. Savvy! The train's in an' I was a-plannin' to nab the money on the way to the hotel. But you guys gettin' nervous like, I . . ."

"Aw, don't talk so loud, Jake! Do ya want them to hear ya in the Springs? Come on. We'll go with ya. Ain't ya promised to divvy up with us? We was only . . ."

"Yeah, we'll go with you, Jake. Honest! I don't aim to see that crooked brother of yourn hold up this here cash down his way. Let's go! It'll be as easy as takin' candy from a baby!"

Jake! Scar Face! Charles Barry! Money in the safe! The words flashed before Marian's reeling thoughts. Oh, what should she do? They mustn't see her! Right now the men were crashing through the dead bushes. She must hide! Then, somehow she must warn Charles!

She dismounted and led the tall Iron Side behind some snow-covered scrub oak. She prayed that they were hidden from the three men whom she could see emerging from among the trees ahead, leading their horses.

It was Jake! Also, that great hulk of a creature was the buffalo-like man whom she had seen in Kit Carson. The third man was small and limped slightly. Then she gasped. The latter was leading Gypsy! Her own Gypsy! A thin, bony Gypsy, streaked with mud, her shaggy hoofs crusted with dirty ice. But she would have known the pony anywhere! A sob rose in her throat—choked her. Poor Gypsy! How they had mistreated her! She must save her!

Breathlessly she watched the men as they galloped off toward Colorado Springs, then she scrambled on her horse and cut madly across country. She must beat them to town!

It was hard going over the rutted, uneven ground. "If only you were Kite!" she lamented to the straining Iron

Side. She felt for the gun that Doctor Frank kept in the holster slung from the saddle, and her fingers touched the chill of steel. Luckily, Doctor Frank had not removed the revolver!

On they raced over the melting snow. Once the mare floundered in a huge drift. Again she stumbled into a treacherous gully, almost throwing Marian over her head.

Over and over her heart and brain hammered the same desperate refrain, "I must save Charles—the money— Gypsy! Hurry—Hurry—Hurry!!"

At last! There sprawled the straggling little town! In a moment she would be at the hotel. She could see its two-story mansard roof towering like a big, brown mother hen among her scrawny baby chicks! A team and wagon was tied to the railing. There was no one on the veranda. Was she too late? Had they come and gone? Were they inside this minute? "Oh, don't let them be— don't," ran her tortured thoughts.

Breathless, clutching the revolver in nervous, shaking hands, she slid from the horse. She ran up the steps and dashed into the silent lobby. Charles looked up from the counter where he was busily writing.

"Marian! Gosh. What's the matter! What is it?" he cried, at the sight of her face and hatless, flying curls.

Marian looked around wildly. "They . . . they aren't here yet?"

"They—who? What do you mean?" cried Charles, hurrying around the counter.

"Jake! He—they're coming! I heard them plan to rob the safe! That money from Denver! Oh, do something. Quick! They'll be here any minute!" cried Marian weakly, the words rushing out in frightened gasps. She ran to the window.

"Gosh! Laurence, did you hear that? Grab your gun! We've got to be ready!"

A man who had been sitting with his heels propped against the iron stove, clattered sharply to the pine floor. He strode to the window beside Marian.

Charles rushed back of the counter and began searching frantically for his gun, muttering, "Where in thunder ... Here, I've got it!" he exclaimed, trembling with excitement.

"They're coming! See them!" Marian cried. "They're crossing Cascade! They ... they're here ..." Marian's voice ended in a whisper.

"Get back here," Charles ordered, pulling her behind the counter. "Now act like you don't suspect anything. And keep your gun handy, Laurence. Be ready to search them when I have them ..." Shuffling, heavy feet crossing the veranda interrupted Charles. Above Marian's head a clock ticked. It thundered into the stillness of the room. Marian clutched her gun tightly.

"Come in, fellows," Jake's voice boomed. "Howdy! Got rooms fer ..." Jake broke off. His surprised narrow eyes were on Marian, who was standing close to Charles.

"What the—— This here's a surprise!" He lunged toward them, his face creased in an evil grin.

"Stay where you are. Drop that gun! We've got you covered ..." Charles shouted, whipping out his revolver.

"The h ... ya say!" Jake's hand darted toward his hip.

Marian's gun roared. Jake grabbed his arm with a yelp of pain. His gun thudded to the floor.

For a minute everything went black before Marian's eyes. There was a string of oaths, a clatter of firearms, a babble of snarling voices.

Had she killed Jake? She hadn't meant to. But he had reached for his pistol. And he would have killed Charles! He was a sure shot, well she knew.

Marian felt weak and sick. She looked up with terrified eyes. Faces blurred before her.

No, she hadn't killed Jake. He was standing there— glaring at her!

Suddenly she wanted to get away—away from those murderous, glinting eyes. To get Gypsy away and take her home to safety. She slipped quickly out of the door. No one noticed. Charles had the men covered. Laurence roped their arms together.

Outside, her knees trembled under her—trembled violently. She caught hold of the porch rail. Then she saw Gypsy! The pony was standing wearily beside old Iron Side.

She ran, stumbling, toward the pony, crying, "Gypsy!

Oh, Gypsy! Don't you know me?" She flung both arms around her neck. "Thank goodness, I've found you at last!" she crooned softly, stroking the mud-spattered shaggy mane.

The pony turned curious eyes upon her. Then it seemed to Marian as if the whole, abused calico body quivered in recognition. A sob burst from Marian. "Gypsy!... You do know me!" she cried.

The pony nickered, and slowly, gently, as she had always done, she rubbed her nose against the girl's shoulder.

XXIV

Quite Grown-Up

Suddenly, Marian cast an anxious glance toward the hotel. Suppose Jake should get loose! She shuddered. She must get away. She must get help for those two in there alone with the outlaws!

Hastily mounting Iron Side and leading Gypsy, she galloped around the hotel and up Pike's Peak Avenue toward home. She yelled at the first man she saw.

"Help—quick! Robbers at the hotel!"

In an instant the man had spread the alarm. Several men began running toward the hotel. Relieved, Marian galloped on. Charles would be safe! Jake couldn't get away now! She and Gypsy would be safe, too, with Jake caught and locked up somewhere.

At home at last, Marian slid from the saddle and ran into the cottage. Father had just ridden in from the ranch and the family was assembled in the tiny sitting-room, discussing the contents of the square envelope which had caused her so much disappointment that morning.

"Everybody! Guess what? I've Gypsy back!" she cried. And then because she was so happy, the tears just would come.

"Gypsy!" came the amazed chorus.

After she had finished her account of what had happened and her family had all trooped out to see the pony, her father looked at her proudly and said, "Marian, you certainly come from the fighting Blanes. My brave little soldier! Not so little, either," he chuckled. "You're nearly as tall as I, now, young lady! To think that you rounded up that scoundrel Jake, saved that money and . . ."

"William!" exclaimed Mrs. Blane who, up to that time, had said very little but whose eyes had glowed with pride, "I think after all this, that Marian should go to the party tonight."

"Of course she shall! I'll take her myself! Pshaw! It isn't everyone that can escort a real heroine to a party!" Father saluted her gravely. "Our little soldier of the plains!"

"Father, don't!" Marian flushed. "I didn't do anything, honest! Why, there wasn't anything else to do. And . . ."

"And you can wear your new Chicago dress," broke in Mother with a smile.

"Oh, I can! And I didn't think there would be a chance

to wear it—ever. Jiminy, but I'm happy to think I can go tonight! I've never been to a big party!''

Catching up the wide-eyed Russell, who, for once, was questionless, Marian swung him gaily around and, much to his disgust, kissed his chubby face. ''I'm going to a party, a party,'' she sing-songed. ''Just think, Russie, Sister's going to a real grown-up party!''

''Aw, grown-ups don't have ice cream!'' Russell mumbled, jerking away.

After supper, Marian dressed with nervous, trembling fingers. Her cheeks were flushed with excitement. ''Suppose I'll look hot and frowsy and horrid!'' she grumbled to Chase, who lay near the chest of drawers. ''I wish to goodness I was lily-white like Auntie!'' Chase, his eyes fixed sorrowfully on every move she made, gave a feeble wag of his tail. He seemed to sense that he was to be left behind.

She admired the loose waterfall of curls that her mother had pinned up in back. Mother had said it was the very latest thing not to wear a net, and somehow Marian's new gown called for a grown-up hair-dress. ''I do like it, though,'' she said, more to her mirror than to Chase. Then quickly Marian slipped into her dress. How soft and silky it felt! Lovingly she ran her hand over the billowing folds. A delighted little shiver ran down to the toes of Mother's borrowed slippers.

At a quarter to nine, Marian put on her copper-toed shoes for the muddy walk down Pike's Peak Avenue. Under her arm she carried her slippers, and about her shoulders was Mother's velvet cloak. Then happily she started out with her father for the party.

The lobby of the Colorado Springs Hotel looked festive with pine boughs and sprays of little red berries from the near-by canyons. It was very different from the room which that afternoon had been filled with gun smoke and the harsh oaths of trapped men.

Marian shivered in remembrance. She hoped that Jake was under lock and key. Then everything else was forgotten as she crossed the long, narrow dining-room which had been cleared for dancing, and found herself in the ladies' parlor. She removed her wraps before a long pier glass framed in walnut. Her eyes admired once more the lovely folds and puffs which enveloped her.

Just then, five chattering women, about Mother's age or older, fluttered into the parlor. "Why, there she is now, Myra," one of them exclaimed. "I was that frightened when they told me. Imagine! Robbers!" The tall woman, with a chin that protruded like a flatiron, hurried over to Marian. "Why, you brave little thing!" she cried.

They were surrounding her, all talking at once, patting her shoulders—smothering her. Marian felt that she would give anything to escape. These women, kind though they meant to be, reminded her of the group of ruffled hens at Crow's Nest when they pecked eagerly—greedily —at a piece of suet. They embarrassed her and made her want to run away and hide.

QUITE GROWN UP

When she managed to break away she found herself in the dining-room full of men. Anxiously she looked about for her father. Young men, old men, bearded men, men dressed in well-brushed working clothes and high boots looked at her. Young dandies in the latest sack coat and gay light trousers, with slick hair brushed smartly forward, beamed their admiration. There was a terrifying silence. Then a wave of talk broke over the room. Helplessly she fingered the folds of her skirt. She could see but two or three women and one of these, framed in a cloud of black silk, sat at the square piano.

Where could her father have disappeared to? she wondered, panic-stricken. Desperately she wished she were home—away from these staring faces—where she could tear off this new dress and get into her outgrown blue flannel in which, at least, she was comfortable and happy!

Then an eager arm grabbed hers and half pulled her out into the lobby, away from the rows of strange faces.

"Thank goodness!" Marian cried. For her rescuer was Charles. His usually tousled hair was smooth and shiny brown, and he had discarded his working clothes for a dark blue suit and soft white shirt. Why, they were the ones he had worn on the train that day that seemed so long ago. "You know," Marian admitted, flushing, "I was ready to run away, I felt so small and scared. I didn't know a party made you feel like that."

"You scared! Why, Marian Blane!" Charles laughed. "Come, sit down over here. I want awfully to talk to you," he cried, his blue-gray eyes serious all at once. "You know," he said, when they were seated beneath the evergreen-festooned windows, "I had to look at you twice before . . . Well, you're so grown-up and different tonight. . . . I'm not sure I like you as well that way."

"It's—it's the dress," Marian stammered, blushing.

"That's it, I guess," Charles answered, his eyes twinkling mischievously. "But seriously, Marian, I can't thank you enough for what you did today. It was wonderful! You saved my life! And all that money! The whole town is talking about it. They . . ."

"But I didn't do anything, really," Marian broke in, her face crimson.

"But you did! And now you needn't worry any more about Jake. He and his friends are locked up over in Colorado City. We put them over there because our jail is so flimsy. Jake confessed they were the outlaws that the whole Territory has been after and told me where the gang holds out south of Pueblo. I bet there's revenge in that confession! I'd be willing to swear he's fallen out with his brother Dan. You see, the reason no one ever caught them was because they always dressed as Indians when they attacked travelers. No one ever knew what they looked like. Jake also told me to whom they sold your Buck."

"Oh, I'm glad they didn't keep him and hurt him!" Marian cried. "Poor old Buck. I hope he found a good home."

"Now, listen to this," cried the young man, his eyes mysterious. "Did you know there's a reward for catching any of Wolf's gang, dead or alive? Well, there is. It's yours! Two hundred dollars!"

"Really, Charles? Oh! I'm so glad! So glad that I helped catch them! But . . . Two hundred dollars!" repeated Marian. "I can't believe it! It's too wonderful to be true!" She stared at Charles in wide-eyed unbelief.

"But I didn't do it all alone, Charles. You two did the most. I didn't do anything, honestly!" Marian argued.

"Oh, no? I suppose saving my life wasn't much! Warning us and everything! But I think it was. So do the manager and Laurence. It was everything to us to save that company money. You'll have to take it!"

Money! Enough to help them through the winter! "Charles, I can't believe it has happened to me! Here I was wondering what I could do to earn money to help out —and now . . . !"

"And now—listen!" cried the young man. "Music! Come, won't you dance? Don't pull away. That's a grand polka. Too good to miss."

"But—but I don't dance. I've never danced! They'll laugh at me! No, sir! I only came to look on."

"Mr. Blane," Charles spoke to her father who was crossing the lobby toward them, "may I have a dance with your daughter?"

"You certainly may, young man!" Father smiled at Marian's flushed, embarrassed face.

Reluctantly she accepted Charles' proffered arm. At the doorway she hesitated, ready to take to her heels. The room beyond was lined with onlookers. A few couples were dancing.

"Come on," Charles whispered.

The next minute he had swung her out on the floor. To Marian's amazement she had no trouble in following his sure, easy steps after the first hesitant ones on her part. Charles was an expert dancer. The music enveloped her in little waves of tinkling sound. It was all so exciting, the music so entrancing that she forgot her feet and the many staring faces. She felt as if she were dancing on air with wings on her slippers.

"Did you say that you'd never danced?" Charles teased.

"Never," Marian flushed.

She gazed about her. There were no girls and but few women in the crowded room. Most of the colonists were men. Some of them came from England where Doctor Bell, one of General Palmer's associates, had interested his friends in Colorado Springs. The Englishmen were waiting to see how the colony turned out before bringing their families West. Nearly all the women present came from the surrounding ranches or from Colorado City.

"Father says they are surveying lots around the Boiling Springs, and that the General is planning a town there to be called La Font," Marian said at length.

"Yes. They're planning to build a hotel there and sell

what they call villa lots. Funny, if some day it should be a great resort. I think the name Manitou would be more appropriate, don't you?''

''Yes,'' Marian replied, remembering Charles' story about the Great Spirit in the Spring.

The dance was over, and Doctor Frank was coming toward her.

''Great guns!'' he cried taking her hand. ''What's this I hear about our little lady?'' he asked teasingly. ''Shooting up bandits, are you—and rescuing young men and . . .''

''Hush!'' Marian laughed. ''There's the music.'' But the dimple in her cheek deepened, mischievously.

''Well, I won't hush! But I'll dance with you,'' the doctor returned, swinging her into a romping square dance.

When, at the close of the dance, they emerged hot and breathless and giggling, the doctor led her to a chair. ''Marian, all joking aside, I'm proud of you! You're the stuff they make them of.''

''Make what?'' asked Marian curiously.

''Oh, these frontier women we hear about.'' Doctor Frank's eyes had grown serious.

''Oh!''

''You know,'' the young man continued, ''I've some wonderful news for you. I was just over to see your mother. Marian, she's better in spite of that setback last month. I think she's going to get well!''

"Honestly?" Marian took hold of his arm and her eyes implored him for the truth. "Are you sure, really?"

"Yes, really." Doctor Frank grinned but his eyes held a solemn promise.

"Oh, I'm so glad, so glad!" Marian's face was radiant. "Now, perhaps when she's stronger she can help in the little school Mrs. Palmer's starting. She's been wanting to dreadfully."

Marian's eyes were bright with happiness when Charles whirled her away in a waltz.

The evening passed so quickly that Marian was surprised to find supper was served. It was midnight! A new year!

Cries and shouts of "Happy New Year!" fairly deafened her. She had danced every polka, waltz, lancers and schottische. She had been besieged with partners, young and old. It was almost over now. All over but for the supper spread before them on the long, evergreen decorated table. A table loaded with platters of thin sliced cold meats, red oozing tarts, quivery jellies and bowls of rich, yellow Charlotte Russe.

"I'm going to propose a toast to you, Marian," Charles smiled, and handed her a plate heaped with good things.

"You wouldn't dare, Charles Barry! I'd hate you if you did!" Marian cried angrily.

"Then I won't! Aloud, I mean." Charles raised his glass of fruit punch and looking across it at Marian said in a stage whisper, "To the Buffalo Girl!"

QUITE GROWN UP

"Silly!" Marian giggled.

A half hour later, Marian and her father walked home along the wide, muddy street. Presently she looked up into his thoughtful face. "Father, wasn't it the loveliest party? I'm so tired but so happy! I know I won't sleep a wink tonight thinking about all the lovely things that have happened."

"Yes, my dear, and I have a feeling that my young daughter was quite the belle of the party, too!" Mr. Blane was silent for a moment. "Marian, something else has happened. I have news for you. There was a man there tonight who will buy our ranch for two thousand dollars."

"Oh!" Marian stood stock-still. "But, Father, you mustn't sell it! You mustn't sell Crow's Nest! Why, now, I can help with this reward money they say I've earned and . . . Besides, where would we live when Mr. Greer returns? It would be lovely there this summer." Marian's pleading eyes sought his. "Please don't, Father!"

"I wondered if you would say that, Marian. I've known this for several days. Mother doesn't wish me to sell, either. Very well, little soldier, we'll stick to Crow's Nest and make it pay! When spring comes and Mr. Greer gets back you can all come out to the ranch. It may be a hard winter, but with my two girls to help me, pshaw, we'll see it through!"

"And Father, Doctor Frank told me Mother'll get well. Isn't that the best news yet?"

"Yes, Marian, the very best!" Father replied reverently.

In the shelter of her own room Marian gazed about with dream-filled eyes. The echo of stringed music and laughter and happiness rang in her ears. The bare, tiny room with its cheap, wooden bed and chest of drawers faded away, and in its place were phantom shadows of luxurious beauty and fulfilled dreams to come. For the first time in her life, Marian really inspected herself in the mirror. She stood gazing for a moment wonderingly at the girl reflected there.

Presently her eyes discovered Lily and John, neglected in their chairs on the trunk.

Somehow the Marian who had wedged them down in that trunk so they would comfort her when she was lonely and bring Lizzie and Chicago near, had disappeared.

Marian knew, now, that it didn't matter whether she ever went back to Chicago. This was home! Colorado Springs—the Crow's Nest—all of it! And she loved it!

"I'll not need you any more, my dears," she murmured as she kissed the dolls tenderly and laid them away in the bottom drawer of the shabby chest.

"Besides, I am quite grown-up now!"

Then, before she blew out the candle, she very gently laid her new blue dress over them.

THE END

310